FABER has published children's books since 1929. T. S. Eliot's *Old Possum's Book of Practical Cats* and Ted Hughes' *The Iron Man* were amongst the first. Our catalogue at the time said that 'it is by reading such books that children learn the difference between the shoddy and the genuine'. We still believe in the power of reading to transform children's lives. All our books are chosen with the express intention of growing a love of reading, a thirst for knowledge and to cultivate empathy. We pride ourselves on responsible editing. Last but not least, we believe in kind and inclusive books in which all children feel represented and important.

The Five Realms series

The Legend of Podkin One-Ear
The Gift of Dark Hollow
The Beasts of Grimheart

Uki and the Outcasts
Uki and the Swamp Spirit
Uki and the Ghostburrow

The Carnival of the Lost series

The Carnival of the Lost

PRAISE … SERIES

'Will entertain everyone: *Podkin One-Ear* already feels like **a classic**.'
BookTrust

'The **best book** …

'Jolly good fun.'
SFX

'I just couldn't put it down.'
Sam, age 11, *LoveReading4Kids*

'Five stars.'
Dylan, age 12, *LoveReading4Kids*

'Great stuff and definitely **one to watch**.'
Carabas

'An original fantasy with . . . **riveting adventure**, and genuine storytelling.'
Kirkus

'**A joy to read** and absolutely **world-class**.'
Alex, age 10, *LoveReading4Kids*

'A **great** bit of storytelling.'
Andrea Reece, *LoveReading*

'Rich with custom, myth, and a little touch of **magic**.'
Carousel

'A story for children who enjoy fantasy, quests (and of course rabbits).'
The School Librarian

THE FIVE REALMS

UKI AND THE GHOSTBURROW

KIERAN LARWOOD

ILLUSTRATED BY DAVID WYATT

faber

First published in 2021
by Faber & Faber Limited
Bloomsbury House,
74–77 Great Russell Street,
London WC1B 3DA
faberchildrens.co.uk
This paperback edition first published in 2022

Typeset in Times by M Rules
Printed by CPI Group (UK) Ltd, Croydon CR0 4YY

A CIP record for this book is available from the British Library

ISBN 978–0–571–34286–0

2 4 6 8 10 9 7 5 3 1

For my parents

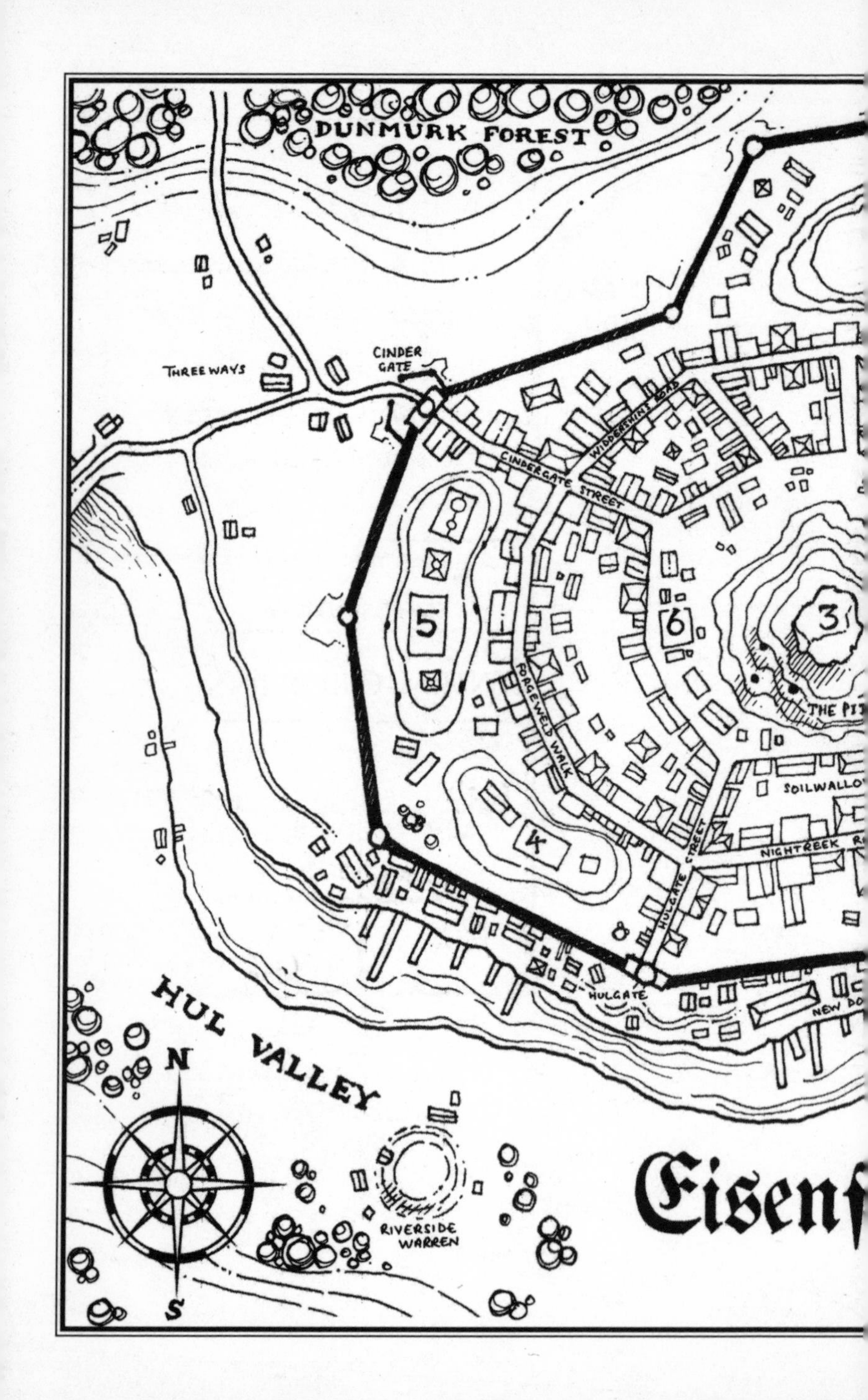

DUNMURK FOREST
THREEWAYS
CINDER GATE
WIDDERSHINS ROAD
CINDERGATE STREET
5
6
3
FORGEWELD WALK
4
HULGATE STREET
HULGATE
HUL VALLEY
N
S
RIVERSIDE WARREN

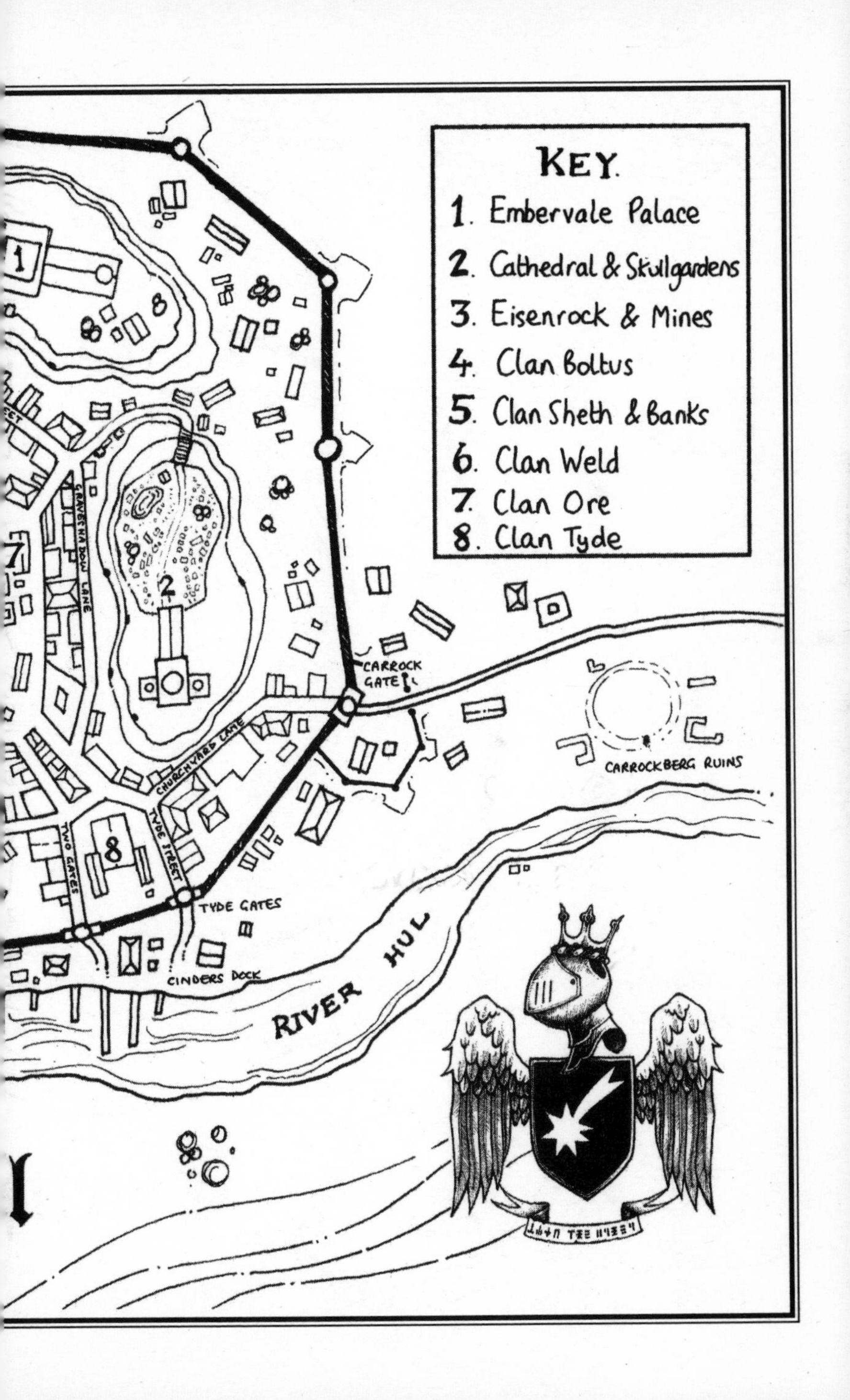

KEY.
1. Embervale Palace
2. Cathedral & Skullgardens
3. Eisenrock & Mines
4. Clan Boltus
5. Clan Sheth & Banks
6. Clan Weld
7. Clan Ore
8. Clan Tyde
CARROCK GATE
CARROCKBERG RUINS
CHURCHYARD LANE
TYDE STREET
TWO GATES
TYDE GATES
CINDERS DOCK
RIVER HUL

Prologue

Stoneaxe is watching.

Hidden behind a stunted, twisted tree that clings to the mountainside, she peeps out from between the branches. Her cloak covers her mouth, so nobody can see her breath steaming. Her fingers clutch the shaft of her best spear as she tries to decide whether to throw it or not. A thin crust of frost has formed on her whiskers, on the braids of her wild, woolly hair. Her ears went numb hours ago.

She has been watching for a long time.

Down on the slopes of the foothills, riding

towards the mountains, is a cart. Pulled by two jerboas, there are four – maybe five – rabbits on board. Too many for such a small vehicle with no proper road to ride on.

As the hills get steeper, the ground rockier and more frosted, the jerboas have begun to struggle. Soon, the riders will have to climb out and continue on foot. Stoneaxe can hardly believe what she is seeing.

Nobody ever comes into *the mountains.*

She shifts the grip on her spear. If they get close enough, she might not need it. She might get to use her axe instead. Slowly, silently, she unhooks it from her belt. It is made from a lump of flint, sanded smooth as a beach pebble, but with an edge sharp enough to cut sunbeams. She tests the blade against her arm, shaving off a small patch of fur.

Four sets of ears to hang over the fire, she thinks. *Maybe five. Four pelts to line my floor.*

It is safe to say the Arukh rabbits don't like strangers.

There is a scrabbling amongst the rocks next to her. A tiny skittering of pebbles as someone – or something – makes its way closer. Stoneaxe rolls her eyes.

'Do you have to make so much noise?' she hisses.

'It was just a pebble!'

Another rabbit flops down next to her, budging her across to share the cover. Stoneaxe glares at the newcomer. Her brother, Brightwing. Only a year younger than her, he shares the same thick mane of brown-speckled fur. The same quick, grey hunter's eyes; the same pattern of black-and-white warpaint on his face.

And now he will want to share the invaders' ears she is about to claim.

'What are you spying on?' he says, nosing through the tree branches. It only takes him a second to spot the cart and its occupants. 'By the crystals! A cartload of idiots! Don't they know what we do to intruders on our land?'

Stoneaxe sighs. Now she will only have two pairs of ears to hang over the fire. Maybe two and a half.

She holds up her axe where Brightwing can see it and smiles.

'Perhaps we should go down and show them.'

Chapter One

Of Moss and Mushrooms

'That's as far as I can take us,' Jaxom says, reining in his jerboas. The fierce trader, the fearless Foxguard agent, looks down at his animals like a worried parent. They sag in the traces, exhausted at having hauled the overloaded cart through such rough terrain.

'There's still quite a way to walk,' says the bard. 'Will we make it in time?' He is cradling a bundle of blankets in his arms. A small white nose, speckled with delicate brown spots, pokes out of the folds.

Jori leans over, pulling the blanket aside to look

at Rue, the bard's young apprentice. His breathing is slow and shallow, his eyes closed as if sleeping. But she knows there is poison coursing through his blood from the arrow of an Endwatch assassin.

She shakes her tattered ears and sighs. 'It doesn't look good,' she says. 'But we're almost in the mountains. I might be able to find some of the ingredients I need. If we stop here a while, I can have a look around.'

'Yes,' says the bard. 'Look. Please. If you are well enough.'

'I'm fine,' she says. Having taken a swig of her toxic dusk potion during the battle in which Rue was wounded, she has been weakened and exhausted herself. But the ride in Jaxom's cart has given her a chance to rest and recover, even if her legs are still a bit shaky.

As Jori limps off, nosing amongst the rocks and grass, the bard climbs out of the cart and sinks to the ground, gently lowering Rue on to his lap. Jaxom takes his panting jerboas some seed and water, while Nikku, the Foxguard leader, fits a string to her bow and nocks a red-fletched arrow. Her eyes scan the sides of the mountains that tower just ahead of them, looking for danger.

'We're sitting ducks out here in the open,' she says. 'We'd better not stay for long.'

'The Arukhs will have the antidote. We *want* them to find us,' says the bard. All the spark in his voice has gone, and his green eyes are full of tears. 'I'd like the chance to speak to them first though. Up amongst the rocks, where they can't use us for target practice.'

There is a scurrying of footsteps and they both jump, relaxing as they see Jori dashing back towards them.

'I've got some!' she says, holding out a pawful of scrapings. 'Purple haircap moss and an eagle mushroom. Well, most of one.'

'Is that all?' The bard looks at the tiny amount of muddy plant matter. 'Will it be enough to cure him?'

Jori shrugs and pulls her pack off the cart. With her other paw, she unlaces it and begins to rummage, dragging out pots, flasks and a tinderbox. 'Not cure, no. We'll need a lot more. But it might slow the poison a bit. Buy us some time, at least.'

'You're not going to start a fire, are you?' Nikku says.

Jori pauses, mid-rummage, a saucepan dangling from her paw. 'I have to,' she says. 'To brew the antidote.'

'Every Arukh in the mountains will see it! They'll fill us full of spears before we can squeak!'

'We need the antidote, Nikku,' says the bard. 'Rue might die without it.'

'We'll *all* die if you light a fire out here. If we're lucky, it'll be *before* we're skinned.'

'I don't think it matters now anyway.' Jaxom, finished with his jerboas, has walked around the cart and is pointing towards the mountains. There, strolling down the slope towards them are two Arukh braves. Both have spears raised over their shoulders, ready to hurl. One also clutches a lethal-looking flint axe.

'That's it,' says Nikku. 'We're dead. Even if I shoot them both, there'll be dozens more up in the rocks, ready to charge.'

'Hold your fire,' says Jori. 'Let them approach.'

'I speak Arukh,' says Jaxom. 'Maybe I can reason with them.'

Jori sets her precious clutch of ingredients aside and stands, holding out her ravaged paws with their bandages and missing fingers.

'This tribe speaks Lanic,' she says. 'And they are more likely to listen to me.'

Jaxom stares at her, wide-eyed. 'What makes you say that?'

'Because I have met them before,' Jori says. 'And I happen to be best friends with their god.'

*

As the braves approach, the bard flicks his eyes over them, taking in all the details of their appearance and filing them away in his memory. It is an old storyteller's habit – noticing everything – and he can't help himself, even when his apprentice lies dying in his arms.

They look quite young, with fur markings that almost match. Brother and sister, perhaps. Their clothes are stitched together from scraps of leather and hide. Simple, but well-made and warm. Their weapons are stone and wood – no metal – but he picks out a copper belt buckle and a silver earring on the girl. Evidence of trade or, more likely, trophies taken from other intruders they have 'met' in the past.

But the most striking thing about them is the warpaint daubed on their faces. Chalk white on the right-hand side, coal black on the left. Half and half, like magpies, or – and at the thought the bard's fur begins to tingle – like a certain legendary rabbit hero from around these parts.

'Uki . . .' the bard whispers. 'Could it be?'

He would ask Jori about it, but she has already started to walk towards them, paws spread wide. When they are about ten metres away from each other, they all stop.

The silence holds for a moment as they eye each other. The points of the raised spears waver a little in the air, picking out juicy parts of Jori that they might land in.

'Please,' she says. 'We mean no harm. We have come to visit your chieftain, Darkfire. I am an old friend of his.'

'Darkfire has no flatlander friends,' says the girl Arukh.

'And we don't like rabbits coming on to our

lands,' adds the boy. 'Except for when we get to kill them and take their skins.'

'Yes, we like *that* part,' says the girl. She smiles like a cat who has just bumped into a particularly plump mouse.

'He is friends with *me,*' says Jori. 'Although he hasn't seen me for many years. The last time I was here, I was with your ... Crystal Holder? Crystal Bearer? The black-and white-furred rabbit. Uki.'

Both Arukhs blink in surprise. Their spear grips falter. 'The Crystal Keeper? What do you know of him?' says the girl.

'How dare you use his name!' The boy tenses, as if about to attack, but Jori keeps her cool. She points to the silver-capped flask at her waist.

'I was one of his companions. Jori. Of Clan Septys. Haven't you heard the tales of us? Don't you recognise my potion bottle?'

The Arukhs narrow their eyes as they take in the flask and Jori's sheathed sword of Damascus steel. Then they turn away and mutter to each other, casting wary glances back.

'How do we know you haven't stolen those

things?' says the girl, finally. 'Or that you are some other flatlander, pretending to be the dusk wraith?'

'I think I can help there,' says the bard, drawing their attention.

'Who is this?' asks the girl, pointing at the bard with her axe. 'And why does he have painted fur and ears?'

'He's a bard,' explains Jori. 'A travelling storyteller. They dye their fur and tattoo their ears. Don't ask me why.'

'It marks us as servants of Clarion, god of tales and poems,' says the bard. 'And I know lots of tales about your Crystal Keeper, Uki. Jori there, too, as it happens. If you let us light a small fire and brew some medicine for my apprentice, I can tell you one. That should prove who we are. Then you can take us to your chief.'

'What is wrong with the young one?' the girl asks.

'Poison,' Jori says. 'Crowsbane. He needs purple haircap and eagle mushrooms. Do you have any at your warren?'

The girl lets out a small laugh. 'Lots,' she says. 'Haircap is used for making dye, and curing toothache. Eagle 'shrooms are good to eat. We have pots and pots of them.'

At this news, the bard's ears prick up. 'Please,' he says. 'We need them to save his life. Why else would we be here, when all rabbits know what you do to trespassers? And we really do know Uki. Jori, myself and Nikku. We can tell you lots about him.'

The Arukhs share another long glance, before the girl nods. They lower their spears and fold their arms – a signal that the bard's offer has been accepted.

'Thank you,' he says. 'Thank you so much. You won't regret it, I promise.'

Jori wastes no time in kindling a fire. Then she hangs a small pot over it on a tripod, throwing the moss and mushroom pieces inside with a splash of water from Jaxom's flask. Soon steam begins to seep from the mixture, along with a bitter, musky smell.

'Hold him up,' Jori says to the bard, scooping out a spoonful of antidote. The bard lifts Rue a fraction, and between them they manage to trickle the gloopy mess into his mouth. The bard gently rubs his throat until he swallows.

'Again,' says Jori, and they feed him the rest. Just a few tiny mouthfuls.

'Will it work?' asks the bard, gently rocking Rue as if he were a tiny kitten.

'Have to wait and see,' says Jori, watching the little rabbit closely. After a few minutes he gives a cough and opens one bleary eye.

'What ... what happened?' he croaks. 'Where are we?'

'Thank Clarion's sacred tuning pegs!' shouts the bard. 'I thought you were dead!'

'He may yet be,' warns Jori. 'That was only a tiny amount of antidote. It will hold off the poison for a few hours at best. He will need a full dose to make sure he recovers.'

The bard looks up at the Arukhs, pleading. 'Couldn't we just go now? It will make no difference to the story ...'

'You promised us a tale,' says the girl. 'One that proves you know the Crystal Keeper. Once we believe you, then we can go.'

‘That was the deal,’ says the boy.

‘A story?’ says Rue, blinking up at the bard. ‘What about?’

‘That’s typical,’ says the bard. ‘Your very life is in the balance and all you care about is hearing another yarn.’

‘But I want to know what happened to Uki. How he fared against Mortix and Necripha.’

‘It seems everyone does,’ says the bard. ‘Very well. Come and sit down you Arukhs. Jaxom, Nikku and Jori too. This isn’t much of a fire, but it will have to suffice.’

The Arukhs share a wary glance before their curiosity gets the better of them. They move closer to the meagre campfire and sit down on one side, just as the others take their places opposite. Even though she is sitting, the girl Arukh keeps her axe to hand. Her eyes twitch to and fro, as if expecting a trap of some kind.

‘Why does she keep looking at my ears?’ says the bard.

‘They collect them,’ says Jaxom. ‘From their enemies. I expect she hasn’t got a tattooed pair.’

The bard gulps, and draws his hood up over his head. 'Then I shall have to make sure my tale is good enough to keep them attached, won't I?'

'It will be,' says Rue, his voice just a whisper. 'Your stories always are.'

The bard gives him a gentle squeeze and then clears his throat, ready to begin.

Chapter Two

The Search for the Drunken Toad

So.

Uki.

For those of you that have just joined (and those that may have forgotten) this particular part of the tale comes towards the end of his first adventures.

As our new Arukh friends clearly know (judging by their marvellous warpaint), Uki was an unusual rabbit. A chimera. A double-soul. Two halves born as one: white fur on one side, black on the other.

Now, while we all think that made him special, his Ice Waste tribe did not. He was cast out, his mother died, and he nearly perished himself.

And that might have been the end of his sad story, in which case, none of us would be sitting here today. Especially not with our faces painted to look like him.

Luckily, for every rabbit in the Five Realms, he was saved from death by a fiery spirit named Iffrit. Saved, and given the task of rounding up four other spirits – or, rather, beings created by the Ancients – who were set on destroying everything they touched. At which point Iffrit vanished, gifting Uki with his strength and his memories.

And so Uki set off and was met along the way by some other heroic outcasts. A reluctant assassin, on the run from her murderous clan (the bard gestures to Jori with a flourish); Kree, a jerboa rider from the plains, along with her tail-less mount, Mooka; and Coal, a blacksmith, scarred and limbless from a mining accident.

Together, they managed to capture Gaunch, the spirit of famine (which was quite easy); Valkus, the spirit of war (which involved stopping two cities from destroying one another); and Charice, the spirit of disease (which nearly ended up with them all dying horribly, several times over).

With each spirit, Uki's powers grew, but it didn't mean anything without the fourth and final enemy. Mortix, the queen of death.

Unless he could trap her in one of the crystal prisms that topped his spears, all his new abilities, including the borrowed life Iffrit had given him, would fade.

As if things weren't hard enough, Uki and his friends were being hounded all the way by an evil witch called Necripha and her hulking servant, Balto. A leftover from the Ancients herself, she had built a network of spies called the Endwatch – their base being the ruined tower not far from here. So, everywhere Uki went, she was close behind, even creeping into his dreams. (They were connected, you see, by the spirits that lived in both of them. A situation that Uki found *most* unpleasant).

At the end of the last tale I told – just before Rue decided to get himself shot – our heroes had been sailing out of the fens, heading south. Uki could feel the pull of the final spirit coming from that direction: a distant tugging at the back of his mind. Capturing her would mean the end of his quest, but he knew it wouldn't be easy. She was stronger than the others, more dangerous. And she had been free for longer, building up her power like a spider weaving its web of steel-strong silk. Watching now, waiting … for Uki to blunder into it.

*

The Gurdle rabbits of the fens had been kind enough to sail Uki and the others down the river to Blacksand Bay, where a trading ship was waiting for them, sails furled. The captain was an old friend of the Gurdles and had agreed to carry them along the coast, dropping them off at a warren called Enk.

They were to be smuggled out by a rabbit who owed Granny Maggitch of the fens a favour. And Granny Maggitch owed Uki her life.

Even though they had just beaten Charice, the third spirit, everyone was still jingling with nerves. There was a particularly nasty clan who ruled the area, known as the Shrikes. They were hunting for

Uki and his friends, and they had a nasty habit of sticking their enemies on giant spikes.

And, even though they had spent much of the last few days on rafts and dinghies, none of them had ever been out to sea. In fact, none of them even knew how to swim.

It was a short but very uncomfortable journey. Riding in river boats had seemed strange enough, but the rocking of the waves made them all very sick. The ship hugged the coast, sailing very close to sharp black rocks. Mooka, Kree's jerboa, *neeked* all the way, and everyone else looked just as miserable. They were almost too busy grumbling and groaning to be scared when they passed by Bloodthorn, the home of Clan Shrike.

It sat atop a granite cliff, a cluster of wood and stone buildings behind a high fortress wall. It was too far away to see clearly, but Uki thought he could make out wooden poles jutting from the battlements all around, some of which seemed to have things spiked on them. Rabbit-sized things.

'Keep yerselves nice and low in the boat,' called the captain. 'Don't want those Shrikeys up there to spot yer. Not unless yer fancy decorating a spike or two. Kether bedamned monsters, they are.'

He spat over the side as they sailed past. Uki and the others ducked low in the boat, keeping as silent as they could.

It wasn't long after that they sailed into another wide inlet. It had broad, sandy mudflats where birds of all shapes and sizes flapped and waded, and beyond it was the familiar sight of the marshes. The ship moored at a rickety wooden jetty, next to a tiny village of a few houses.

'This is Eelbury,' the captain said. 'Yer need to follow the road upriver until yer reach Enk. Can't miss it. Big place on stilts. Safe journey, and perhaps I'll have yer as passengers again soon.'

'Not turnipping likely,' Kree muttered under her breath, along with some words in Plains that sounded very rude.

The road was on a high earth bank that wove beside the edge of the salt marshes. By late afternoon they had made their way along it to Enk, which was indeed a 'big place on stilts'.

Jutting out above a broad lagoon, the town was

built on a platform raised up by many thick oak logs. Wooden houses clustered all over it, and at high tide the water must have lapped against the edge of the wharf. But the tide was low now and the place seemed to teeter in mid-air, a mirror of its houses and smoking chimneys reflected on the surface of the lagoon beneath.

They paused at the sight of it, knowing that it would be crawling with Shrike soldiers on the lookout for smugglers, and quite possibly them too.

'Can you remember where we're supposed to meet Granny Maggitch's friend?' Kree asked.

'Behind the Drunken Toad inn,' said Uki.

'The place looks very crowded,' said Jori. 'Perhaps we could just go around?'

'Can't,' said Coal. 'There's thick marshes on one side, the lagoon on the other. Besides, the only way across the Thorn river is the floating bridge, and that runs out of Enk.'

'We'd better just get on with it,' Uki said, swallowing his nerves. 'I'm sure we'll be fine.'

They walked into the town with no problems, although they did catch several glimpses of Shrike soldiers in their crimson armour amongst the traders and fisher-rabbits that thronged the narrow streets.

Enk was a squashed-up, claustrophobic place. Every scrap of space on the wooden platform was used. Buildings were tall and thin, with first and second floors jutting out further and further, jostling for position amongst all the other structures. The narrow streets in between, dingy from the lack of sunlight, were packed with market stalls and street sellers all shouting out their wares. It was a slow, cramped effort, getting from one side of town to the other. They pushed and squeezed, trying to fit Mooka through tiny gaps, all the while looking out for the sign of the Drunken Toad.

It was impossible to find. There were tailors, smiths, bakers, grocers and pawnbrokers. There were several inns – the Three Pikes, the Dragonfly Arms ('But dragonflies don't *have* arms,' Kree kept saying), the Drowned Badger – but no mention of a toad, drunken or not.

Eventually, they found themselves in the shadowy space at the back of three houses, hopelessly lost.

'Are you sure it was the Drunken Toad?' Kree

asked. 'Couldn't it have been the Tiddly Newt or the Hammered Frog?'

'We haven't seen those either,' Jori pointed out, casting a pointed glance at the blacksmith. 'Don't *you* know where it is, Coal? You're supposed to be our guide.'

'I've only passed through Enk a couple of times,' said Coal. 'I don't remember the names of any taverns. Granny did say it was near the waterfront . . .'

'Oh dear.' A voice came from the shadows between two buildings, followed by the sound of swords being drawn. 'Are we lost? Did my dearest cousin forget to bring her guide scroll?'

'Venic!' Jori leapt into a fighting stance, sword swishing from her sheath. Three grey-cloaked figures padded out into the alleyway. One was almost a mirror-image of Jori: her cousin, who had betrayed them back in Nys, before they had entered the Fenlands.

The other two were black-armoured Septys rabbits, their free paws resting on the dusk-potion flasks at their belts. Uki had been told Venic was searching for him, back when he was struggling against Charice's curse in the marshes. But so much had happened since then he'd forgotten all about it.

'I knew we'd run into each other again eventually.' Jori's cousin Venic had ice-blue eyes in contrast to her grey. He sneered at them all, the point of his sword moving between their faces. 'And it seems you've picked up a new friend to go with your collection of outcast ragamuffins.'

'Watch your tongue, boy.' Coal spoke with a growl, lifting his hammer-arm, ready to strike. Kree had drawn her adder-fang dagger. Uki pulled a spear from his harness. Both sides stared at each other, breath held, waiting for someone to make the first move.

Instead, there was a clattering noise, seeming to come from every direction at once. Before anyone could turn to face it, a squad of crimson-armoured Shrikes appeared, blocking every exit from the alley.

'What have we here?' One of the Shrikes spoke with a voice as mean and wheedling as Venic's. 'A bunch of brigands wanted for helping a known smuggler escape the Emperor's justice *and* three trespassing Septys agents. Must be our lucky day. I'm not sure we have enough spare spikes at Bloodthorn to fit you all. I hope some of you smaller ones won't mind sharing.'

Uki stared as the Shrike leader removed her helmet to reveal none other than Captain Needle, the rabbit who had scared him so much back at Reedwic.

Venic in front of them, Needle surrounding them . . . poisoned blades and spikes on every side. They were trapped, outnumbered and helpless.

*

Uki stepped backwards, bumping into Jori, Kree and Coal, who had all done the same. They were now squashed into an outward-facing circle around the trembling Mooka, staring at a wall of swords, spikes and spears.

'What do we do, Uki?' Jori whispered beside him. Her paw was resting on the flask of dusk potion at her belt. Would she have time to unclip it and drink? No, the Shrikes had shuffled even closer, the glistening barbs of their armour only a metre away.

Uki's mind raced. There were too many of them.

They were penned in. Could he use his strength somehow? Batter them an opening to run through?

Even if they escaped, they would still be lost in the cramped alleyways. It would only be a matter of time before they were caught again.

But that wasn't his only power now. He had Charice's too. He remembered how Jori had been exhausted by dusk potion. What if he could reverse that ... give her the speed of the mixture without even drinking it?

His senses reached out to her, feeling the flow of energy from the thousands and thousands of nerves and connections in her body. So many, so complex. It was like looking out at the wild sprays of stars in the night sky above the Blood Plains. He had no idea which ones to alter, where to make the right changes. What if he hurt his friend by mistake?

But he did remember what had happened to her *after* the potion. When her body was all used up and full of pain. If he could make everyone threatening them feel like that ... maybe they would have time to escape.

'Put your weapons down,' Needle was saying. 'If

you come quietly, we will make the spiking quick. Well, as quick as possible. We wouldn't want to spoil *all* the fun.'

While her guards were busy laughing, Uki closed his eyes and reached out. A field of energy spread from him, mapping the bodies of everyone in the alleyway. He could sense, without even looking, which rabbits were his enemies and which the familiar shapes of his friends. He could feel their breath, their heartbeats, the buzz of their thoughts, the blinks of their eyes.

Carefully, like his mother shaping clay with her clever paws, he began to mould the shape of Jori's dusk-drained body into each enemy. He sucked the strength from their muscles, the air from their lungs. He squeezed the blood vessels in their brains as tight as they would go. He made their hearts pound, their bones ache, their jaws clench until their teeth cracked.

He took the symptoms that had almost knocked Jori out and made them ten times worse, turning the rabbits' own bodies against them.

And then he opened his eyes again.

Every single rabbit surrounding them toppled to the floor.

The Shrikes clattered and rattled against each other. Venic and his men crumpled under their cloaks, swords tumbling out of their weakened paws. All of them lay, groaning and whining, clutching at their heads and stomachs in agony. And in the middle stood Uki and his friends, completely untouched.

'*Nam ukku ulla*,' Kree said. 'Uki, did *you* do that?'

'Charice's power,' Uki said, his voice almost a whisper. His friends were staring at him with horrified faces. Like he was some kind of monster. Like the rabbits in his tribe used to stare, just before they threw stones or screamed at him.

'I'm sorry,' he said. 'I didn't know ... I just wanted to stop them ...'

'Don't apologise,' said Coal. 'You've just saved our hides! What are we standing around for? Let's get out of here!'

Jori and Kree snapped back to themselves. They grabbed Uki's paws and turned to run. But just as they were starting to sprint down an alleyway, another rabbit blocked it, heading towards them.

'Not *again*,' said Jori. She drew her sword but, as the rabbit came closer, they could see she wasn't Shrike or Septys. Just an ordinary fen rabbit with a patched yellow cloak and a look of relief on her face.

'*There* you are,' she said, panting for breath. 'I been waiting for you at the Toad, but you didn't turn up. Then I saw a great posse of Spikers go running past and I figured they be after you.'

'Are you Granny Maggitch's friend?' Jori asked.

'Aye,' said the rabbit. 'And you need to come with me, hoppity-quick. I's got you a place on a caravan, heading south. But you have to go *now*.'

'We're ready,' said Coal. 'Show us the way.'

The fen rabbit turned and ran back down the alley with everyone close behind her. In and out of the buildings she wove, ducking under drying fishing nets and dodging market stalls. In a few minutes they were at the wooden wall that ran around the edge of the town.

As they paused for breath, Uki looked to his left, seeing the town gate further down. It was manned by at least six Shrikes checking everyone who went in or out. If they tried to leave through there, they'd be caught instantly.

'Don't worry,' said their guide. 'We's not going that way. There's a secret door here, if you'll help me push.'

She put her shoulder to the wall and began to shove. Uki joined her and the cracks of a doorway appeared in the thick wooden planks. It swung outwards, revealing the road outside and, beyond that, the open river. A cluster of wooden carts, each pulled by one or more rats, were gathered just beyond the door.

'By Gollop,' said the rabbit, staring at Uki. 'You're a strong one! Now listen quick – see that bunch of fellows there with the carts? That's a travelling show. My sister rides with them and they's said they'll take you as far as you want to go. You run across now and hide where they tells you. You've got to get across the floating bridge before you're safe from the Spikers.'

'Thank you,' Uki said. 'Thank you for helping us.'

'Any friend of Granny Maggitch is a friend of mine,' said the rabbit. 'And she'll be thanking me herself with a nice barrel or two of elderberry wine. Run now. Before them Shrikes see the door open!'

Before any more could be said, they dashed across the space between the town wall and the carts. When Uki looked back a second later, the door was already shut, as if it had never been there.

Then they were in amongst the carts and a crowd of new rabbits were greeting them.

*

There were three covered wagons, the canvases patched all over and every scrap of bare wood painted with splashes of colour – daisies, stars, butterflies. Sleek grey-furred rats stood between the traces, their bridles decorated with silk ribbons and posies of wildflowers. A strong-looking rabbit with a broad chest, thick beard and a topknot of hair was talking to them, casting wary glances over at the Shrikes by the Enk gate.

'Well met,' he said. 'My name is Cascade and this is our group of performers. The Greenwood Strollers is our name. There will be time for proper introductions later, but Minnow's sister tells us you need a quick getaway.'

'Yes, please,' said Uki. 'If it's not going to get you in any trouble.'

'We shall see,' said Cascade. 'But we can take care of ourselves, if it comes to that.'

Uki noticed the three daggers tucked into his belt and wondered if this group of performers were all that they seemed.

Cascade was speaking quickly, giving orders to the others. 'That jerboa of yours – fine beast, by the way – he can go in the traces with old Twilight there. He sticks out like a sore ear at the moment, but we'll put some saddle blankets over him. He should look like an ordinary rat when we've finished. Then you'd best get hidden in the caravans. The big fellow with the hammer can ride with me and Minnow, the children can burrow in amongst the puppets. Groff and Melodie will look after you.'

The Strollers listened carefully to his orders and then moved to obey them as soon as he had finished, more like soldiers than minstrels.

Two sandy-furred rabbits with enormous, dish-like ears led Mooka away, cooing and clucking to him. He was swiftly hitched up to their caravan behind a grey she-rat and draped with patchwork quilts and knitted blankets.

Coal was taken to the lead wagon by a bard rabbit with tattooed spirals on the inside of her ears and painted swirls on her fur. *That must be Minnow*, Uki thought, *the sister of the rabbit who helped us escape.*

Even as Coal was clambering aboard, two long-furred angoras were tugging at Uki's cloak, beckoning him to climb into their wagon. Jori and Kree were already inside, so Uki hopped after them, finding himself in a tent-like space that was crammed on all sides with puppets. String puppets, hand puppets, rolls of painted backdrops and bits and pieces of scenery. Carved, painted wooden heads stared at him with their lifeless eyes. Princesses, warriors, gods and goddesses from every tale Uki had ever heard, and more besides. There were badgers, weasels, frogs and snakes. Even winged dragons with golden scales and clouds of flaming breath. It was like stepping into a jumble of fairy tales. Like peeping inside the head of a dreaming bard.

'Quick, get hidden,' Jori hissed at him, as the

wagon juddered and began to move. The puppets nodded their heads and waved their arms as they rocked with the motion. It was as if they had all suddenly come to life at once.

Dodging dangling strings and spiked tails, Uki found a spot in between a fierce-looking forest rabbit with horns and an evil creature all covered with twisted iron. Its dull red eyes seemed to glare at him as he crouched in the shadows. He glared back, taking out one of his spears and clutching it ready, in case they were found by the Shrikes.

Next to Uki's head was a small hole in the canvas covering. He put his eye to it and peered outside.

The wagons had joined a queue of carts and pedestrians who were headed out of Enk. They followed a dirt road down to the river, where a large wooden raft was floating. Several rabbits were guiding everybody on to it, pointing and shouting as the deck gradually filled up. As they rolled down the bank, Uki spotted a pair of Shrike guards on the raft who seemed to be watching the whole process very carefully. The Strollers were the last to be loaded, just squeaking on to the edge of the floating platform.

One of the guards stepped up to the lead wagon and spoke to Cascade. Uki held his breath, just waiting for him to look inside and spot Coal. The other Shrike began to walk along the caravan, passing the disguised Mooka, then on to the puppet wagon. Finally he stopped, right by the hole Uki was peeking from.

Only a paw's breadth away, Uki could see the stitching on his crimson leather armour. The way his whiskers moved every time he breathed.

Don't look in the wagon, Uki silently prayed. *Please don't look inside.*

And then, back up the line, the first Shrike was laughing at something Cascade said. He stepped away and waved, before walking towards his comrade. The pair of guards hopped off the raft, leaving the bridge rabbits to begin hauling on the rope that would drag it across the river.

Uki let out his pent-up breath in a long sigh, and finally began to relax as the city of Enk grew smaller and smaller in the distance. They had escaped. They were on their way.

Chapter Three

Witherwitch

As the moon rose that night, they pulled up their caravans and camped by the roadside. They sat around a roaring fire with their hosts, eating a feast of flame-grilled parsnips, bubbling tomato and bramley apple soup and flagons of the finest honey mead.

After their victory and escape, the food tasted finer, the flames crackled brighter and their songs were merrier.

Cascade led them all in renditions of 'The Bard with the Bright Blue Ears', 'My Lovely Rat' and 'Fiddletwitch the Ploughman', while an old, brown-spotted rabbit strummed along on a lute. In between songs they spent a lot of time laughing and clapping each other on the back, going over their past adventures and their narrow escapes.

'You should have seen Uki's face when I popped up out of those maggots!' Kree kept shouting.

'And the look on Ma Gurdle's when I told her I was going to heal the Maggitches!' Uki added.

Jori shook her head and smiled. 'I can't believe we did it again. Twice now, we've squeaked our way through when we should have been doomed.'

'That's because we're unstoppable!' Kree whooped, dancing by the fire with a jug of sloshing mead in her paw. 'We're the unstoppable outcasts! Look out, Hulstland– we're invince-a-bubble!'

Coal, now firmly a part of the group, gave a chuckle. 'It's "invincible", pipsqueak. I think, perhaps, you've had too much mead.'

But Minnow the bard came to top up their flagons and start another song, leading the dancing on into the night.

And so it went on. Their time with the Greenwood

Strollers was the most carefree and relaxed of Uki's life so far. No mention was made of why the Shrikes had been looking for them. There were no demands for answers or payment or chores of any kind. Cascade and the others just accepted them as they might old friends or long-lost family.

They wandered leisurely along the road, stopping at each small warren to give performances. Great Deeping, Herongate, Larkswell ... and then the wagon turned south and started heading towards the vast mass of trees on the horizon that was Dunmurk Forest. And also – as if Uki was being guided by fate – towards the cold swell of pulsing evil that was Mortix.

The days were long and lazy and, to fill the hours, each of them found their own unique place within the troupe.

Kree liked to help groom and care for the Strollers' rats, along with Mooka. She walked alongside them as they pulled the wagons, led them to patches of juicy grass and dandelions when they paused to rest, and brushed their fur every evening. Karim and Naia, the two huge-eared rabbits who performed as 'Inferno', usually took care of the animals and were pleased to have some company.

Jori found that she liked to help Groff and Melodie, the puppeteers, with their creations. She sat for hours in the wagon, untangling strings, oiling squeaky joints and freshening up coats of paint on the tiny figures.

Coal and Cascade had struck up a friendship and, every chance he could, the wounded blacksmith stood by as the juggler practised throwing his knives, staring as they went up and up, ever higher, before tumbling down end-over-end, always just a whisker from chopping off his fingers.

And as for Uki, well, he just watched. Watched and enjoyed the quiet moments of not having anything to do. Nobody to save, nobody to fight and, best of all, nobody trying to kill him.

So it went on, life on the open road, until they came to the planted fields and hedgerows that told them a warren was near. Then they would start preparing for a performance.

The routine for each show was always the same. They would arrive in the morning or afternoon, and spend a few hours setting up the stage, with its painted backdrops, rows of lanterns and strings of bunting.

Then they would wander through the village or warren in costume, calling out the wonders that would be performed that evening, a crowd of small children following them like lost ducklings.

And, finally, there would come the show.

Uki loved this part most of all.

Minnow, the bard, would begin as soon as it grew dark, the twirling patterns on her fur lit in rainbow puddles of coloured light from the strings of paper lanterns, the bright stars twinkling in the sky above, as if they were watching too.

She would start with a tale: 'Beobunny' or 'The Fisher Rabbit', perhaps, or a legend about Lord Bandylegs. Clave, the musician, played along on his lute or panpipes, matching the mood, occasionally breaking into a flurry of notes whenever Minnow paused for breath.

Next came Cascade with his juggling act, sending knives and flaming torches soaring up into the air in spirals. Another tale or poem, and then Melodie

and Groff would send their puppets on to the stage to act out an epic adventure – 'Sir Bracken and the Dragon' was a favourite. Or the one about the three young rabbits who fought off the monstrous Gorm.

To finish, Karim and Naia stepped up with their fire-eating, sword-swallowing, stilt-walking extravaganza. The night sky would be filled with blazes of light, echoing with whoops and cheers from the audience. As the applause went on, Uki, Jori and Kree would go out with pots and buckets to collect coins.

The best thing about that bit, Uki thought, were the masks they had to wear. Carved wooden faces, painted in gaudy, vivid colours. Dragons, fierce badgers and wolves.

Nobody could see him underneath. Nobody knew he was Uki. He was just a blue-scaled monster or a long-nosed fox. Two eyes peeping through cut-out holes.

It made him feel unknown, safe from all the forces that hunted him. And, because nobody could see his fur, he could have been the same as any other rabbit. Ordinary. Normal. A simple child – one without the fate of the whole Five Realms resting on his shoulders. It was like having a holiday from being himself.

But, as we all know, holidays don't last.

*

The further they went from the Fenlands, the worse Uki began to feel. It was just a niggling uneasiness at first, but it grew and grew into a black cloud of a mood that seemed to follow him, even when he was doing things that had previously made him feel happy.

His dark voice didn't help, of course. That tiny part of Uki that always nagged and whispered every worry, every fear. Long ago, back when he was a bullied scrap of a rabbit in the Ice Wastes, he had given it a name. At the time he remembered thinking, *My fur is split in two halves, so why shouldn't everything else be?* Now it was always there, ready to ruin any pleasure he might get with its negative moaning.

It came to a head one afternoon, while the Strollers were pulled up for a break by the roadside and the others were busy with their chores.

Uki would have liked to make himself useful too,

but his bleak mood wouldn't let him. He couldn't help worrying about the last part of his task: capturing the final spirit. That and what had happened back in Enk with the Shrikes.

He sat by the roadside, looking at a small stream that babbled past. There were clusters of reeds along it, and it reminded him of the fens. Made him think about his time there, and how the place would now be healing over – carrying on with the slow rhythms of life, just as it had before.

If only *he* could spring back so quickly.

The last spirit, his dark voice kept telling him. **Mortix, she's the worst yet. The toughest, the sneakiest, the deadliest. How can you hope to defeat her? How can you keep your friends safe from her clutches?**

Uki knew it was true. He had Iffrit's memories of her when she was trapped in the prison crystal: a small, thatched cottage on a bare island under that endless pink sky. How the fire guardian would fly above, looking down on the thin, veiled figure below and feel a shudder of unease. If she scared Iffrit himself, what chance would *he* have?

And then there were his new powers. It had felt good to heal the Maggitches with them, but when he hurt those rabbits in Enk . . .

You're just as bad as Charice was, his dark voice kept saying. Uki shuddered. He knew it was right. Using his powers to hurt other rabbits . . . he felt as though he had betrayed himself somehow.

'A carrot for your thoughts?' There was a rustle from behind, as Jori came striding through the grass to sit beside him.

'Oh,' said Uki. 'You wouldn't want them. They're a bit . . . dark.'

'What are you worrying about? The next spirit?'

Uki nodded. 'That and what happened back in Enk.'

'When you crushed those rabbits that were about to kill us? You saved us all, Uki.'

'I know. But I still feel bad about it. I don't think my power should be used that way.'

Jori plucked a purple clover from amongst the grass and began tweaking out the petals, sucking the sugary nectar from the bottom of each before flicking them into the stream, where they whirled away like miniature boats. She was silent for a good few minutes before she cleared her throat and spoke.

'Then don't do it again,' she said. 'It's as simple as that. Make yourself a vow. That's what I did. I know three hundred and forty-two different mixtures of plants that can kill a rabbit stone dead. Melting your stomach, boiling your blood, making your skin fall off . . . I can do it all. But I've promised myself never to use any of it. I want to help rabbits, not bury them. You can choose to do the same.'

A choice. Uki hadn't thought of it like that. And he'd never considered how Jori might look upon her past training either. He nodded, feeling at least part of the weight on him begin to lift.

'By the Goddess,' he said, 'I swear never to use Charice's power to hurt another rabbit. Only to heal. And I also promise not to eat any more of Jori's cooking.'

As Jori laughed and pretended to punch him, Kree came wandering over. She plopped herself down next to them.

'Those performing rabbits,' she said. 'They have some amazing stories to tell. Did you know they once travelled around Gotland fighting evil creatures made of iron? And then their two best fighters were kidnapped and they had to leave. Amazing.'

'I wouldn't believe everything they tell you,' said Jori. 'They are all actors, you know.'

'And fire-eaters and jugglers . . . What an exciting life to have! I think I might teach Mooka some tricks and join them. After we finish our quest, that is.'

'Yes,' said Uki. 'The quest.'

'Uki is feeling anxious about the next task,' said Jori. 'I'm trying to convince him he's being dumb.'

'*Nam ukku ulla,* of course he is!' Kree reached over and gave one of Uki's ears a tug. 'Why are you worried? You have us beside you! And that ugly lump, Coal. We've captured three spirits already! We've beaten Endwatchers, *two* clans, snakes, plagues and a whole ocean of disgusting maggots. We're amazing!'

'But Mortix . . .' Uki began.

Jori stopped him with a paw on his arm. 'It doesn't matter, Uki. However tough or strong she is, we will beat her. All of us together. We're family now, remember?'

'Yes, I remember,' Uki said, feeling a warm glow spread through him. 'Family.'

*

His spirits had begun to lift again after that. At least until they got to Witherwitch, the last warren before the southern road was swallowed up by the shadows of Dunmurk Forest. It sat on a low hill by the roadside, surrounded by fields of ripening wheat and corn.

'There's only about thirty rabbits in the place,' Cascade had grumbled, as the wagons crawled along the dusty road towards it. 'Maybe we should just push on. The city of Eisenfell is just on the other side of the trees.'

'We might as well stop,' Minnow had urged. 'It'll take us two days to travel through the forest, and we need to buy supplies. Besides, we had a good turnout last time we were here, remember?'

Uki sat between them on the riding board of the wagon, listening in. He silently hoped they did stop. The sense of Mortix was growing ever stronger and he knew she couldn't be far from the edge of Dunmurk. Maybe in Eisenfell itself. This might be his last chance to see the troupe perform. His last chance to be the secret, masked rabbit before his quest had to continue.

'Oh, all right, then,' said Cascade, shaking his bearded head. 'But you have to buy us a jug of elderberry ale each afterwards, right Uki?'

Uki laughed, or at least tried to. There was an ominous aura about the tiny warren. Worrying. As if the place was a bad omen.

Stop being silly, he told himself. *You've been listening to your dark voice too much lately. You're starting to sound like it yourself.*

Still, he couldn't shake the feeling and, as they pulled into the village, it only got worse.

*

'This place doesn't feel right,' Jori said, as they began unpacking the wagons and building the stage. Uki gave her a look, wondering whether she had picked up the same hunch as he had.

'I know,' said Kree, helping them lift down a piece of rolled-up scenery. 'But I can't work out what it is. That forest over there? All dark and gloomy?'

'No,' said Uki, who found the sight of the endless bank of trees soothing, inviting. 'It's the warren. It seems . . . too *quiet*.'

'That's it!' said Jori, looking around. 'Where are the children?'

Uki looked too, and noticed that the troupe were all alone in the village square. Usually there would be a gaggle of young rabbits standing nearby, watching their every move, bubbling with excitement. He could only see one hunched rabbit shuffling past with a basket of turnips. Apart from that, every door was closed, every window shuttered.

They were just about to help Groff and Melodie unload their puppets, when an elderly rabbit with a wispy grey beard hobbled over to them and cleared his throat.

'Greetings!' Cascade strode up to him, holding out one of his broad paws in welcome. 'You're the mayor here, aren't you? I remember from the last time we visited.'

'Yes, yes. Mayor Runce,' said the old rabbit, as Cascade took his paw in an iron grip and pumped it up and down. 'But I'm afraid there's no point in you performing here tonight. I thought I'd better tell you before you unpack all your things.'

'No point?' Cascade frowned down at the frail mayor with a gaze that made him wince. 'Are you saying we aren't welcome in your warren?'

'No! Not at all!' The mayor flattened his ears in worry and waved his paws in the air, close to tears. 'We had a wonderful time at your last performance. It was magical, truly … it's just that … well … there's nobody here to watch you.'

The Strollers looked around the silent warren with its closed-up houses and burrows. 'Nobody?' Uki said, a sick feeling beginning to bubble in his throat. 'But where have they all gone?'

'Left,' said the mayor, and this time he really did cry, silent tears running into his beard. 'All but ten of us who are too old to walk. They packed up in ones and twos and headed north. Now the place is like a ghost warren.'

'But why?' Jori asked. 'This seems like a nice, quiet spot. The fields are full of crops. Why would they leave?'

'Ask *them*,' said the mayor. He pointed towards

the forest where a large group of rabbits had appeared, trudging along the road from Eisenfell, passing close to the village itself. When they turned back to the mayor to ask him what he meant, he had wandered off, heading back to his lonely longburrow.

'Well, bless my juggling clubs, this is strange,' said Cascade.

Uki watched the group of walking rabbits as they came closer. There were thirty or more and he could now see they were pushing handcarts laden with everything they owned. The adults carried sacks stuffed with possessions on their backs, struggling under the weight.

'It looks like they're running from something,' he said. **Mortix**, added his dark voice. **You know very well it's her they are fleeing.**

'Maybe we should take the mayor's advice and ask them,' said Jori.

'Good idea,' Cascade nodded. 'And while you're at it, see if you can persuade them to come and see a show. We could use the coin.'

The Strollers sat themselves down on their half-built stage to wait as Uki and his friends walked over to the road and the crowd of laden refugees. As they got closer, Uki could see the looks on their faces. They all bore the same expression: sad, tired … *beaten.* As if all hope had been stolen from them.

What has Mortix done? he wondered. *How can it be worse than Charice and her plagues?*

The first rabbits he came to were an old couple, pushing a handcart full of freshly made clay pots. Jars of glaze teetered in stacks on top, and the man had a wooden potter's wheel tied to his back with lashings of twine. Usually, Uki found it difficult to speak to strangers without even being introduced, but there was something familiar about these two. Especially the woman. The shape of her eyes, the way she held her ears … Uki felt as though he almost knew them.

'Um … excuse me,' he said, waving a paw.

The pair stopped in the road, the potter taking the chance to mop his brow with a clay-stained kerchief, pulled from a pocket. The other walkers shuffled around them and kept on moving, even as Uki, Coal and Kree walked amongst them, asking questions of their own.

'Yes?' said the lady. 'How can we help you?'

'I was just wondering why you and these other rabbits are walking this way?' Uki asked. 'And why are you carrying all your things?'

'We come from Eisenfell,' said the potter, as if that was an answer.

'Yes,' Uki continued. 'But what … I mean to say … *why* are you all leaving? What happened there?'

The pair blinked at each other for a moment, before looking back to Uki. 'Kether count and preserve us,' said the woman. 'Where have you been for the last few months? Haven't you heard what has happened?'

'No,' said Uki, confused. 'I've been in the Fenlands. And before that, in the north. I haven't heard any news about Eisenfell.'

The potter huffed in disbelief and shook his ears. 'Then you should think yourself lucky, young lad. The place has become a living nightmare. Anyone with half a brain is leaving. We're off to Gotland, where we came from originally. Now that the Gorm have gone, the place is a hundred times safer than here.'

'Eran, you old fool, the boy wants to know what's happened to the city, not our life history. You're confusing him.' The potter rolled his eyes and went back to mopping his brow as his wife continued talking. 'It's Emperor Ash,' she said. 'He's gone bad. Claims he's become a god now. The God of Death, if you please. He's turned all the guards and soldiers into some kind of army. Breathless, he calls them.'

'Deathless,' corrected her husband, rolling his eyes again.

'Whatever. Anyway, he's declared *himself* the new religion – would you believe it – and has got all the clan lords in Eisenfell to follow him. Worshipping Kether is against the law now. As is singing, dancing, feasting, and just about everything else you can imagine. And if you so much as whimper in disagreement . . . well, nobody ever sees you again.'

'Hundreds have vanished,' said the potter. 'Smiths and carpenters, mostly. One morning they're there, the next their houses are empty.'

'So many of our friends . . .' said the woman and began to sob into her apron.

'I'm sorry,' said Uki. 'I didn't mean to upset you.'

'It's not your fault, poppet.' The woman dried her eyes and gave a sniff. 'But if you're with that acting troupe there, you had best turn around and run for the hills. They'll be snaffled as soon as they set foot in Eisenfell.'

'Shame,' said the potter. 'I love a good puppet show, I do.'

'I'll tell them,' said Uki. 'Thank you for your time.'

The potter nodded, and his wife ruffled Uki's ears as they carried on their way. The rest of the crowd had all passed by, and Uki could see his friends standing a bit further up the road, waiting for him.

Before he even got to them, Kree began jumping up and down.

'Did you hear the same thing we did?' she squeaked. 'It's Mortix, isn't it? It has to be! The spirit has taken over Emperor Ash himself!'

'I don't know why you're so excited about it,' said Jori. 'It means we somehow have to attack the Emperor of Hulstland. The most powerful, well-protected rabbit in the whole of the Five Realms.'

Uki had begun to feel the same wave of dread. 'Yes, it must have taken Ash. Or the God of Death, as Mortix wants him to be called. Is he really that difficult to get to?'

'The Ash I knew was,' said Coal. 'From what I just heard, though, it's going to be even harder now. Sounds like he has layers upon layers of guards. The clan lords, his elite soldiers. Even the old Eisenfell City Watch. He seems to have turned them into something much more sinister.'

'I found out much the same,' said Jori. 'The city has been transformed into a giant fortress, the inhabitants its prisoners. Anyone who breaks the new decrees gets dragged off. Nobody knew exactly what happened to them.'

'Vanished,' said Kree. 'That's what I was told. Anyone who so much as sung a bedtime lullaby to their young ones.'

'That doesn't bode well for the Strollers, then,' said Coal. 'We'd best tell them not to go near the place. Looks like our days as performers are well and truly over.'

Uki sighed. He had known it would finish soon, but

he'd expected a few more days of the travelling life. Rolling through the forest on the wagons, looking up at the leaves. A happy farewell on the road beyond as they followed on the spirit's trail. Now it sounded as though Mortix was almost untouchable. A powerful god-emperor locked inside an impenetrable fortress.

With heavy feet, they walked back to the Strollers to break the news.

*

Cascade and the others were as horrified as Uki had been. The looks of fear and dread on their faces matched those of the refugees.

'The mayor was right, then,' said Minnow. 'We should pack up and leave.'

'Gotland sounds very attractive right now,' said Groff.

'Then maybe on to Enderby after,' added Karim. 'Silverock mead and Applecross cider.'

'Anywhere but here,' said Melodie. 'If folk are leaving their homes behind now, it's only going to get worse.'

Cascade nodded his head, fixing Uki and the others with a long, serious stare.

‘I’ve never asked why you fellows have been travelling with us,’ he said. ‘Or even where it is you’re going to. But I’ve got a feeling you’re heading straight for the place that everyone else wants to escape.’

‘We are,’ said Uki, after getting a nod from Jori. ‘At first we were just heading south. But now we know our destination. We’re going to Eisenfell.’

‘And I suppose,’ said Cascade, ‘that there’s nothing I can do or say that would change your minds?’

‘There isn’t.’

The burly juggler puffed air from his cheeks and shook his head. ‘It’s none of our business where you go or what you do, I suppose. But we Strollers have grown fond of you. We wouldn’t want to see you come to harm. Not if we can stop it.’

‘We can take care of ourselves,’ said Jori.

‘*Bulu Jibba!*’ said Kree. ‘Even Emperor Ash – or whatever he calls himself now – should be scared of us!’

Cascade laughed. ‘I’m sure of that. But you will be careful, won’t you? And if there’s anything we can do to help . . .’

'Actually,' said Uki, 'there might be.' His mind had been racing all the while the others were talking. If Eisenfell had indeed become a deathly fortress, they would need a way to get in. And the Strollers seemed like the sort of rabbits who might know about that.

'I don't suppose,' he said, 'that you'd know a secret entrance to Eisenfell? A trick to getting in unseen, that is?'

'I suppose I might,' said Cascade. And he tried to smile, although it came out as more of a grimace. One already filled with regret.

*

Cascade knew a rabbit named Locke, a boatbuilder at the docks just outside the city walls. Part of the same smuggling network that Granny Maggitch used, he had access to secret tunnels. If they could follow the river and get to the docks without being seen, Uki and the others would be able to get inside the city without having to go through any of the gates.

After Uki and Jori had carefully memorised Cascade's instructions, the Strollers invited them to spend one last night together. A farewell party, of sorts, although nobody was much in a festive mood.

Still, they ate corn bread and baked potatoes and drank the last of their honey mead together. Clave played along on his flute, and Kree even danced on the half-built stage as Mooka, her jerboa, looked on, making quiet *neek* noises of encouragement. Coal stomped along, trying his best to keep up as his crutch got tangled with his good leg, much to Kree's amusement.

One or two of the old rabbits who had remained in Witherwitch came out to watch, and Cascade, Karim and Naia did a spot of fire eating and juggling for them. They even earned a few copper fenkles.

But for Uki and Jori, it was a very bittersweet evening. Neither of them had grown up with many friends or much to celebrate. It made them appreciate moments of warmth and happiness like this all the more, but at the same time filled them with sadness at the thought of losing them.

'Do you think we might find the Strollers again, after all this is over?' Uki said, as the pair sat amongst a jumble of puppets beside the stage, sipping their mugs of mead.

'Maybe,' said Jori. 'That would be nice, wouldn't

it?' But there had been a pause before she answered. One filled with all the worry that Uki felt himself.

'I know what you're thinking,' he said. 'There's a good chance we won't succeed. Or even if we do, some of us might not survive.'

Jori gave him one of her dark looks before nodding. 'I don't like thinking of pleasant futures for myself. It's hard when you have a clan of assassins hunting you. My family still want me dead, don't forget. And besides, this spirit is going to be different from the last two, Uki. They were hard enough, but the Emperor of Hulstland . . .'

'What makes him worse than the mayor that Valkus controlled?' Uki asked. 'He was an important person. He had guards and things around him.'

Jori laughed. 'Syn was a tiny place. I know it seemed big to you, but compared to Eisenfell it was just a scrappy wooden fort with a handful of rabbits in it. The city is another thing entirely.'

'In what way? Surely, it's just like a bigger version of Syn, isn't it?'

'It's nothing like it.' Jori drew her sword and began to sketch in the mud at her feet with its point.

A squiggle that might be a stream and a small circle next to it. 'Although it might have been similar, nearly six hundred years ago. Before the meteor struck. It came out of the sky and landed close by the river Hul. Made a crater as deep as a mountain, with the great lump of rock and sky iron in the centre.'

She added a bigger circle around it. 'The chieftain of the nearest tribe was called Cinder. He quickly claimed the land surrounding the crater and built a warren there. Then he discovered how to use the metal from the meteor to forge steel. After that, there was no stopping him. He became king, then emperor, spreading his lands further and further until he controlled all of Hulstland itself.'

'So, the emperor is powerful,' said Uki. 'The people Valkus and Charice controlled were too, in their way.'

'Not power like *this*,' said Jori. 'Since Cinder, each emperor has built Eisenfell bigger, using their steel tools to cut and carve stone. They've stacked the place higher and higher, one layer on top of the other. There's nowhere else like it in the whole Five Realms.

'And as the city has grown stronger, so have the rabbits that rule it. The clans that surround Emperor Ash are rich and powerful, and all they care about is getting even *more* money, even *more* power. Each clan has its own small army; the emperor has his Elite Guard; the city has its Watch . . . there's troop after troop of danger, all blocking our path to the emperor.'

Uki's mind reeled, trying to imagine it. It was a universe away from the paltry village of huts he grew up in. 'Is there anyone else in Eisenfell except soldiers and builders? It doesn't sound like there could be.'

'Well, you just saw some of them,' said Jori. 'Rabbits flock there from all over. The city draws them in with the hope of a better life, more money . . . or just a chance to see wonders like the cathedral and Embervale Palace.'

'Have you seen those places?' Uki asked.

Jori nodded. 'I've visited court twice before, with my father.' At the mention of his name, Jori shuddered. 'I wasn't very old. I just remember ceilings higher than the sky. Stone columns everywhere, like cold, dead trees. And windows full of coloured glass . . .'

Uki stared into space, trying to imagine it. It was the perfect place for Mortix to plant herself, to grow her power. But what was her plan? Why make the emperor declare himself a god and drive everyone away from the city?

Whatever it is, he thought, *it can't be anything good. We have to stop her, no matter what stands in our way.*

'Uki?' Jori tapped him on the shoulder, bursting his bubble of thoughts. 'I've been thinking. Do you have any idea where Necripha is in all this? You said she'd mentioned Mortix when you were in that pit. Do you think she could have had a paw in what's happened?'

Uki shrugged and shuddered. The shrivelled old witch-rabbit with her three eyes. She was really a leftover from the Ancients as well: a guardian of knowledge who had once been a sister to Gormalech and the others. Her thirst for secrets had made her start the Endwatch. Now she and her spies watched from the shadows, waiting for the moment they could seize power for themselves.

Uki had a connection to her, thanks to his own bond with Iffrit. It meant he could sometimes see through her eyes, although the visions were always horrible and disturbing.

'I know you don't like to use the link,' Jori pressed, 'but it might give us a clue. At least we would know whether we have to worry about her as well.'

Uki shuddered. 'I suppose I could try,' he said.

Jori nodded and looked at him expectantly. Realising he didn't have much choice, Uki closed his eyes and began to focus, reaching for the invisible cords that joined him to his enemy.

Straight away he could sense Mortix. Closer now than ever, and with the other spirits trapped in their crystals, her presence blazed in his mind. It was cold and dark. An icy void, an emptiness. Not a scrap of life or emotion – so alien to everything Uki loved and cherished that he almost turned away in terror.

No, he told himself. *Forget Mortix. You need to find Necripha. She'll be here, too, somewhere.*

Sure enough, as he looked closer, he spotted a purple thread, almost lost behind the glaring presence of Mortix. Necripha. He recognised the feel of it from his encounters with the three-eyed rabbit. It seethed with bitterness, greed, spite. Gritting his teeth, he forced his mind to follow it, seeking out its owner . . .

A familiar flash of pain jolted through Uki's head and he toppled forwards, clutching at his temple. Snippets of visions passed before his eyes: a great chair that gleamed like silver on a tall platform; rows of rabbits with blank metal faces, bladed spears held in their paws; a building like a mountain range, spires higher than treetops; and a flag, a ball of white flame with a black heart in the centre . . .

'Why, hello, my young friend. My saviour.'

The voice echoed in his head, even as the flashes of vision faded. Uki had connected with Necripha before, but this time it felt different. Wrong. Like she was inside *his* head, instead of the other way around. He could feel her, burrowing behind his eyes – an itching, burning, maggoty sensation.

'Trying to spy on me, are you? Using our secret bond to get some clues?'

Uki squirmed, trying to break free of the link, to throw Necripha out of his head. He could feel her there, like a worm in an apple, writhing about, digging through all his thoughts and secrets.

'Well, it won't work any more. I've made a new friend and she's shown me a trick or two. I can tell when you're peeking through my eyes now, and I know how to stop it. I can even take a little look through yours. *Let's see . . . where are you? Near the forest? And what's this . . . puppets? How sweet . . .'*

'How . . .? How are you doing this?' Uki managed to force the words out, even though his head felt like there was a thunderstorm boiling inside.

'I told you. I have a new friend. I'm sure you'll see her soon. She's dying *to meet you . . .'*

Uki heard the horrid cackle of laughter, and then Necripha's presence was gone. His head was blissfully empty, his nose full of the smell of dry earth and sawdust. At some point he had toppled over and was now lying on the ground amongst the puppets, with Jori bending over him.

'Uki! Uki! Are you all right? Who were you talking to?'

He sat up with a groan, feeling like he had just been kicked by a jerboa. 'It was Necripha. I think she's in Eisenfell already. Is there a big chair there? Made of metal?'

'The Cinderthrone,' said Jori. 'Yes, in the palace.'

'Then she's with Mortix.' Just saying the words made Uki's stomach sink. 'And she's told her all about us. They know we're coming. They'll know what I look like.'

He half expected Jori to shout or curse, but instead she narrowed her eyes. She looked over to where Kree and Coal were dancing and cheering with the rest of the Strollers, oblivious to what had just happened.

'More rabbits looking for us,' she muttered. 'We must be the most hunted creatures in the Five Realms.'

'What are we going to do, Jori?' Seeing the worry on his friend's face made Uki's fears surge. He could almost hear his dark voice laughing at him.

Jori forced a smile, trying to bring back her usual rock-solid calm and confidence. 'Relax,' she said. 'It's not like this is anything new for us, is it? We'll just have to hope Cascade's smuggler friend is good at their job.'

Uki nodded. He turned to watch the singing and dancing too, sensing it might be the last carefree moment they would know for a long while. And wishing, just wishing, he could follow the Strollers west in the morning instead of walking into Mortix and Necripha's web.

Chapter Four

Goodbye, Mooka

They parted at dawn, clasping hands with each of the Strollers in turn and watching as their caravans rolled north, off to the pass that would lead them through to Gotland.

'Ukku neekneek bu!' said Kree. 'Part of me wishes we were going with them.'

There was an awkward silence, as everyone agreed with her but didn't want to say it. Instead, they turned south and faced the deep-green cloud of trees that was Dunmurk Forest.

'This is it, then,' said Kree.

'Yes, this is it,' agreed Coal.

Uki pulled his cloak hood over his head, making sure his ears were tucked inside. They were still a long way from Eisenfell, but he couldn't shake the feeling he was being watched.

'Do you really think they'll be searching for us out here?' Kree asked, looking around her with nervous eyes.

'Who knows?' said Coal. 'But if Uki's right, and this Necripha knows we're coming . . . well, we're not a hard bunch to spot.'

'There's plenty of trees to hide in up ahead,' said Jori. 'But we will have to be careful when we reach Eisenfell. There will be many eyes looking for us. Guards, imperial agents, Endwatch spies . . . maybe members of Clan Septys, too. Hoods and cloaks for everyone.'

'Maybe I should . . .' Uki began, but Kree interrupted him.

'If you're going to suggest going alone again, you had better stop right there,' she said. 'We're in this together, remember? And never mind Jori worrying about everything. Just remember all the amazing feats we have done!'

Uki nodded, filled with yet another swell of gratitude for having such friends.

Jori took a deep breath, steeling herself, and gave his shoulder a squeeze. 'A journey of a thousand miles begins with a single hop,' she said.

Uki looked up at her, nodded, and they set off, into the forest.

*

Dunmurk was mostly filled with oak trees, each one probably hundreds of years old, with trunks wider than his old village hut. Their wide branches reached out, twining over each other above, but leaving wide areas of space on the forest floor.

It was unlike any other woodland Uki had been in. The air was filled with a soft, green light, and you could see far into the depths where herds of deer ran, squirrels scampered and birds swooped and chattered. News about the God of Death clearly hadn't reached the forest animals. The place was full of them, chirping, cooing and scuttling about in their tree-filled world.

The road south was wide and well used, with deep ruts from thousands of cartwheels passing up and down. Clearings were dotted along the way for camping. Some even had troughs for rats (and jerboas) and neat piles of chopped firewood that thoughtful travellers had left for those following them.

'How long will it take us to get through the forest?' Uki asked Coal after they had been walking all morning.

Coal scratched the torn stump of one of his burnt ears. 'At this pace . . . around three days, I should think. It's a big old patch of trees, you know.'

'And quiet too,' said Jori, nibbling her lip. 'Don't you think we should have bumped into someone by now? Traders or merchants at least, surely?'

'That we should,' said Coal. 'It's starting to get me worried.'

Uki hadn't mentioned it but he was worried as well. He swore he could feel the air growing colder with every step he made towards Eisenfell, but he didn't know if that was just his imagination playing tricks on him.

But Dunmurk wasn't completely deserted. Late afternoon on the first day, they saw another group fleeing north. Kree spotted them in the distance, when they were just a moving shadow between the trees. This time, rather than talk to them, they left the road and hid deeper in the forest, waiting for them to pass.

They looked just as hopeless and beaten as the rabbits they had seen at Witherwitch, dragging what few belongings they could carry as they escaped. Uki wondered just how bad things must be to flee the place you had been born, had lived in for all your days. Even though life in his village had been close to unbearable, it was only when he and his mother were in real danger of being killed that they had finally run.

Just how terrible is it in Eisenfell? he wondered. *What kind of nightmare are we walking into?*

Someone else passed them during the second night of camping. They were in a clearing beside the road, sleeping next to their fire after a supper of mashed chickpeas and grilled mushrooms. Kree had sung them to sleep with a Plains lullaby, and Uki had taken the first watch. He had been awake about an hour, looking up through the trees at the lonely stars above and trying to spot constellations he knew, when he heard the unmistakeable scuff of footsteps on the road.

His first thought was of the Endwatch, sending their agents out to spy on him. Then he thought it might be Venic, Jori's cousin, or Captain Needle of the Shrikes. Finally, he wondered if it might be the giant horned rabbits that haunted the forest – a half-remembered legend his mother used to tell him.

Look at you, scared out of your fur, his dark voice whispered. **Have you forgotten that you've got powers the gods themselves would kill for? You could squash a giant rabbit and use its horns as toothpicks. How can you expect to lead the others when you don't use the gifts you've been given?**

Powers. Of course. Uki remembered the new talent he had gained from Charice. The ability to sense living things all around him. He reached out with it now, tracing the invisible threads of the forest creatures. The sleeping forms of his friends, lost in their dreams; Mooka, curled up next to Kree; roosting birds, slumbering squirrels. Even teeming patches of life amongst the roots that must be nests of ants or bees.

And there, on the road, two figures walking. He

could *see* them even in the dark, like glowing, rabbit-shaped beacons of light. And he could also sense what they were feeling: hearts pumping, adrenaline surging, every muscle tense with fear.

They were young, too, maybe the same age as him. Travelling by night so they wouldn't be seen, trying to get as far away as possible from whatever terrors pursued them.

Uki relaxed and sat silently as they passed. Calling out might only scare them more, even if it was just to offer them some leftover mushrooms and a warm place to sleep. Instead, he whispered a quick prayer to the goddess to keep them safe, then returned to watching the smouldering embers of the campfire.

*

It was only as Uki and his friends neared the edge of the forest that they saw something truly frightening.

On the afternoon of their third day of walking, Mooka's ears suddenly pricked up. Kree spotted it and called back to them. 'Somebody's coming, up ahead!'

Uki reached out with his senses, picking up a creature – big, slow and stupid.

'It's a rat, I think. But I can't sense anyone riding it. Are there wild rats in the forest?'

'Not that I've ever heard of,' said Coal. 'Perhaps we had better get off the road again.'

As quickly as they could, they headed into the trees, deep enough to be hidden from the road, but close enough to see what was approaching.

Crouching behind tree trunks and bushes, they peered back at the track they had just left, with Kree trying her best to keep Mooka quiet. It wasn't long before they could hear the scrabbling of claws and the rat appeared – it definitely wasn't a wild specimen.

The beast was saddled and bridled and covered in studded leather armour. A caparison of black cloth was draped over its body, edged with white embroidery and a flaming white star. It was a military rat – a beast used by a soldier of Eisenfell.

But the thing that made Uki tremble in fear was its rider.

A rabbit, dressed in black leather armour, with a blank, featureless steel helmet completely covering its face: no eyes, no mouth. It clutched the reins of the rat in one paw, and the other rested on the handle of its sheathed sword.

As the pair passed them by, Uki could see the rider turning its head from side to side, scanning the forest, searching.

'Are we far back enough?' Kree whispered. 'Is it going to spot us?'

'I don't think so,' said Jori, although her own paws had gone to her sword and the flask at her belt. 'At least, I hope not.'

'How can it even see?' whispered Coal. 'There's no eye slits in that helmet. Just blank metal . . .'

Uki didn't even hear them. He was straining with his new senses, trying to read the life source of the rider. The rat was there, gleaming brightly, as were he and his friends. But the rider was a complete blank. It didn't show up in his mind's eye at all.

As if – even though he could see it moving – as if the rabbit were actually dead.

*

They stayed hidden amongst the trees until the rider had passed, then waited a while longer, just in case.

Sure enough, they saw the rat return the way

it had come, disappearing down the road towards Eisenfell.

'Patrols,' said Jori. 'And they were looking for somebody. If that was indeed an Eisenfell guard, we were lucky it didn't spot us. They are not rabbits you want to mess with.'

'Was it searching for us, do you think?' Uki asked. He had kept his discovery about the rider being dead to himself for the time being. At least until he understood what it meant.

'Could be. Or maybe they're just looking for rabbits that have escaped. If folk keep leaving the city, soon there'll be nobody left there except soldiers.'

Coal grunted. 'Either way, I think we should probably disguise ourselves from here on in. Just to be on the safe side.'

They all pulled their hoods over their heads and tied their cloaks tight around them. Jori hid her flask under her jerkin and Kree – after much sulking – agreed to wash off her red stripes of fur paint.

'But what about Mooka?' she said, once she had been thoroughly scrubbed and cleaned. 'I can't hide the fact he's a jerboa. Will he stand out in Eisenfell?'

'Afraid so,' said Coal. 'I can't recall seeing a single one the whole time I was there.'

'Nor I,' said Jori. 'And don't forget, this particular creature is quite easy to spot.' She pointed to his missing tail.

'I think I might have an idea,' said Coal. 'But the pint-sized shouty one isn't going to like it.'

'*Nam ukku ulla!* I definitely am *not* going to like anything *he* suggests!' Kree stood in front of Mooka, hands on her hips, while the jerboa blinked his big, dark eyes up at Coal.

'Maybe we should hear the idea first?' Uki suggested.

'It's nothing bad,' said Coal. 'There's a farmer who lives just outside the city. I stopped at her place once or twice when I was a travelling blacksmith and did some odd jobs for her. She's very nice. She keeps a few rats in a stable ... perhaps we could leave Mooka there?'

'No!' Kree shouted, throwing her arms around Mooka's neck. 'Where I go, Mooka goes!'

‘That’s actually not a bad idea,’ said Jori. ‘The city won’t be much fun for him, and at least he’ll be safe.’

‘And,’ Coal added, ‘we’re likely to be sneaking around in some pretty tight spots, especially if these friends of Cascade are smugglers. Mooka won’t be able to fit down tunnels or climb rooftops.’

Uki watched as Coal spoke softly to Kree, gently explaining his plan, making it clear that there was no choice. He knew just the right words and exactly how to say them. **Now that’s what a *real* leader looks like,** his dark voice whispered.

Kree buried her face in Mooka’s fur for a long while. Finally, some muffled words drifted out. ‘Is it a nice farm? Will he have space to run?’

‘Absolutely,’ said Coal. ‘Big fields. Lots of rats for company.’

‘And we’ll come back and collect him as soon as we can,’ Uki added.

Kree gave a reluctant nod and they carried on their way. Uki could hear her singing quiet songs in Mooka’s ear as they walked and felt a sour pang of guilt. But Coal was right. The city was no place for a jerboa and leaving him behind would make the rest of them harder to spot.

And at least he won't die, added his dark voice. **Like the rest of you probably will.**

*

A few hours later, they noticed the forest had begun to thin a little. The gaps between the trees showed daylight in the distance, instead of soupy green shadows. They had come to the edge of Dunmurk.

'Ladies and gentlemen, bucks and does,' Jori said, as they walked the last few steps. 'I present to you . . . the city of Eisenfell!'

The treeline seemed to end abruptly, leaving them standing on a steep hillside of green grass that stretched down to the curve of a wide river. Small burrows and farm buildings were dotted here and there amongst fields of crops and grazing flocks of rats and sheep.

But Uki saw none of that. His eyes were drawn instantly to the walls, the towers, the spires . . . the thrumming *mass* of stone and brick that nearly filled the valley below him.

'What . . . ?' he stammered. 'How . . . ? Is that . . . real?'

'Pok ha boc,' Kree whispered, her mouth hanging open like Uki's.

'Impressive, isn't it?' Jori said.

Impressive wasn't the word. In fact, there wasn't one in Uki's vocabulary that could have described it.

When he'd seen the wooden walls of the twin cities of Syn and Nys, Uki had been amazed that rabbits were able to build structures so big. Now he realised that place had been nothing more than an anthill. A toy. A speck.

The walls of Eisenfell alone were a marvel. From up on their hill they could see almost the full circle of them, towering up like the sheer rock faces of mountains, higher than Uki would ever have thought possible. Slabs of grey stone, somehow cut and sliced into blocks, then stacked to form towers, gatehouses, turrets and buttresses.

How does it all stand? Uki wondered. *How does it not come toppling down like one of the dams I used to build?*

And then his gaze drifted *inside* the colossal walls, making him gasp again.

The crater was there, in the centre, just as Jori had

described. But it was nothing like he had pictured it in his mind's eye. A *canyon* might have been a better word for it. A god-sized scoop out of the earth, a hole big enough to fit the entire Icebark Forest inside, with room to spare.

And in its middle – thronged with ladders and scaffolds and tiny moving specks that must be rabbits – was the meteor.

Despite the hundreds of years of mining, the endless tons of iron that had been taken and forged into armour and weapons, there was still a chunk the size of a small mountain. It was rugged and knobbled, and Uki could see the glints of metal that ran through its rocky crust like veins.

That thing came from the sky, he marvelled. *From space. It's not even a part of this whole world.*

'What's that building?' he heard Kree ask. 'With the pointy bits all over?'

'The Cathedral of Kether,' said Jori, pointing. 'And there is Embervale, the emperor's palace.'

Uki followed her finger and saw, raised up on separate hills beyond the crater, two ornate and complex buildings.

He blinked.

He rubbed his eyes and looked again.

'Those are . . . made?' he squeaked. 'Did rabbits actually *build* them?'

Having lived most of his life in a tiny roundhouse of stone and straw, seeing anything bigger tended to leave him in awe. But even the *idea* of these things being put together brick by brick . . .

'Each took many years to finish,' said Jori. 'The hills they stand on are rabbit-made, too. All the ground around them was mined out in search of sky iron. And if you think they're big from here, wait until you're standing right next to them.'

Uki couldn't even imagine how tall they must be. Higher than any tree he had seen, that's for certain. Maybe even as tall as the Arukh mountains he used to marvel at from his home in the Ice Wastes.

And all built by paw. Spires and arches and steeples, both buildings were covered with them. Windows were everywhere, some tall and narrow, some shaped as circles or crosses. And the glass inside glinted with every colour of the rainbow.

Finally, as if that had not been enough, Uki cast

his eyes over the rest of the city. Down below the hills of the palace and cathedral, ringing the top of the crater, were throngs of buildings in all shapes and sizes. Every scrap, every inch of space inside the walls had been piled up with houses, shops and smithies, stretching up and up into two, three, four storeys. And each with a chimney trailing out a haze of smoke.

From up on the hillside, it looked like a sea of roofs, a lake of slate and thatch, dusted over with a grimy mist. Hundreds, maybe thousands of houses, and all with a family or more living inside . . .

'How many rabbits live in this place?' he said, trying, but failing – to imagine.

'Kether knows,' said Jori. 'The city teems with them. Or at least it did, before they all started leaving.'

'There will still be many thousands,' said Coal. 'Only the most desperate will have run. Or the ones lucky enough to escape. See how much smoke there is? Eisenfell remains full to bursting.'

Uki remembered that Coal had once lived here, until the mining accident that scarred him and took his limbs. He imagined how he would feel himself, returning to his village after having been driven out. Whether seeing familiar sights would balance out the bad things that had happened to him.

'How does it feel to be home?' he asked.

'Home.' Coal made a low noise that might have been a growl or a chuckle. And then he didn't say any more.

'Come,' said Jori. 'We should find this farm, leave Mooka, and then get to the docks. The night watch always used to start patrolling at sunset. They were never the nicest rabbits before – Kether knows what they're like now.'

Uki nodded, and began to follow his friends down the road, gawping at the walls of Eisenfell as he went. It felt like he was walking into some strange dream, some other world of stone, brick and mortar. One where rabbits didn't truly belong.

*

Coal led them towards a cluster of thatched houses and barns at a junction of roads not far from the city walls. The simple buildings were dwarfed by Eisenfell looming behind them: a brick avalanche – a stone thundercloud – chewing up the horizon.

He walked up to the door of the first house and gave it a knock with his wooden crutch. It creaked open a moment later and a grey-furred she-rabbit in a patched smock poked her head out. Her brow was furrowed, her ears tucked tight to her head, but when she saw Coal's face, peering out from under his hood, she relaxed.

'Charcoal! It's you!' she said, sighing with relief.

'I thought you might have forgotten me, Daisy,' said Coal.

'I'd recognise that eyepatch anywhere,' the farmer said. 'I thought you wouldn't be back this way, but here you are. And you've brought some friends with you.'

'We're not stopping,' said Coal, as Uki and the others smiled and waved. 'But I'm afraid I have a favour to ask.'

He explained about Mooka and how they needed a place for him to stay out of sight while they went into Eisenfell.

'Of course,' said Daisy. 'I've a small herd of rats he can be tucked away in. I owe you that much for fixing my plough and not taking a copper for it. But are you sure you want to be going into Eisenfell? With these children? It's not a fit place for anybody, right now . . .'

'Could you tell us what's happened?' Jori asked. 'We've only heard bits and pieces, you see.'

'Is it really that terrible?' Uki added, half hoping it would all turn out to be an exaggeration.

'I'm afraid so,' said Daisy. 'I don't go near the place no more. Some while back, the emperor decided he was a god. With the power to control death. He put word out that all who followed him would live forever. All who disobeyed him would disappear. Then came lists of rules – things you weren't supposed to do no more. I got word of it all from taking my crops to market, you see.'

'We've passed many rabbits leaving,' said Coal. 'What's happening in the city now?'

Daisy shook her head. 'Most of the clan lords have joined Ash's new religion. The night watch and the city guard, too. They've formed a new army called the Deathless. They march around the place with those blank metal faces, snatching off rabbits to Kether knows where. It's miserable, from what I hear. No wonder rabbits are fleeing. I sees them go past at all hours of the night, but most of them get caught and dragged back.'

'Why haven't you gone?' Jori asked. 'You could easily get into the forest from here.'

'I could,' said Daisy. 'But I got my herd of rats here. I can't bring all of them with me, and I refuse to leave them here for them monsters. Still, if things get any worse, I just might have to take my chances.'

Kree let out a horrified wail and clung to Mooka's neck in fright.

'Oh, don't worry, young one,' said Daisy. 'I promise I won't take off while your jerboa is here. He'll be waiting for you when you get back. He's a fine creature, by the way.'

Her words comforted Kree a bit, as did the way Mooka nuzzled Daisy's hand when she went to pet him. Together they led him to the stable and saw him fed and groomed. But it was still a sad moment when they finally had to leave.

'Goodbye, boy,' said Kree, kissing him on the nose. '*Uk noo ha.*'

'Neek!' Mooka replied, twitching his big, dish-sized ears. He knew something was wrong but didn't understand.

'I promise we'll be back for him,' Uki said to Kree, gently taking her hand. 'And he'll be much safer and happier here.'

'*I* won't, though,' said Kree, blinking away tears. Still, she allowed Uki and Jori to gently lead her away from the stable, down the road towards the river, all the while glancing back until the thatched farm had dwindled to a tiny dot.

*

The river Hul curved in from the west, sweeping around the stone hulk of Eisenfell on its way down to the sea. The docks were on the other side of the city, sandwiched between Eisenfell's walls and the wide ribbon of water.

Following the river bank, Uki and his friends merged with groups of merchants and travellers on the muddy road. They kept their hoods pulled low, peering out from beneath until a cluster of buildings came into view, crowded together between walls and water like a horde of greedy children fighting over the last sugared carrot. Warehouses, workshops, market stalls, shipwrights, cranes and taverns, they squashed into every inch of the narrow space, pushing against each other until it looked as though the whole mess might just slip off the bank with a splash.

Piers and pontoons jutted out into the river, and tied up at these were a mass of boats, their bare masts and rigging stretching up into the sky. The spindly branches of an alien, floating forest.

Uki had seen docks before, at Reedwic, but these were a hundred times bigger. And a hundred times busier.

Rabbits from all over the Five Realms were scurrying about like worker ants, carrying crates and barrels off boats on to land, or from the land on to boats. As they walked closer, Uki could see all the different styles of dress, all the different colours, shades and lengths of fur.

There were dwarf rabbits swinging through the rigging; lops with long, dangling ears; angoras with wild manes of fur. There were rabbits with turbans and headscarves, some wearing leather armour, others with kilts or brightly coloured silk robes. And the boats were just as varied: longboats, barges, sloops – even some enormous ships with layers of decks and three or four towering masts.

Teams of dockhands poured off the boats in trains, carrying the crates to warehouses and waiting carts as traders and ships' captains yelled at them. Wooden cranes swung backwards and forwards, lifting pallets stacked high with rolls of fabric, bales of wool and boxes of food. And amongst it all ran packs of children in ragged clothes, patched and tattered and smeared with mud. They dodged in between legs and clambered over crates like tiny acrobats. Whether they were running errands or just playing, Uki couldn't tell.

'Doesn't look like whatever's happening inside the city has affected the docks much,' said Jori, as she stepped aside to avoid three of the sprinting ragamuffins. 'They're as chaotic as ever.'

'None of these are Eisenfell rabbits,' said Coal. 'They're just here to buy and sell. And coins don't worry themselves about gods and tyrants.'

The sight of the teeming dockside had taken

Kree's mind off Mooka for a moment. 'What's a tyrant?' she asked. 'Is it a kind of insect?'

'It's an evil ruler,' said Jori. 'One who is consumed with power.'

'Or who has been captured by an evil spirit,' Uki added. He wondered again what Mortix's plan was. Whether it didn't involve all these rabbits outside the walls, or if she just hadn't got around to dealing with them yet. He wanted to stop the children and tell them about the danger they were in. Tell them to run for the forest and not look back.

He almost got the chance when one stumbled and fell in front of him. A half-starved thing in clothes that were held together with patches, she caught her foot on the side of a turnip box and rolled, sprawling in the dust.

Uki was there in an instant, stretching out a paw to help her up. Forgetting his strength, he almost lifted her clean off the ground– she was light as air, nothing but fur and bone.

'Ta,' she muttered, staring into the shadows under Uki's hood. She must have noticed his mismatched fur and eyes, because she blinked in surprise for an instant before turning and dashing off, lost in seconds amongst the bustle and noise.

They stood watching for a while longer, until a loud whistle sounded, marking the end of the working day. The last pieces of cargo were loaded on to the boats and tied down with rope and tarpaulin. The sailors and dock workers said their goodbyes and drifted off towards the taverns for their supper and a mug or six of ale.

'We had better find this Locke,' said Jori. 'We've still got a few hours before sunset. But we'll have to be careful. If Mortix's soldiers are looking for us, they're bound to be checking here as well.'

'Cascade said he had a boatyard, right next to the river,' remembered Uki. 'With the sign of a key.'

'Like that one?' said Kree, pointing to a carved wooden key dangling from a post. It stood next to a low wooden building with a tatty thatched roof.

'Well spotted!' Uki slapped her on the back. 'I thought it would be like trying to find the Drunken Toad all over again.'

'I have eyes like a hawk,' said Kree, puffing out her chest. 'Ears like a fox, strength like a buffalo and the speed of . . . of . . . *a jerboa*!' and she burst into tears.

'Is this going to happen every five minutes until our quest is done?' said Coal, rolling his eye.

'I miss him!' Kree wailed.

'There, there.' Uki put an arm around her and made an awkward attempt at patting her back. 'He'll be fine. We only left him a few minutes ago . . .'

'Can we just get on and find Locke?' Jori was casting nervous glances at the bustling sailors around her. 'We're starting to attract attention.'

With Uki ushering Kree along as gently as he could, they crossed the yard in front of the building and ducked inside the open doors. They found themselves inside a long, narrow hut, with a half-built boat on a wooden framework in the middle. Stacks of planks lined the walls, and there were tools scattered all over the floor, but the place seemed dark and empty, the shutters all closed and bolted.

'Here's a lantern,' said Coal, and stood back as Jori struck a flint to light it. She held it up, shining it into the hut's corners, peering underneath the boat scaffold.

'No sign of anybody,' she said. 'Cascade said Locke was black-furred with white speckled ears. Said he'd be easy to recognise.'

Uki looked at the hammers and nails dotted all over the floor. They looked as though they might have been dropped in a hurry. As if their owner had suddenly been interrupted . . .

'Can I help you?'

A voice called from the doorway, making them all jump at once. Jori spun round, shining her lantern on an old she-rabbit leaning on a staff and peering in at them.

'We're . . . er . . . we're looking for Locke,' she said, when she had recovered. 'He doesn't seem to be here.'

The old rabbit took a good look at the street around her before answering. When she turned back to them, Uki noticed her eyes were wide with fear.

'They took him,' she whispered. 'Four weeks or more ago. Just like the others . . .'

'Who took him?' Uki asked. 'What others?'

'The Deathless. Guards from the city. Them with no faces. Came and snatched him one night. And they've taken more, too. Carpenters, shipwrights . . . they come in the dark and then . . .'

Her voice trailed off and she wiped a paw across her eyes. Uki could see that her fingers were trembling, as if she were truly terrified. He shared a nervous look with Jori. How were they supposed to get inside the city now?

Jori cleared her throat. She moved closer to the old rabbit so she could whisper.

'We were supposed to see him about entering the city. We were told he knew a way.'

The old rabbit blinked at them for a minute, and then began to shake her head.

'I don't know nothing about that,' she said. 'I only come here once a week to sweep up sawdust. I was friends with Locke's grandmother and he always made sure he looked after me. I didn't pry into his business, though. I don't know nothing . . .'

Jori sighed and hung the lantern back on the wall before blowing it out. 'I see,' she said. 'Thank you anyway.'

The old rabbit's paw suddenly shot out and grabbed Jori's arm. She pulled her close and stared into her face with wild eyes. 'Don't go into the city!' she hissed. 'It's not safe! Anyone who can run is leaving . . . the living dead! The faceless ones!'

Uki was about to ask her what she was talking about when there came a shout from outside the hut. He ran to the door and looked out, instantly wishing he hadn't. There, standing in the yard, their blank metal masks pointing right at him, were three of the Deathless.

'You, rabbits! With the hoods! Come out and present yourselves!' one of them yelled, his voice muffled, metallic.

'They're here! They're here!' the old rabbit screamed.

Uki looked at his friends, seeing matching expressions of horror on all their faces.

'They've found us!' he shouted. 'Run!'

Chapter Five

The Hulside Howlers

Before anyone could even move, the Deathless began to charge towards them, armour clanking, blank steel faceplates gleaming. Then the old she-rabbit was amongst them, waving her staff and wailing, tangling them up for an instant.

Uki sparked into action. The powers given to him by Iffrit kicked in, and he felt time slow to a crawl. The guards were barrelling forwards, knocking the old rabbit aside, coming straight towards him. But their movements were sticky, slow as snails. He could see the specks of dust puff up as their feet struck the dry mud of the yard; he watched the old rabbit's staff begin an end-over-end topple as it flew from her paw.

The slowness didn't affect him, though. His fingers snapped towards the last two short spears in his harness, but he realised he didn't want to waste one if he could help it.

Instead, his eye caught on a wooden mallet lying on the workshop floor. In a blink, he had snatched it up, then flung it at the approaching rabbits.

Uki watched it spiral – graceful, deadly – until it connected with the lead guard's blank silver faceplate. The metal bent in with an echoing *claaanng!* sending the rabbit toppling backwards into his squad, knocking them all to the floor in a scrambling heap.

And then Jori slammed the workshop doors shut, cutting off the scene from sight.

'We have to find another way out!' she shouted, as Uki's sense of time popped back to normal. They all began to dash around the darkened hut, searching for another door or window.

'Here!' Uki heard Kree yell. 'There's a hole under

this door at the front. And a path out . . . but it goes into the river!'

They all ran to the end of the workshop, where two big, double doors stood. A gap at the bottom exposed a slope, full of lapping river water.

'A slipway,' said Jori. 'For Locke to launch his boats.'

'Blistering beetroots,' said Coal. 'I'm not great at swimming. In fact, I think sinking is all I'm good for.' He raised the heavy hammer that had replaced his right arm.

'We'll only have to wade,' said Jori. 'We can go out this way and climb up the bank.'

'Hurry!' said Uki. He could hear the Deathless beginning to batter at the other entrance.

Kree ducked through the gap between the door and the slipway, splashing into the river. She yelped as she plunged into the water. '*Neekneek poc!* It's cold!'

'It's better than a sword in your squidgy bits,' said Coal, shouldering the door open. Jori squeezed through the gap, then Uki. His bare feet sank into the river, feeling the sloping ground beneath them.

Kree had already clambered out onto the bank and was peering around the corner of the workshop.

Just as Coal had stepped out and closed the door behind him, there came the sound of splintering wood.

'They've gone in,' Kree whispered.

'Quick,' hissed Jori. 'Up the bank. We've got a few seconds to lose them in the crowd before they realise we're not there.'

Scrabbling one after the other through the mud, they clambered up the bank next to the workshop. Uki and Jori reached back to help the struggling Coal, and they found themselves in the yard again. The old she-rabbit still lay tumbled on the floor next to the unconscious guard with the dent in his helmet, shouting and screeching at the top of her voice. The other Deathless had all rushed into the boatshed, searching for their quarry.

'This way!' Jori shouted, heading back to the cobbled road that wove in between the dock buildings. All the commotion had attracted a big audience, and the street was packed with sailors and workers trying to see what the fuss was all about.

'Into the crowd!' Uki called, as they ran. He readied himself to begin pushing rabbits out of their way, but was surprised when they all parted for them, leaving a clear path deeper into the docks.

It was a stroke of good luck as, just at that moment, the two remaining guards burst out of the workshop. 'There they are!' one shouted, and they ran in pursuit.

Uki and his friends sprinted through the crowd, hearing yells of protest from behind them. He risked a glance over his shoulder and saw that the wonderful dock rabbits had closed ranks behind them, making it hard for the guards to follow.

'Clear a path! Clear a path, in the name of the god-emperor!' he heard one guard bellow. It was met with jeers from the crowd until Uki heard the unmistakeable sound of a sword being drawn.

Now they'll let them through, Uki thought. But the dock workers' bravery had bought them valuable seconds.

They pelted past warehouses, fish markets and taverns, rows of sailors and bargemen staring at them as they ran. They wove around buildings, dodged under teetering stacks of crates and bales of wool, until they had no idea of where they were or which way they were going.

Finally, they turned a corner into a narrow alley and found themselves up against the hard, stone wall of Eisenfell itself.

'Dead end,' said Kree, leaning against the brickwork and panting for breath. Everyone else was gasping too, especially Coal, who leant heavily on his crutch, sweat pouring down his face.

'Have we lost them?' Jori said, when she had recovered a little.

Uki went to the mouth of the alley and peered out. All he could see were more buildings, but he could hear shouts and crashes from somewhere else amongst the docks.

'I can't tell,' he said. 'This place is too squashed-up.'

'It's only a matter of time until they find us here,' said Coal. 'We need to keep moving.'

Uki nodded. He made to step out of the alley when he caught a glimpse of light gleaming off metal in the distance. *A guard's faceplate!*

'It's them!' he whispered, jumping backwards. 'Just a few buildings away!'

Everyone rushed to the back of the alley, looking for a gap or hole they could slip through. There weren't any. They were trapped like fish in a barrel.

'Don't panic,' said Kree. 'Uki can do his thing, like he did in Enk. Make them all crumple to the ground.'

'I don't think I can . . .' said Uki.

Jori gripped his shoulder. 'Look. Forget what I told you about not using Charice's power. If they catch us, it's over!'

'It's not that,' Uki said, wondering how to explain it. 'It's the Deathless. There's something *wrong* with them. When I tried to sense the one in the forest, I couldn't. They don't have any . . . *life*.'

'Try again,' said Jori. 'You might have been mistaken.'

Uki shrugged, knowing in his bones it was no use, but trying anyway. He closed his eyes and reached out with his newest power, trying to feel the life source of everything around him.

He was instantly overwhelmed with a thrum of information. Scores and scores of rabbits filled the buildings all around, blazing out their energy like beacons. The glow of light was dazzling, but in amongst it all were two patches of darkness. Two spots that were a complete absence of anything. Holes. Vacuums.

Uki knew they were the Deathless because they were moving. Edging closer and closer to where he and his friends hid. He tried to use his power on them, to twist their own bodies against them, but there was nothing there to grab hold of. It was as if they didn't actually exist.

'It's no use,' he said, opening his eyes. 'I can make out where they are, but I can't touch them.'

Coal grunted. 'It's a fight, then,' he said, hefting his hammer-arm. 'Knock them out before they can call for reinforcements. Then get out of the docks any way we can. Meet back at Daisy's farm if we get separated.'

'How are we going to get into Eisenfell, though?' Uki asked.

'Not this way,' said Jori. She had her flask in one hand, sword in the other.

'I *knew* we shouldn't have left Mooka behind,' said Kree, drawing her dagger. 'We could have ridden him out of here in a flash.'

Uki reached for a spear and braced himself. He could feel the not-rabbits getting closer and closer. Soon they would step into the mouth of the alleyway . . .

'Psst!'

The sound of someone whispering. Uki looked at the shadows in the alley corners, up at the roof tops.

'Psst!'

Where was it coming from? He peered at the wooden walls of the buildings, then at the ground itself . . . and that was when he saw it. A trapdoor, covered with mud like the path around it, levered up a few inches. And in the gap was a pair of eyes.

'Down here!' the eyes' owner whispered. Uki looked closer and recognised the urchin rabbit from earlier. The child he had helped up when she fell.

'Quick!' the urchin called. 'Follow me!'

Uki didn't wait to be asked again. The Deathless would be on them any second. He flipped the trapdoor open and jumped in, finding himself in a narrow tunnel that wound its way between the foundation posts of the building above. The urchin rabbit was already disappearing down it, clutching a lantern to light her way.

As the others began to jump down after him, Uki followed her, keeping his spear drawn just in case. He heard a grunt as Coal squeezed himself into the tunnel, then a thump as the trapdoor shut, plunging them into darkness. The only glimmer of light came from the urchin up ahead.

'Are you sure this is safe?' Kree asked, peering down the narrow passage.

'What choice do we have?' Uki replied. Wondering who the urchin was and where the tunnel might lead, Uki began to follow the glow.

*

The way was narrow and the walls roughly scraped out. In places Uki had to squeeze sideways to get through. Chunks of mud and drizzles of sand pattered down on their heads. And all the while, the urchin rabbit dashed ahead with her light, making them struggle to keep up.

Finally, out of breath and fed up with soil showering down on him, Uki shouted 'Wait! Hold on a minute!'

The flickering light paused, and then grew brighter as the urchin came back to them.

'What?' she said, sounding quite annoyed.

Uki caught his breath and shook the mud from his hood. He could hear Coal and Kree both muttering curses behind him.

'Thank you for saving us,' said Uki, 'but could you please tell us why you did it? And where you're leading us?'

The urchin huffed, then reached into the pocket of her tattered trousers. She pulled out a crumpled, much-folded piece of parchment and shook it open, holding it in the lamplight so Uki could see.

There, amongst the rips and stains, was a printed woodcut of a rabbit with half white, half black fur. A crude picture of Uki himself – it had to be. Above it, in blocky runes, were lines of writing.

'What does it say?' Uki asked. 'I can't read Hulst runes.'

Jori poked her head over his shoulder and frowned at the parchment. 'It says: 'Wanted: black-and-white furred rabbit. Fifty hod reward. By order of God-Emperor Ash.''

'Fifty hods?' Uki said. 'Is that a lot?'

'A hod is a gold piece,' said Jori. 'For that amount, I might think about turning you in myself.'

Uki gave the urchin a wary look. 'Is that where you're taking us? To be arrested so you can get the reward?'

'What?!' The urchin scrunched the parchment up and shoved it back in her pocket, glaring at Uki with her teeth bared. 'You think I'd do the deadheads a favour, just for a bit of gold? You think I'm some kind of traitor?'

'No, no . . .' Uki waved his paws, trying to calm her down. He had said the wrong thing again. 'It's just . . . we're very worried. You can imagine. And we don't know where we're going . . .'

'What he means to say is' – Jori stepped in, much to Uki's relief – 'we would really like to know where you are taking us. So we can be certain we are out of danger. My name's Jori, by the way, and this is Uki.'

'Scrag,' said the urchin, which took Uki a second to realise was her name. 'And we're going to the Howlers' burrow. That all right with you?'

And before Uki could say any more, she was off again, slinking through the narrow tunnels like a very speedy mole.

*

Uki didn't dare interrupt her again, she seemed so fierce. Instead, he concentrated on trying to keep up with her, trying to piece together clues as he went, to see how much trouble they were in.

She was obviously used to being down in these tunnels, that much was clear. And judging by the look of her, she was in need of a good bath and a full meal. *Perhaps she lives down here?* he thought. *And she couldn't have dug all this on her own. Maybe there are lots of them?*

Remembering the group of children that had been running around amongst the dock crowds, Uki wondered if they had all made these tunnels their home as well.

She seems to hate the guards, at least. That means she probably isn't *going to turn us in for the reward.*

Unless that's what she wants you to think, his dark voice added.

That might have been enough to make Uki panic, but in the end there wasn't time. Up ahead, Scrag turned a corner and, when Uki caught up with her, he found himself in an underground room with a low roof lit by scores of candles.

After the darkness of the tunnel, the light hurt his eyes and he stood squinting for a moment. The others stumbled out into the open behind him, also blinking and peeping between their fingers.

'*Pok ha boc,*' Kree said. 'It's so *bright* . . .'

When Uki's eyes had adjusted, he could see the room was only five or six metres across. Several other narrow tunnels fed into it and the walls were stacked high with sacks of vegetables and seeds, stolen from the docks above he presumed.

Sitting in the room's centre were five new rabbits, all children. At the sight of Scrag's guests, they jumped up, weapons in hand. All except the smallest, a scrap of a thing with brown fur and big eyes, who hid behind the others.

'Easy,' said Scrag. 'Put them bashers away. I brung the special one! See?'

She pointed at Uki and motioned for him to remove his hood. Uki gave the young rabbits a careful look first.

They were tatty, filthy scraps of things, just like Scrag. Two of the girls were identical: bigger and stronger than the rest, with muscles showing through the torn holes of their shirts and copper rings through their ears. The others looked like they could be knocked over by a strong breeze without Uki even having to use his powers.

Their weapons were nothing more than sticks with sharp pieces of glass and stone tied to the ends, although one of the big ones had an iron crowbar.

All in all, Uki decided they were probably harmless. He reached up and pulled his hood back, showing off his neatly split fur. Scrag unfolded her parchment and held it up beside him, for effect.

'Kether's forty-eight whiskers,' said a boy with white-and-brown piebald fur. 'It *is* him.'

'The Bonegrubbers will want to know about this,' said the girl with the crowbar.

'*Everyone* will want to know about this,' said her twin.

'Excuse me,' said Uki, 'if you don't mind … Could someone please explain to us what's going on?'

'And why you keep speaking those stupid words that don't make sense?' Kree added.

'That's gang talk,' said the piebald. 'So the deadheads can't understand us.'

'Deadheads?' said Kree.

'Deathless. The guards and soldiers.' The piebald tapped his head with a finger and waggled his ears, as if he had just been extremely clever. Kree was not impressed, judging by the rude Plains words she kept mumbling.

'We are the Hulside Howlers,' said Scrag. 'And this is our base.'

'Where are your parents?' Coal asked. 'Do they know you're playing soldiers in some badly dug tunnels under the docks?'

'Our parents are *gone*,' said Scrag, the fierce look back on her face. 'And we'd be too, if we hadn't dug out this place. We're trying to *survive*, down here. It's no game. No game at all.'

'Coal's sorry if he caused offence. Aren't you?' Jori nudged him in the ribs, and he muttered what might have been an apology. 'And we're very grateful for your help. We were looking for a rabbit called Locke. He was going to get us inside Eisenfell. Perhaps you've heard of him?'

'Locke's gone too,' said Scrag. 'Same as our folks. They've taken all the carpenters, smiths and builders. Nobody knows where.'

At this, all the Howlers looked very sad and worried. Uki felt deeply sorry for them. He knew just what it was like to be without parents . . . that sense of complete helplessness, of being isolated and alone.

'Are these Locke's smuggling tunnels?' he asked, thinking it a good idea to change the subject. 'Do they lead into the city?'

'They's *our* tunnels,' said Scrag. 'The Howlers dug them. We know where Locke's are, too, but the deadheads are watching them. And don't worry . . . we're taking you into the city. Right now.'

'What if we don't want to go with you?' Coal growled, brandishing his hammer-arm.

'Then we'll make you,' said the rabbit with the crowbar. The Howlers raised their weapons again. It wouldn't take Coal five seconds to knock them all out but Uki didn't want anyone harmed. They were just lost children, after all. Lost, like him.

'Wait!' he shouted, raising his paws, palms outstretched. 'We don't want any trouble. If you can get us inside Eisenfell, we'd be happy to go with you, wouldn't we?'

Jori and Kree both nodded, doing their best

to look friendly. Gradually, the Howlers lowered their clubs and sticks, but they kept casting wary glances at Coal.

'We'd better get going, then,' said Scrag. 'Stow will run ahead to call the parliament.'

A rabbit with black fur and piercing blue eyes nodded, and dashed off down one of the tunnels, not even pausing to take a candle. The others all busied themselves with lighting lanterns and packing food and water into sacks to take with them.

'Can I ask where we're going?' Uki said. 'And what exactly is the parliament?'

''The Parliament of Underfell,' said Scrag, handing him a lantern. 'The gathering of all the gangs.'

'And the place we're taking you,' said the piebald with a sinister grin, 'is called *The Ghostburrow.*'

Chapter Six

The Ghostburrow

The journey through the tunnels seemed to last for centuries. It was difficult to tell how far they had walked, winding this way and that in the darkness, but Uki guessed it was at least a mile, maybe more.

The Howlers chatted as they marched and, through listening in, Uki learnt that the maze of tunnels beneath the city was known as the Underfell. Whoever, or whatever, had lived down here in the time before Mortix's arrival, it was now the home of several tribes of child rabbits. Ones much like the Howlers themselves.

He also learnt the names of his new allies. The piebald rabbit (who Kree seemed to have taken an especial dislike to) was called Lurky. The twins were Crowbar and Heaver. Stow had run ahead on her mission, and the brown-furred rabbit was Decker.

Somehow, Uki knew that those weren't their real names. Just as this underground scurrying and hiding wasn't their real life. When their parents had vanished, everything they knew disappeared too. They'd had to build a new world for themselves, just like him. One in which nothing seemed certain any more, and there was nobody to tell you it was all going to work out, that everything would be fine.

Except for your friends. That's what they are for. Yes. Uki had forged himself a new family. And so had these children. It made sense that they had renamed themselves when you thought of it like that. They were new rabbits now. Stronger. Tougher. And the world would never again be the safe, friendly place they had once believed it to be.

*

Just when Uki was getting sick of squeezing his way through the Howlers' hastily dug tunnels, they suddenly popped out into a much wider passage. It had thick beams along the walls for support, and a ceiling of planks. The wood was iron-hard and stained dark by time, but still sturdy and strong.

'What's this place?' Uki asked, shining his light across the packed-earth walls.

'An old smuggling tunnel,' said Scrag. 'We're inside the city walls now.'

'Anything you recognise?' Uki asked Coal, remembering he had worked in Eisenfell, before his accident.

'Never been here before,' said Coal, running his paw down one of the support beams. 'I was a miner, not a smuggler. This shaft is old, too. Hundreds of years, maybe.'

'Actually, it's one of the first ones ever dug,' said Lurky. 'It was the very edge of the crater, once upon a time. This had been sealed off for centuries. Until the Underfell claimed it back.'

'What are you, some kind of tour guide?' Kree rolled her eyes at him.

'No. What are you? Some kind of grumpy pixie?'

Kree took a deep breath, ready to launch into a torrent of insults, until Jori clapped a paw over her mouth.

'This ghost burrow you're taking us to,' she said, trying to change the subject. 'Why the scary name? Is it really haunted?'

Scrag laughed. 'It looks like it should be. It's a chamber in the Bonegrubbers' territory. They live underneath the Skullgardens.'

Just the name was enough to send a shiver through Uki's fur. 'What are those?' he whispered to Jori.

'It's what they call the graveyard, on top of the hill next to the cathedral,' she said. 'All the rabbits in Eisenfell get buried there. The rich ones, at least.'

A burrow amongst the graves. Mortix the spirit of death. Uki shook his head. This final part of the quest was growing darker every step they took.

'And what do they want with Uki?' Coal asked. He seemed to be on edge, as if the path their adventure had taken had unnerved him somehow.

Lurky made a grovelling gesture with his paws. 'He's the special one, don't you know? The 'Grubbers have got a soothsayer who says the black-and-white rabbit is important. We've all been looking out for his royal highness. As if we didn't have anything better to do.'

'He *is* important,' said Kree, pulling Jori's paw away so she could shout. 'He's the most important rabbit in the whole Five Realms!'

Uki felt his cheeks burning crimson under his fur. To distract everyone's attention, he began to trot ahead down the tunnel, beckoning them on. 'Let's get moving, shall we?'

With a final growl at Lurky, Kree began to follow, and they started to make their way along the shaft.

*

Strolling through the old passageway was a lot easier than squeezing around in the Howlers' tunnels. And a lot safer, too. Even though being underground should come naturally to Uki, he had lived his whole life on the surface. He usually found the earthy darkness quite soothing, but when the tunnels you were crawling through looked so badly made, it was hard not to think of all the tons of dirt above your head waiting to fall down and crush you.

Every now and then they saw an object that gave them a glimpse into Eisenfell's past. An abandoned wooden bucket, all rotted into splinters. A name or a simple picture carved into the hardened mud of the wall. Tiny clues from a world long gone, hundreds of years in the past. A time and place where rabbits didn't have to worry about ancient spirits and their evil, when this shaft was full of rabbits sneaking back and forth with carts brimming with goods, talking, laughing, and singing. Uki tried to picture them here as he walked along, imagining the dark, cold tunnels packed with life once more.

He was just staring at the rust-covered head of a broken pickaxe – still in the spot where it was thrown away, centuries ago – when Scrag stopped short. She was shining her lantern at a spot on the wall where a rough symbol had been carved. Fresher than any of the markings around it, it looked like a simple face with X marks for the eyes.

'We're on Bonegrubber land now,' she said. 'There should be a tunnel just up ahead, off to their burrow.'

'Do you all have your own patches, then?' Uki asked.

'We do,' said Scrag. 'And we mostly keep to them. But finding *you* is a special occasion. The 'Grubbers will be pleased we're here.'

Uki wondered how many gangs there were in the city. The place was certainly big enough for hundreds of them. He was about to ask, when Lurky pointed out two narrow holes scraped out of the wall next to one of the wooden supports. One was marked with the face again, the other had a straight line with two dots on either side.

'What's that other symbol mean?' Uki asked.

'It's a T for trap,' said Lurky. 'Can't you read Hulst runes? The tunnel is rigged to collapse if anyone tries going down it. Just in case the Deadheads come here, hunting for us.'

'Kind of you to mark it so obviously,' said Kree, rolling her eyes. 'As if they wouldn't be able to work out that T means trap.'

'Well, *you* didn't know,' said Lurky. He stuck his tongue out at her before vanishing into the Bonegrubber tunnel.

'Here we go again,' muttered Coal, as the rabbits began to squeeze in, one by one. If Uki felt claustrophobic in the gang tunnels, it must be horrible for the big blacksmith. *And* he had to manage without an arm and a leg.

'Can I carry your crutch for you?' he offered.

Coal smiled and put a paw on his shoulder. 'That would be very kind of you,' he said. 'Sorry if I've been a bit snappy. All this sneaking around with gangs is not how I imagined coming back to Eisenfell.'

'Don't worry about it,' said Uki, smiling back. 'It will be all right though, won't it?'

Coal watched as Jori, then Kree disappeared up the cramped tunnel, a frown on his scarred face. 'I hope so,' he said. 'I really do.'

*

Luckily, there was only a short length of tunnel to wriggle through. After a few metres of squeezing, they emerged into another open space. One full of cold, damp air and a smell of fossilised dust that hit Uki's nose like a hard slap.

Standing up and raising his lantern, he found he was in a large chamber with walls of stone. Columns like tree trunks rose up to the ceiling, where they curved over to meet in arches. Tendrils of roots had snaked through cracks in the brickwork and hung down, twining and plaiting themselves together like ghostly bunches of hair.

'What are all these stone boxes?' he heard Kree ask, her voice echoing around the room. Turning his attention to the ground, Uki saw rows and rows of granite platforms, each one with the carved statue of a figure lying on top. Most of them had crumbled with age, but he could make out rabbit ears and suits of armour on some. Stone rats or other creatures lay at their feet, and all of them were draped in thick shrouds of clotted, dusty cobwebs.

'Tombs,' said Scrag. 'The graves of the first families of Eisenfell.'

'You mean . . . dead bodies? Inside those things?' Kree edged closer to Uki, staring around with wide eyes.

'Yes,' said Lurky, in a deep, spooky voice. 'And bones and worms and ghosties!'

Kree scowled at him. 'Would *you* like to be buried down here as well?' she said.

Jori, ignoring them, was looking up at the ceiling, deep in thought. 'But we must be below the city level

still. And if we're under Cathedral Hill as well, then we're miles beneath the Skullgardens.'

'We are,' said Decker. It was the first time Uki had heard the brown rabbit speak. 'This is the lowest of the tombs. And the oldest. There are stacks of them under the hill, all built on top of each other.'

'You could easily get lost here and never come out,' said Scrag. 'Just one more pile of bones in a place stuffed full of them.'

Uki peered at the worn statue on top of the nearest tomb. What remained of the crumbled face looked stern. He wore a suit of elaborate plate armour, and his paws rested on his chest, clutching a sword. There was some kind of snarling badger curled under his boots, missing most of its snout, and there were faint traces of runes, running around the edge of the lid. Who had this rabbit been? Uki wondered. What kind of life did he have? Was he fierce and cruel, or brave and kind? There was nobody left alive to say. Anyone who might have come here to remember him was long dead as well.

'What's to stop us getting lost, then?' Coal asked, sounding less pleased than ever.

'Signs,' said Scrag. She shone her lantern into

a corner of the chamber, where another dead-eyed face had been scraped into the stonework. Next to it was a metal gate, all ornate scrollwork, now coated in rust. Crowbar and Heaver went over and dragged it open, causing the ancient hinges to squeal like a pair of dying mice.

Wincing at the noise, and the thought of who – or what – might hear it, Uki hurried through, with Jori and Kree close behind him. He almost thought he saw the lid of one of the tombs move, imagined the bones of a long-dead lord clambering out to complain about his rest being interrupted.

Judging by how quickly all the others followed them, they must have been thinking similar things. The place was so creepy you couldn't stop your mind playing evil tricks on you.

They stepped out into a corridor of carved marble. Once upon a time, it must have been very grand, but now it was bricked off at both ends. Piles of brown dust and skeletal stalks lay like snowdrifts either side of the doorway. It took Uki a moment to realise that they must once have been bouquets of flowers, left by those mourning the dead inside.

Scrag led them along to the corridor's sudden end and pointed at another Bonegrubber sign, chalked onto a corner of the brickwork. Peering closely, Uki noticed the mortar was missing from a section of wall. The stone blocks were just stacked loosely in place.

The Howlers set about pulling them free, piling them neatly to one side and exposing a hole big enough to crawl through. One by one they wriggled into the gap, emerging into another chamber full of tombs, much like the first.

And so it went on, mausoleum after mausoleum. Chamber after chamber. Always following the scratched signs, always clambering slightly higher and higher.

As they moved closer to the surface, Uki noticed the graves became gradually less ancient. The carvings weren't so worn, the cobwebs not so matted. Sometimes the wreaths and piles of flowers were almost intact, although they crumbled to fragments if you brushed them with a paw.

They must have walked through twenty or more crypts, pasts the remains of hundreds of rich, important rabbits, before Scrag finally stopped before a grand, oak door.

'Behold,' she said, with an exaggerated flourish, 'the Ghostburrow.'

Pushing the door open, she revealed a room far bigger than any of the others. Thick columns stretched up fifteen metres or more to a vaulted ceiling. Marble tiles covered the floor. At one end was a hearth, complete with a roaring fire, all carved out of cold, lifeless stone. And set out before it was a long, granite table, chairs lining either side, each one filled with the statue of a rabbit.

Uki stared at the place, mouth open. His feet froze at the doorway, as if stepping inside would be wrong, somehow. It was so grand, so elegantly constructed, and yet buried beneath the ground where nobody would ever see it. A perfect, private, secret thing. A space that belonged to some other world. The world of the dead, perhaps.

'What is this place?' he whispered. 'Why is it here?'

'This was built by Emperor Cinder's son, Flame,' said Lurky. All trace of cockiness had gone from his voice, as if he, too, was overcome by awe. 'It's to remember his father and the lords of the first clans that made the empire.'

'The first lords?' Jori said. She was peering at them closely. Then she took a breath and stepped over the threshold, walking up to them and staring at each one in turn.

'What are you looking for?' Uki hissed, not yet brave enough to follow.

'Lord Nightshade,' Jori replied, stopping by the statue of a hooded rabbit. 'Kether above, this is him.' She reached out a paw to brush the carved folds of his cloak, staring up at his stern face in silence, in awe.

He actually does look a bit like Jori, Uki thought. *The same glare, the same frown line on his brow.*

'What's so important about Nightshade?' Kree asked. She hopped into the room and went over to the seated stone figure. Uki – tiptoeing – followed too.

'He's my ancestor,' Jori said, pointing to a stone flask, carved onto the rabbit's belt. 'He was the first Lord of Clan Septys. The first to discover the use of dusk potion. He built the clan warren in the Coldwood and spent his life inventing half the potions they still use today.'

Her voice was hushed: sad, even. Uki thought he might try to cheer her up. 'I'm sure he would be proud to have you as part of his family. If he's looking down from the Land Beyond, I mean.'

Jori gave a bitter laugh. 'I doubt it. I'm an outcast from Clan Septys, remember? I refused to follow all his teachings. He'd probably want me dead, like the rest of them.'

Uki bit his tongue, even though he wanted to tell Jori how brave she was, turning her back on all that history, all those expectations that had weighed down on her. She had stood up for her own beliefs, when it meant losing everything. If only she could take pride in that herself.

He was about to change the subject and ask who the other stone lords were, when a crackling noise from the other end of the room broke the musty silence. Orange light burst outwards from a freshly lit campfire, flaring throughout the chamber and casting sharp shadows across its stone counterpart in the fireplace opposite.

Uki and the others jumped, paws on weapon hilts, spinning round to see another group of rabbits – living ones, this time – silhouetted against the flames.

'Who goes there?' a voice echoed around the cavernous crypt.

'The Hulside Howlers,' Scrag called. 'Here for the parliament.'

'Ah. Welcome,' the voice replied. 'Come and join our fire.'

'Thank Kether,' said Lurky. 'It's cold enough to freeze the nipples off a hedgehog in this place.'

'How rude,' said Kree, although Uki suspected she was just annoyed Lurky had made a crude comment before she could. Keeping a wary eye, they left the lords to their endless stone banquet and went to meet the other gang.

As they drew closer, Uki could see several rabbits huddled around a small fire that was burning inside a circle of broken rubble. Most of them were children of various ages, although there was an elderly lady rabbit in the middle and, off in the shadows, what looked like an adult soldier. Unless, of course, it was just another statue.

'Hello, Bonegrubbers,' said Scrag, as they reached the fireside. 'I see Stow must have passed on our news.'

Uki noticed the black-furred Howler who had run ahead. She was curled in a piece of old sacking and looked very relieved to see her friends again.

'She did,' said the elderly rabbit, waving a paw in Stow's direction. Uki noticed her eyes were filmed over and cloudy. The way she tilted her head made him realise she was blind. 'Did you bring *him* with you?'

'He's here,' said one of the rabbits sitting next to her. They were all staring at Uki as if he were an exhibit in a zoo. He stared back, noting the dusty shrouds they were wound in and the smudges of black paint around their eyes. They looked like creatures who had crawled out of the stone tombs, like dead things come back to life.

'Lovely place you've got,' said Lurky, breaking the silence. 'Really cosy.'

'Ignore him,' said Scrag. 'He's got a habit of being annoying.'

Kree snorted back a laugh. 'We noticed.'

'We thank you for bringing the special one,' said one of the shrouded rabbits. 'And we welcome you to the Ghostburrow. I am Rattle, and these are my fellow gang members. The old lady is Rilda. She reads the bones.'

When Rattle mentioned bones, Rilda emptied a leather pouch of painted knucklebones on the floor next to the fire. She waited until they had finished tumbling and then traced her fingers over them, humming to herself.

Uki looked over to the corner, where the figure of the armoured soldier stood. His new senses picked up the tingle of life coming from it, and from another source hidden in the shadows. He was about to ask who *they* were, when the noise of tramping feet came from outside the chamber.

'The others arrive,' Rilda said, pointing a shaky finger to a grand doorway next to the carved fireplace. From outside it, the glimmer of lanterns could be seen, soon followed by the silhouettes of several rabbits.

Uki held his breath, hoping the blind rabbit was right, and that it wasn't a squad of armoured guards. He was relieved when a crowd of twenty or so children appeared, bundling into the room, nudging and jostling as they went.

They walked up to the fire and stood, gathered in three groups. Even if they hadn't been standing next to each other, it would have been easy to spot which gang they belonged to. Like the Bonegrubbers with their shrouds and face paint, they each had a kind of uniform.

'The Toffs are here,' announced one rabbit from the group that wore odds and ends of badly fitting, luxurious silk clothing.

Rattle stood and gave her a bow. 'Greetings, Rainna.'

'And so are the Scrappers.' A squat, broad rabbit from the second gang spoke up. He had thick coal dust and mud matted all over his fur, a dented copper helmet on his head and he carried a wooden pickaxe handle.

'Welcome, Grit,' said Rattle.

'Don't forget the Stinkers,' said one of the third bunch. Their uniform was simply a layer of filth covering them from head to toe. Great, gooey clods of muck that stank of rot, dung and grime. You could almost see the air around them turning green.

'As if we could.' Rattle gave them a nod, while trying to keep his nose pointed in a different direction.

'Well, then,' said Rainna of the Toffs. 'Are you going to tell us why we've been called?'

The newly arrived rabbits were staring around the Ghostburrow, paying particular interest to Uki and his friends.

'Hey, I recognise you!' One of the Scrappers pointed to Uki, elbowing his friends to get their attention. 'Your face is on posters all over the city! You're the one the guards are looking for!'

Excited murmurs began to spring up around the chamber, until Rattle cleared his throat to get everyone's attention.

'This is Uki,' he said. 'And these are his friends. He is indeed the rabbit that the guards are seeking. Our soothsayer, Rilda, saw his coming in the bones. She knew he would be at the docks, and so we asked the Howlers to keep watch for him, which they have done.'

There was quiet for a moment as every pair of eyes stared at Uki again, making him squirm. *This is the time to say something important,* he thought. *This is when I should make an inspiring speech of some sort.* He opened his mouth, but found his mind had suddenly emptied itself of every single word he knew.

'Well,' said Rainna, when the awkward silence had gone on a bit too long for comfort. 'He's here. Now what?'

Everyone's attention turned to Rilda the soothsayer, much to Uki's relief. She was still tracing her long fingers over the knucklebones on the floor.

'I have asked the bones many times,' she said, her cracked voice wavering. 'But they cannot tell me. All I can see is that he is important. That he will save us.'

'How's he going to save us?' Lurky poked Uki's shoulder with a podgy finger. 'He's only a child, just like the rest of us. Can't be more than eight years old.'

Kree slapped the piebald rabbit's paw away, snarling up at him. 'I told you before – he's the most important rabbit in the Five Realms! He has powers, you know. Magic ones. Tell them, Uki!'

'I . . . er . . .' Everyone was staring at him again. This time he took a deep breath and decided to just explain everything from the beginning.

'I know I don't look like anything special,' he said. 'And I'm not. Not really. I'm just a rabbit from the Ice Wastes. One who lost his parents, like all of you, I suppose. But then, just after my . . . my mother died . . . I met this creature. A spirit. He was made of fire, except he wasn't really there . . .'

He could see the gang rabbits frowning at him, as if he was talking nonsense. But before the words could dry up, he felt Jori give his arm a squeeze and Kree waved him on.

'He was made by the Ancients, you see. And he had been guarding four other creatures like himself in a prison made of crystal. Except the crystal broke, and they escaped. So, he gave me the job of finding them again, and trapping them in here.' Uki tapped the three crystals on his harness as they glowed softly in the darkness: yellow, red and green.

'And there's one more left. One last spirit. I think she's here, inside the body of your emperor. That's why he's changed . . . why he's calling himself a god and why all your parents have been disappearing. If I can find out for sure, and if I can trap him in one of my spears . . . then things might go back to normal.'

'You can get rid of the deadheads?' said Rainna.

'You can stop the emperor?' asked Grit.

'Sounds like a load of weasel dung,' said one of the smelly rabbits. 'And we should know. Spirits? Crystals? Ancients? How are we supposed to believe all that?'

'Because it's true.' A voice came from the shadowy corners of the room. A young girl's voice, clear and confident. There was movement in the darkness as the speaker made her way to the fireside, followed by the sound of clanking metal as the armoured soldier walked up behind her.

As she stepped into the light, Uki saw she was around the same age as Jori. She had black velvet fur, deep brown eyes and small ears held back from her head with a band of silver. She was dressed in a heavy cloak lined with crimson silk, and beneath it swished a dress made from layers of cloth embroidered all over with gold thread that sparkled and glinted where the firelight caught it. She held herself with a proud confidence – similar to that which he admired in Jori – as if everything she did or said was going to be important.

The soldier behind her was just as impressive. He was taller than Coal even and clad in a suit of plate armour made from shining steel. A tabard of black cloth covered his breastplate and it bore the imperial crest: a white falling star. The pauldrons on his shoulders were decorated with swirls of metal, and his paws were encased in heavy gauntlets, spiked at the knuckles. At his belt hung a broadsword at least three times as long as Jori's blade, and with a ruby on its pommel the size of a chicken's egg.

Uki marvelled at how much sky metal must have been used to forge his outfit and how much it cost. You could probably have bought half of Hulstland with it, and still had some change left over.

Above the suit, the soldier had long, brown fur, neatly trimmed into a pointed beard. His sharp, blue eyes darted across the faces of all the gang rabbits, lingering for a long while on Coal and his hammer-arm, before darting off again, constantly moving.

He's guarding her, Uki thought. *And she's very important. But who is she, and why is she down here with all the orphans and runaways?*

His questions were quickly answered. As soon as the girl stepped forward, Jori gasped in surprise, then knelt on the floor, bowing her head. Many of the other rabbits copied her – even Coal attempted a bow, his eyes wide with astonishment.

Uki and Kree just stood there, staring, wondering what under earth was going on.

'Please,' the girl said. 'Everyone, stand. There's no need to be formal.'

'Your Highness,' said Jori, getting to her feet. She nudged Uki in the ribs and glared at him, as if he had just been terribly rude.

'Have we met?' the girl asked Jori. 'You look familiar.'

'Once or twice,' replied Jori. 'When I was at court, and when you visited my clan warren.'

'I'm sorry,' said Kree, butting in, 'but are we supposed to know who this is? Is she some kind of princess?'

'She's *the* princess, you dunderwit,' said Lurky.

'Princess Ember, daughter of Evil Ash— I mean the god-emperor. No offence, Your Highness.'

Uki swallowed. *Royalty.* Here in front of him. Should he kneel now? Or was it too late? He hoped he hadn't upset her, or made himself look like some kind of bumpkin again.

Wait until she finds out you want to jab a spear into her father, his dark voice added, making him squirm even more.

Ember didn't seem to have noticed his rudeness. She was smiling at Kree. A small, sad smile that hid a great weight of unhappiness.

'Please,' she said. 'I don't want any special treatment. Down here I am just the same as you.'

'Except *you've* got a great big pet bodyguard,' said Kree, pointing at the armoured soldier.

Ember smiled again. 'This is Sir Prentiss.' She laid a paw on the soldier's arm. 'He's been looking after me since I was a kitten. I wouldn't feel safe without him.'

Sir Prentiss nodded and raised a paw to salute everyone. Ember's description of him as a nursemaid wasn't fooling Uki. He still looked as though he could slice his way through every rabbit in the room without breaking into a sweat.

'Tell me,' Ember said to Uki, 'do you really think you could save my father? How will you manage to get this . . . spirit . . . out of him?'

'Well, I, er . . .' Uki's mind raced, trying to think of a way to explain it. In the end, he decided to show her and reached for one of the spears in the quiver on his back.

In a blink, Sir Prentiss had drawn his sword. A whistle of steel, a flash, then the blade was hovering at Uki's throat. Coal growled in reply, raising his hammer and stepping in front of Uki. The two adult rabbits stared at each other, tensed and ready to fight.

'Wait!' Uki cried. 'I wasn't going to hurt her! I just wanted to show her the crystal on my spear!'

'Hold, good Sir Prentiss,' said Ember. She reached across and pushed his sword down with her paw. 'These rabbits don't mean us any harm.'

'Just being careful, my lady,' said the knight. He sheathed his weapon, but his eyes never left Coal. The blacksmith stayed where he was, hammer poised to strike.

'Here,' said Uki. He – very slowly – drew one of his two remaining spears and offered it to Ember, haft first. She took it in her paws and looked at the shard of pink crystal slotted on to the end.

'It's a piece of the prison they were trapped in,' Uki explained. 'It looks just like a bit of glass, but it's really made by the Ancients. When the spirits are inside, it's like there's a whole world there. They lived on islands in an ocean, locked away so they couldn't hurt anybody.'

Ember touched the point of the spearhead, her eyes full of tears. 'And do you have to . . . kill my father with it?'

'Oh, no!' Uki was horrified at the thought. 'I just have to get close enough to jab him. The spirit, Mortix, will be drawn into the crystal. The rabbits I saved before both survived.' He tapped the crystals on his chest.

'That's good to know,' said Ember. 'Although . . . although I think my father will die anyway. Whatever took control of him also stole his life away. It does it to all those who choose to follow him. Lords, guards . . . everybody.'

Jori cleared her throat. 'Perhaps ... Your Highness ... perhaps you could tell us what happened to the emperor. It might help us decide what to do next.'

Ember nodded, her eyes sadder than ever. When she spoke, her voice was quiet. Almost a whisper.

'It started a few months ago. The guards captured a rabbit who was trying to sneak into the palace. A ragged, half-starved thing. His feet were raw from walking and the bones were poking out of his fur. They said he must have come all the way from the Cinder Wall.'

'*Nurg*,' Kree whispered in Uki's ear. 'Or one of those other rabbits from Nether the spirits took over. It has to be!'

'They threw him in a dungeon, but he kept insisting he had a special message for my father. In the end, he was brought into the throne room. And that's when I saw it happen.'

'Mortix?' Uki said. 'You saw the spirit of death?'

'I don't know what I saw,' said Ember. 'There was some kind of shimmering light. It passed from the ragged rabbit to my father ... swirled about his head, then oozed inside him. The next moment, the stranger had fallen down dead and my father was taken ill.'

'Mortix took control of him,' said Uki. 'She went into his head and pushed him aside. These things the Ancients made can do that. They can control us like puppets.'

Ember nodded. 'Whatever happened, it didn't take long. Within days my father was well again but he was . . . different. He hardly seemed to know me, or any of his lords. And then he started proclaiming that he had become the God of Life and Death. He made new laws that he should be worshipped instead of Kether. He promised everyone who followed him that they would live forever.'

'And did many join him?' Jori asked.

Ember nodded. 'Most of the clan lords did. And all of the guard. He started holding ceremonies where they were given his blessing.'

Uki thought of the faceless masks of the guards, that sense of lifeless emptiness beneath. 'What happened at these ceremonies?'

'They took place in the throne room,' said Ember,

her ears beginning to tremble. 'My father … or whatever he now is … took the rabbit's paws in his. Then his eyes glowed with a horrible light. It spread to the rabbit in front of him, drawing something out. And when it was done they were … different. Silent. Dead, almost, even though they still moved and breathed.'

That would explain it, Uki thought. *Mortix's power sucks the life from her victims and makes them her slaves.* It was similar to the way that Charice created an army of diseased servants, or that Valkus made rabbits turn against each other. They all used rabbits to fight for them – spreading their will like a virus.

'And then …' Ember began to sob as she spoke. 'And then he said he wanted to do it to *me*. Sir Prentiss, too. He wanted to turn *us* into those mindless monsters!'

'So, did you run away from the palace? From your father?' Uki asked.

'Yes.' Sir Prentiss answered for Ember, who was now crying into his tabard. 'I smuggled the princess out of the palace to the cathedral. The bishop is ... *was* ... a friend of mine. I knew he hated what had been going on and thought he might help us. Except he had already been taken. Instead of him, these young rabbits were waiting for us when we arrived. They led us to the tunnels and safety. Of a kind.'

'See that in your bones, did you?' Lurky said to Rilda.

'I did indeed,' the soothsayer replied.

Talking about the palace reminded Uki of Necripha, of that glimpse of her before the Cinderthrone. Might Ember have even met her?

'Before you left,' Uki asked, 'did you see any strange visitors? An old woman with a scarf tied around her head? Maybe with a big, muscly guard?'

Ember lifted her head from Sir Prentiss's chest and nodded. 'Why, yes. Yes, I think so. I remember seeing someone like that, just before I ran away. Are they part of your quest as well?'

'Kind of,' said Uki with a shudder. Now he knew who was responsible for all the posters with his face on. And who would be waiting for him to make his next move.

Grit, the leader of the Scrappers, stepped forward to speak.

'Three months ago. That was when our parents started disappearing. Did your father – the emperor – have anything to do with that?'

'He gave an order. For builders and smiths to be gathered from the city. But what he wanted them for or where he sent them I'm afraid I have no idea.'

Grit gave a grunt and scratched under his helmet. A small shower of dust pattered over his shoulders. 'We think we might have the answer to that,' he said. 'We found a new forge or factory, built right under the Eisenrock itself. Got a ton of guards outside the door, so we couldn't get near. Chipper here has been living in the old mines for a year or more. She says it definitely wasn't there before.'

He pointed to one of his gang who might have been a white-furred lop rabbit, but it was difficult to tell under all the mud, coal dust and the oversized helmet that hid her eyes.

'That's right,' she said. 'A new forge. A big one. And they're working it night and day.'

‘What are they building?’ Coal asked. Grit and Chipper shrugged at the same time.

‘Can’t get close enough to find out,’ said Grit. ‘Not without getting snaffled by the deadheads.’

Uki’s fingers played over the buckle on his harness. ‘That’s interesting,’ he said, thinking aloud. ‘But I’d like to get a look at Mortix first. Just to see how difficult it will be to capture her.’

‘It will be next to impossible,’ said Sir Prentiss. ‘The amount of guards you would have to get past . . . A gnat wouldn’t be able to bite Emperor Ash, let alone someone throw a spear at him.’

‘All the same,’ said Uki. ‘I need to see. Is there a way to sneak into the palace?’

A snickering came from Rainna and her band of Toffs. ‘A way in? Where do you think we live? Our base is right under Embervale, in all the old mining tunnels and the secret rooms and passages.’

‘You *live* there?’ said Kree. ‘Right under the guards’ noses? Are you stupid?’

‘We prefer to think of ourselves as brave,’ said Rainna. ‘And we can take you right to the throne room itself. We have a peephole there where you can see everything.'

Uki gritted his teeth and nodded. 'Then that's our first step,' he said. *You never know,* he thought. *We might just get close enough for me to finish this with one spear jab.*

Is anything ever that easy? He could almost hear his dark voice laughing at him.

No, he sighed. *Nothing ever is.*

Chapter Seven

Embervale

Uki was glad to escape the Ghostburrow, with its icy echo, its stink of lost centuries and the never-ending banquet of the stone lords.

Most of the gang members remained behind, wanting to discuss the secret forge and the chance that their parents might be trapped inside. They cast wary glances at Uki and his friends as they prepared to leave, still wary of the things they had heard about him. He wasn't sure if the fear in their eyes was because of him, or if they were worried he might not come back. Perhaps a bit of both.

For their trip to the palace, Rainna chose a guide – her 'best scout' – a young rabbit called Nikku. A fierce little thing, she wore her brown hair in a plait and was dressed in a white silk shirt with the arms torn off and an elaborate pair of baggy, striped trousers that were held up with a piece of rope. She was armed with a sharpened silver butter knife, its handle decorated with the imperial crest. Despite being clothed in odds and ends stolen from the palace laundry, she still looked like a rabbit you didn't want to mess with.

As well as Uki, Jori, Kree and Coal, Lurky the Howler had volunteered to tag along (much to Kree's annoyance). He had never been to the palace and wanted to see 'how them posh folk live up there'. Luckily, none of the Stinkers had asked to come. It was hard enough to breathe with them in the spacious Ghostburrow. Goddess knew what it would be like all squashed up in a tunnel together.

Scrag handed them some lanterns, a flask of water and some chalk.

'Mark the walls as you go,' she said. 'In case you get lost.'

'They won't get lost with *me* around,' said Nikku, puffing out her chest.

'Yes, but if *you* get killed, we're all done for,' said Lurky. He meant it as a joke, but nobody laughed.

'Good luck,' said Ember, as they headed out of the chamber. 'And be careful.'

'We will,' Uki called over his shoulder, trying to sound brave.

The truth was, he couldn't seem to shift the feeling of dread that had begun to follow him around like a stormcloud.

He didn't know if it was the dark, creepiness of all the tombs or the looming presence of Mortix, but every step he took closer to the palace made him feel colder, more steeped in dread. It was as if the marrow in his bones had turned to ice. As if a creeping frost was edging up his spine, into his brain. And there, too, was the thin itching of Necripha's hatred. Was she peering through his eyes right now? Did she know he was closing in on her?

He shook his head to clear it and concentrated on following Nikku as she led them out of the Ghostburrow and into another maze of passages.

Behind him, he could hear Lurky and Kree trading insults. At least they weren't affected by the gloom of this death-filled place.

'This is the last of the crypts,' Nikku was saying, as they climbed through a hole chipped in the ceiling. They came out in an octagonal room, the walls lined with shelves, each one holding a lead coffin.

'Thank Kether for that,' said Jori, helping Coal clamber up. 'I was getting sick of the smell of old bones.'

'I know,' said Nikku, wrinkling her nose. 'No wonder those Bonegrubbers are so odd. Our hideout smells of pastry and bread. It's just under the palace bakery.'

'You can't beat the fresh river air,' said Lurky. 'That's the aroma of our base.'

'Except for when you're around,' said Kree. 'Then it smells of a dead ferret's sweaty kneecaps.'

'Give it a rest, you two.' Coal heaved himself up, then arranged his crutch beneath his arm. 'It's bad enough listening to Kree's mouth running away with itself, let alone giving it an echo. You're like an old, married couple.'

‘Married!’ Kree made a retching sound. ‘I’d rather marry a pile of Mooka’s fresh dung!’ From her bristling fur and the way she avoided looking in anyone’s eyes, it was obvious she was blushing like a bonfire.

Lurky looked just as embarrassed. He quickly tried to change the subject. ‘Who, or what, is a Mooka?’ he asked.

‘The most beautiful animal in the world,’ Kree replied. Then all the feisty energy seemed to drain out of her in an instant. Her bottom lip poked out, and her eyes filled with tears.

‘Come on,’ Uki said, taking her paw. ‘Let’s get to the palace. The sooner this is over with, the sooner you can get back to him.’

Kree gave a sad nod, and they watched Nikku as she pushed at a brick in the wall next to one of the coffin shelves. There was a soft *click* and the shelving swung backwards, exposing a long, brick tunnel.

‘This goes right under the cathedral and on into the palace cellars,’ she said. ‘I think one of the emperors had it built because he didn’t like getting his fur wet when he went to church.’

'That would be Emperor Furnace,' said Jori. 'He was one carrot short of a bunch.'

'Don't the guards know about it?' Uki asked. He had visions of meeting a patrol halfway down and having nowhere to escape to.

'It was bricked up, centuries ago,' said Nikku. 'We found it by chance when we were trying to find a way into the vegetable pantry.'

Uki couldn't imagine what it must be like, sneaking around the walls of the palace, inches away from your enemy. 'Why do you stay there?' he asked. 'Aren't you worried about getting caught?'

Nikku shrugged. 'Our parents were all palace folk. We grew up there. Been playing in the tunnels and caves ever since we could walk. Besides, if the guards saw us, they'd probably think we were just servants. The worst we'd get is a clip round the ear.'

Or your life sucked out of your body, added Uki's dark voice. For once, Uki couldn't help but agree.

*

The passageway ran straight as an arrow, all the way to the tallest hill in Eisenfell, the one with Embervale palace perched on top like a sleeping dragon.

Every inch of the tunnel was lined with neat, red bricks, and the floor was paved with flagstones.

All this work, Uki marvelled, *just because an emperor didn't like getting his whiskers wet.*

The hardest thing to understand about this city, this empire, was just how much wealth and power was floating around. Not to mention the effect it had on rabbits. The village Uki grew up in was made of a few rocks, chipped out of the frozen ground. The rabbits there hadn't even seen a piece of gold, and they counted themselves lucky every time they managed to scrape their way through winter. If the chief had demanded a mile-long tunnel be built, just on a whim, he would have been laughed out of the tribe. Or, more likely, staked out on the glacier as an offering for Zeryth the Ice God. Uki's relatives were quite fond of that sort of thing.

He wondered what would have happened if they had suddenly discovered an asteroid filled with iron on their doorstep. The same thing as here, probably. The Ice Wastes would be full of castles and cathedrals and secret passages before you could twitch a whisker.

‘We’re under the palace now,’ said Nikku, breaking his chain of thought. By instinct, he started to tiptoe, even though nobody could possibly hear anything outside this brick tunnel, through the hundreds of feet of earth and stone above.

They soon came to the passage’s end: a flight of worn steps leading up to a solid brick wall. As in the tombs of the Skullgardens, the mortar around a whole section had been carefully chipped away. Nikku began to slide the bricks out, stacking them neatly beside the hole she made.

‘How far is it to the throne room once we’re in?’ Jori asked.

‘It’s quite a climb,’ said Nikku. ‘Lots of squeezing through narrow nooks and crannies.’

‘Great,’ said Coal.

‘Perhaps you shouldn’t eat so many sugared turnips,’ Lurky and Kree said, at exactly the same time. And then glared at each other in shock.

‘See?’ Coal smirked as he knelt to crawl through the hole. ‘Married couple.’

*

If creeping around beneath the city, or through ancient crypts, was strange, sneaking about a busy palace was even weirder.

Nikku led them from the tunnel (after meticulously replacing the bricks) through a series of dark, musty cellars. All so old that they had been forgotten about, filled with stacks of crates and barrels quietly rotting away in the gloom.

From there, they crawled through some more deserted mineshafts. Nikku explained how the entire area that Eisenfell now covered had once been filled with clumps of iron, blasted through the layers of earth and rock when the asteroid collided with the ground.

Over the centuries, it had all been dug away, piece by piece, and the rabbits had covered everything over with their houses and castles. The only remaining iron was in the mines surrounding the lump called Eisenrock, smack-bang in the centre of the city.

One day, that too would run out. Then the rock itself would be devoured. And then what would the noble clans use for their steel? The natural iron of the Five Realms was poisoned by

Gormalech – completely unusable. Uki supposed they would start trying to steal metal from each other. Some kind of great war would start, or perhaps the emperor would simply seize it all, crushing everyone in his path . . .

Unless you fail to capture Mortix, his dark voice said. **Then none of it will matter anyway**.

Uki shuddered. Just thinking of her name made him realise how close they were. He could feel a chill, pulsing outwards from somewhere above. A cold like the worst winter in the Ice Wastes, except that, instead of freezing your ears and whiskers, it seemed to start inside your own chest, leaching into the very blood that pumped around your veins.

Nikku had reached the end of the mineshaft they were in and was whispering instructions. Uki expected to see her breath steam in the icy air, but nobody seemed to be feeling the cold except him.

'After this shaft, we're inside the palace walls,' she was saying. 'We'll be using the secret passages that were built for spies and sneaking. They're usually empty, but you never know who you might bump into. Best keep your weapons handy.'

Uki and Jori shared a nervous look. The last thing they wanted was to meet one of Mortix's guards and have to fight their way out of the palace. The only advantage they had was the element of surprise.

Scarcely daring to breathe, they followed Nikku up into a narrow stairway, squeezed between two stone walls. The spiders of Embervale certainly enjoyed the secret passages. They were draped from floor to ceiling in cobwebs. Before long, thick strands of dusty webbing clung to everyone's fur, hanging down like white, hairy wigs. Uki had to keep clawing the stuff from his eyes, blinking as it tickled his nose, threatening to make him sneeze.

From the other side of the wall, they began to hear voices. First, there were muffled shouts and some kind of metallic clanging ('The kitchens,' Nikku explained), then there was the tramping of booted feet that must have been a patrol of guards, and finally the mournful sound of a musical instrument – some kind of flute – playing a sad, lonely tune.

'That will be Lady Sheth,' whispered Nikku. 'Her husband was ... *changed* ... by the emperor. Now she sits alone in her chambers all day, playing music to herself.'

'Do you know all the rabbits in the palace?' Uki asked.

Nikku nodded. 'Most of them. From these tunnels you can watch them in secret. You find out all sorts of things. Here, I'll show you.'

They crept up a few more steps and paused on a small landing. Nikku put a paw to the wall, where there was a tiny wooden hatch. She gently moved it aside to reveal a peephole, shining with torchlight.

'Put your eye to that,' she whispered.

Filled with a kind of guilty curiosity, Uki did as she said, peering through the peephole with his left eye. He found himself staring into a rich chamber, thick carpets on the floor, tapestries covering the walls, and a towering four-poster bed taking up much of the space. A fire blazed in the hearth and a candelabrum hung from the ceiling, filling the room with light.

As his eye adjusted to the brightness, Uki saw two rabbits. One – a lady dressed in robes of ice blue, covered with silver embroidery – sat on the edge of the bed, her head in her paws. The other – a fierce-looking man in fine ceremonial armour – was walking back and forth by the fire, clearly worried about something.

'But, Blain,' the lady was saying, 'if you go through with it, you will never be the same again! All the other lords have become so . . . different. So . . . *dead.* It's as if they don't even remember who they were before!'

'I know, I've seen them!' Blain's voice was cross, but also tinged with fear. 'I don't want that to happen to me. I'm not hungry for it, like Sheth and Boltus were. But how can I refuse the offer? The emperor would see it as a terrible insult!'

A sob came from the lady, and her shoulders shook as she cried. 'Can't we just leave? Can't we go home to the mountains? We can hide in our warren until this all goes away. Until everything is back to normal again!'

'And what if it doesn't return?' Blain said. 'What if every single clan lord accepts the emperor's blessing and gets changed? What if I'm the only one left?'

'Then we can run!' The lady jumped off the bed and clutched her husband, squeezing his paws in hers. 'We can escape to Gotland or Enderby. Anywhere to get away from this horrible, lifeless place!'

The two held each other, both crying, and Uki pulled his eye away. Somehow it felt very wrong, watching such a personal, private moment. Spying on rabbits who didn't know they were being watched.

'Who are they?' he asked Nikku.

'Lord and Lady Frost,' she said. 'They came to visit court a while ago. They're not happy with what's going on. I suspect they'll be off very soon.'

'I hope they're allowed to leave.' Uki slid the wooden cover back over the peephole, wishing there was some way he could help the poor rabbits on the other side.

'I wouldn't bet on it.' Nikku turned away, leading them further up the stairs, deeper into the hidden walkways of the ancient palace. The muffled sound of crying followed them, until it vanished into the clouds of dust and cobwebs.

*

The passage spiralled around inside the walls for another age, until Nikku finally stopped and turned to face them. They had arrived in a cramped room, only just large enough for them all to squeeze in. Three of its walls were the same smooth, grey stone as the rest of the palace. The fourth had large window frames carved all along it, but instead of glass, some kind of dusty fabric covered them. Strands of coloured wool poked out all over, and there were holes everywhere, as if a swarm of moths had stopped by for a feast.

Nikku snuffed out her lantern and motioned for the others to do the same. Once the room had been plunged into darkness, thin beams of light crept in through the punctured cloth.

'We're behind a tapestry,' Nikku whispered. 'On the other side is the throne room. This is just one of the many places built to spy on it, but it's so old, we think it must have been forgotten.'

'Excellent,' said Coal, moving to put his good eye to a peephole. Uki would have followed, but he was overwhelmed by a sudden surge of icy air. A cold presence was in the room beyond. Timeless.

Lifeless. Freezing. As empty and dead as the black space between the stars.

Mortix.

He felt Jori at his side, her strong paw on his back. 'Is it her?'

He nodded, blinking against the cold. It felt as though his eyeballs were turning to ice. A chill so great, it made the winter blizzards of his childhood seem like a summer's breeze.

'Think of Iffrit,' Jori said. 'He was stronger than her and he's a part of you now.'

She was right. He pictured the little creature he had met, all those moons ago in the forest. He remembered the bright flames that had licked over Iffrit's body as he hung in the air, telling him a bizarre tale about crystal prisons and deadly spirits. That, in turn, unlocked one of Iffrit's own memories: of how the guardian used to soar over the world Mortix had been imprisoned in, with giant wings of orange fire.

The remembered blaze warmed Uki. Iffrit's power kindled inside him, thawing through the deathly chill of Mortix, curling through his blood as it flowed around his body. It was like drinking a hot cup of cream, honey and cinnamon. His paws twitched as they came back to life, his ears prickled with pins and needles as they slowly unfroze.

'You should come look at this,' said Coal, eye still pressed to the tapestry.

Lurky and Kree had already found peepholes of their own, and their quiet gasps at what they saw made Jori and Uki hurry over to the wall of cloth.

Leaving Jori to the higher holes, Uki squatted down and peered through a tear the size of a pebble. He expected to find himself looking into a room similar to that of Lord Frost's, so he wasn't prepared for the sheer scale of the throne chamber. It made his head spin with vertigo.

The tapestry they were spying through was high off the ground. *Very* high. Fifteen metres or more. As if they were perched on a cliff edge, looking down at mouse-sized figures below.

From up there, they had a view of the whole room. They could see the way it stretched off into the distance: a chasm of paved marble large enough to hold an entire warren inside.

How? Uki marvelled. *How do the walls hold up so much stone? Why doesn't the ceiling come tumbling down?*

The answer must have been the columns – rows and rows of towering trunks of white marble that stretched up to the roof and then arched over, interlacing like the branches of a forest canopy. There were even bunches of leaves carved out of the stone. Imitating life, just like the frozen fire in the Ghostburrow.

'The windows,' he heard Kree whisper. 'They're alight!'

Running the length of the far wall were a series of stained-glass windows. Almost as tall as the ceiling themselves, they were filled with intricate patterns of coloured glass. Every shade of the rainbow. The golden light of summer sunset that flooded into the room lit them, made them blaze. It was an explosion of colour that burned across the stone floor, bringing life to the cold, grey tiles.

And to the rabbits that swarmed all over the room.

From their secret vantage point, they looked like toy dolls, posed in groups amongst the columns. Uki could see rows of Deathless, the tinted sunbeams gleaming off their silver faceplates in sparks of violet, crimson and orange. They stood, stiff as statues and just as lifeless, in regimented lines everywhere. In between were huddles of courtiers, all dressed in long robes, heads tilted towards one another as they whispered. Servants moved amongst them, carrying trays filled with crystal goblets and plates of food.

Important-looking rabbits with staffs ushered others here and there, herding them like lost sheep towards the centre of the room, towards the dais of steps that held a tall metal chair draped with swathes of black silk. To where a velvet-furred rabbit sat, dressed in a suit of pure sky metal, staring at all those around him with a cold, heartless gaze.

'There's the emperor,' said Nikku. As if she needed to point him out.

Uki could *feel* who it was, even from up in their hideaway. The icy waves were pulsing out of him and, as Uki stared, his senses gave him a glimpse of the spirit who was living inside. Just as with Valkus and Charice, Uki could see the wispy, transparent form of Mortix floating in the air around Emperor Ash. A ghostly image, like someone had painted over reality with lines of fog. Invisible to anyone but Uki.

She took the form of a tall woman, wisp-thin, with pale, chalky skin. Her ebony hair drifted in waves around her head, as if she was swimming at the bottom of some chill ocean, and her eyes were pure, glistening black. A tattered robe hung from her slender frame, and her long fingers were tipped with talon-sharp nails. Like her brothers and sister, she had round, stubby ears on the side of her head and no trace of fur. *Just like the Ancients,* Uki thought. *The ones who made her.*

'Do you think you could hit the Emperor with a spear from here?' Kree asked. 'If you used all your strength?'

Uki shook his head. He might be strong enough, but there was no way he could strike such a tiny target from so far away. It would just be a waste of his precious spears. He only had two left, after all.

'Who's that next to the Cinderthrone?' said Jori. 'Could it be Necripha?'

Tearing his eyes away from Mortix, Uki peered

into the shadows next to the iron chair. There was indeed somebody there. A hunched, shrivelled figure in a hooded robe. He couldn't see her face from this distance, nor whether she wore a scarf around that revolting third eye on her head, but he could sense the bitter spiteful aura that swirled around her. It couldn't be anyone else.

'That's her,' he said.

Next to him, he felt Coal tense. 'Where? That bent old thing beside the dais? That was the one you were trapped in the hole with?'

'Yes.' Uki remembered those awful hours, stuck in the bottom of a muddy pit with the dying rabbit and her servant. He could have left them to rot, but he saved their lives and now here they were, trying to ruin his quest and get him captured.

If only you'd listened to me, said his dark voice, **Mortix might not know we were coming. You could have walked right up and caught her.**

Not that it would ever have been that simple.

And anyway, why was Coal so interested in her? Uki remembered how he had shown the same fascination back in the Fenlands. What did he know about the Endwatch that the rest of them didn't?

Uki was about to ask, when he heard Jori give a strangled, shocked gasp. She clutched at the tapestry, making the whole thing wobble.

'*Pok ha boc!*' Kree hissed. 'What are you doing? If the cloth falls down, everyone will see us!'

But Jori wasn't listening. Her eyes were fixed on the throne-room floor below, her ears pressed tight against her head, visibly trembling. 'It's *him*,' she whispered. 'It has to be.'

'Who?' Uki scanned the chamber, trying to spot what had upset her. A procession of some kind was making its way along a black carpet toward the throne, two familiar-shaped rabbits at the front.

One was dressed in a grey cloak, draped over padded leather armour, dyed a deep shade of shadow-black. His fur was dusky grey, with black tips on his ears. Almost an exact match for his best friend, Jori.

'It's Venic!' Uki whispered. Jori's cousin, who had ambushed them in Enk.

'What's he doing here?' Kree said.

'Following us,' said Coal. 'And it looks as though he's about to get blessed by the god-emperor.'

Uki knew what *that* meant. He pulled at Jori's cloak, trying to tug her away from the peephole, but she wouldn't budge.

'The other rabbit,' said Kree. 'It must be Needle.'

Putting his eye back to the hole, Uki looked at the rabbit beside Venic. She wore crimson armour, spikes jutting out along her forearms. The fur around her eyes was painted with a thick, black stripe.

'They've teamed up together,' said Coal. 'How sweet.'

'I don't think we need to see this,' Uki said. 'Come on, Jori.'

'No.' Jori almost growled the word. 'He's my cousin, my blood. My clan. I have to watch. I owe him that, despite everything we've both done.'

'And I *want* to watch,' said Lurky. 'Has anyone got any radishes? Some parsnip chips, maybe? I like a good munch when there's a show on.'

'How about we make a show of you falling from this window and splatting on the floor, you *bulba boodah*?' Kree grabbed Lurky by the collar and Nikku had to separate them both.

'Be quiet, all of you!' she whispered as loud as she dared. 'If they see or hear us, we're dead!'

A brooding silence filled the room as they all placed their eyes back at the peepholes, watching as God-Emperor Ash bestowed his 'blessing' on their enemies.

They saw Venic and Needle walk up the steps to the Cinderthrone and kneel, taking the god-emperor's paws in their own. Uki though, with his unique sight, could tell what was actually happening. Mortix, gleaming ghostly white over the spot where Ash sat, had surged towards the kneeling rabbits, a look of dark hunger in her eyes.

Words were being said, although Uki was too far away to hear. But he could see Mortix's wide grin of triumph, her hungry fangs and the glow of blinding white light that began to pour from Venic and Needle, flowing like a waterfall of smoke towards the Ancient spirit's mouth.

She's drinking them, he thought. *She's eating up their life, swallowing it like wine.*

Charice had given him the power to sense living energy, and he could feel Venic and Needles' now. It was ebbing away, disappearing. And at the same time, that of Mortix was growing stronger.

'The light,' Kree whispered. 'It's all around them.'

'What can you see?' Uki asked, wondering what the scene looked like to someone without his spirit-sight.

'There's a glow coming out of them,' Kree said. 'And it's lighting up the emperor.'

'He really *is* blessing them,' said Lurky, his voice full of awe. 'It's magic.'

'It's not magic,' said Uki. Although he could see how it would look that way. But Mortix was a *thing*, made by the Ancients. And they themselves had just been living creatures, not that different from rabbits. What was happening, down there in the throne room, was just a creation going horribly wrong. Like a wagon losing its wheel and crashing, except much more complicated.

'Venic . . .' Jori's whisper was almost too quiet to hear. Finally, she turned away, looking at Uki with tears in her eyes. 'He's gone, isn't he?'

‘I think so,’ said Uki. There were no words he could say. Instead, he took Jori’s paw and squeezed it tight, hoping that was enough to show he was there, that he understood her pain. That their friendship meant she was not alone.

Down below, the empty shells that had been Venic and Needle were standing, shuffling off, out of the throne room, led by two of the faceless guards. Another pair of rabbits had stepped up to take their place, kneeling in front of the god-emperor.

But something was happening. Instead of taking their paws, the figure on the throne had turned to the hunched old rabbit beside it. Uki could see the ghostly shape of Mortix, bending her head and listening as Necripha whispered.

And then, to his utter horror, both of the vile creatures turned and stared upwards, across the room, straight at the tapestry where Uki and his friends were hidden.

Even from that distance, he could see the looks of hatred on their faces. He could see Necripha’s gnarled hand as she raised it and pointed a bony finger.

The evil witch had used the link she shared with

Uki to find him. She had traced it, as he had done before, across the throne room and up to the tapestry. They had been pinpointed, and any second the guards would be after them.

*

'We have to run!' Uki turned from the tapestry, pulling Kree and Jori with him. 'We have to go *now!*'

Nikku stared at him for a moment, eyes wide with fear for an instant, before snapping back into control.

'This way,' she said, running out of the room and down the stairs. The others all followed, Lurky – silent for once – huffing and puffing as he sprinted, and Coal swinging himself down the steps on his crutch as fast as he could.

Slipping and stumbling, tangling themselves in cobwebs, they reached the small landing where Uki had spied on Lord Frost. Now, instead of the sound of crying, the echo of heavy boots on stone could be heard, growing closer and closer.

'They're in the secret passage!' Kree shouted. 'They're going to find us!'

'Not if I can help it,' said Nikku. She put her shoulder to the wall and pushed. Uki leant across to help her and a door opened. It had been made out of the bricks themselves, invisible amongst the gloom and dust.

'Passages within passages,' said Coal, as they all bundled through.

'Embervale has more secret corridors than real ones,' said Nikku. She forced the door shut behind them, sealing them in complete darkness. 'We can't risk a lantern. We'll have to feel our way with our paws.'

They began to shuffle forwards, reaching out to brush the walls with their fingers, testing the ground with their toes.

As the sound of guards marching on the steps went past them, they found another staircase in the darkness and began heading downwards.

'Where does this go?' Uki whispered as loudly as he dared.

'It comes out in one of the feasting halls,' Nikku replied. 'And then there's another passage in one of the fireplaces that will lead us back to the cellars.'

Down, down they went, in blackness that was so complete, Uki began to wonder if he would ever see again.

His paws ran over the cold stone brickwork, rasping against the dust, bumping over the lines of mortar that held the palace together. His toes felt for the steps, feeling the glassy edges where centuries of booted feet had worn them away. *Step, step, step,* he made his way ever downwards, until he went to put his foot down and instead met a flat, solid flagstone.

The jolt travelled up his body, making him bite his tongue. Judging by the several sounds of 'oof' and 'ow', he realised the same thing must have happened to everyone else, too.

'We're at the bottom,' Nikku whispered. 'I just have to find the catch for the door.'

Uki could hear her tapping at the walls with her paws, trying to find the hidden stone or lever that would spring the catch. He reached out himself, expecting to run his fingers over the brickwork, and instead feeling soft fabric. And underneath that, the firm warmth of a rabbit's body. One taller and broader than him.

'Jori?' he whispered. 'Coal?'

They both grunted, their voices coming from

behind him. Neither of them was the rabbit his paw was touching.

His fingers moved some more, tracing out the shape of a belt with a pouch, the scabbard of a sword.

He swallowed, the fur on his neck beginning to prickle.

'I think,' he said, trying not to let his voice shake. 'I think there's someone else in here with us.'

There was silence for a moment, and then the scraping of steel on flint as Nikku lit her lantern.

Sparks flew, light flickered then bloomed, chasing away the darkness and revealing who it was that Uki's paw had found.

A ghost! That was his first thought. For the *thing* was draped in long black robes and had a skull for a face – gleaming white bone, carved all over with whorls and spirals.

The others must have thought the same, as they all jumped backwards, pressing themselves up against the passage wall.

It was only as Uki leapt back himself that he noticed the skull-face was just a mask. Grey eyes peered out from the sockets, and a pair of black-furred ears poked from the top. The rabbit had a paw on the sword hilt at its belt, ready to draw, but before it could, a second rabbit poked its head out from behind it.

This one looked less scary. He had familiar spirals and patterns dyed into his fur. His ears were heavily tattooed and pierced with two large, wooden discs and there was a silver ring through his nose.

A bard! Uki realised. *Like Minnow. Except with more decorations.*

'Well!' the bard said, his eyes twinkling with amusement. 'Fancy meeting some fellow travellers, and in such an unusual spot! I don't suppose you chaps know a way out of the palace, do you? Preferably one that doesn't involve being caught and killed by those metal-headed guards?'

'Who . . . who are you?' Uki managed to stammer.

'My name is Yarrow the bard,' said the tattooed rabbit. 'And this scary specimen is Zarza. She's a bonedancer, don't you know.'

'That means I'm an assassin.' When the masked rabbit spoke, her voice was as cold as a Skullgarden grave. 'I'm here to kill the emperor. And any other rabbit that gets in my way.'

Interlude

'His eyes are closing.' Nikku leans close to Rue, who still lies in the bard's arms, propped up and wrapped in blankets.

'I'm awake.' The little rabbit fights to keep his eyes open. He smiles at Nikku and reaches out with a paw to touch her face. 'You are in the story! I knew you were important when I first met you.'

'I am,' Nikku smiles back. 'In the story, that is. I wasn't all that important, in the scheme of things.'

'We wouldn't be here without you,' says Jori. 'The guards would have caught us in the palace walls, and it would all have been over.'

The bard looks over to the Arukhs, who are still staring at him, wide-eyed.

'Well?' he says. 'Have you heard enough? Will you take us to your chief for more medicine?'

The pair pause to look at each other, then turn back to the bard, eyes hungry for more of the tale.

'First you tell us more,' the girl says. 'Then we will take you.'

'There's not much time,' says Jori. 'I can scrape another tiny spoonful of antidote from this pot, but it won't last long. We need to start walking now.'

'Right,' says the bard. 'We go now, or no story. And if Rue dies, I will *never* tell you another word. Even if it means losing my spectacular ears.'

The Arukhs look like they are about to protest, but the story has its hooks in them. They *have* to hear more, have to know where it goes. The bard has got them, and he knows it. A good story is better than a worm on a hook for bait.

'We will take you,' says the boy rabbit, standing up with a grunt.

'Thank the Goddess for that,' Jori mutters, just

loud enough for the bard to hear, and she spoons the last of the antidote into Rue's mouth.

'Is it far?' the bard asks, struggling to stand up with Rue in his arms.

The boy Arukh shakes his head. 'Not far,' he says. 'But it will be too steep for your cart. I can carry the child, if you like.'

The bard is reluctant to let these fierce rabbits touch Rue, but he also knows that his knees and back might crumble to pieces if he tries to walk with him in his arms. With an order to be careful, he tenderly passes his apprentice over to the Arukh brave.

Just as they are about to leave, Jaxom clears his throat.

'I really hate to do this, but my jerboas . . . I can't just leave them.'

'Of course.' The bard nods his head. There are wolves in these mountains. And probably hundreds more Arukhs, besides.

'I'll wait here until you come back,' Jaxom says.

'No,' says the bard. 'You get back to Gant in Melt. Send out more sparrows to the Foxguard, just in case.'

Jaxom's eyes widen, his ears flick back. 'I'm not *leaving* you!'

The bard walks over and puts his paws on Jaxom's shoulders. 'It's fine. I've got an idea we might not be coming back this way. You'll be stuck out here waiting for nothing.'

'We'll be all right, Jaxom.' Jori pats the flask on her belt and nods towards Nikku's bow. 'Besides, I know Darkfire. Once we see him, we'll be safe.'

'I can't . . .' Jaxom says. 'I won't . . .'

'Go,' says the bard. 'Send the sparrows. I'll reply back to you when I can. That's an order, by the way.'

Jaxom tries to protest again, but both Nikku and Jori have a quiet word with him. Finally, he agrees and climbs up into his cart, holding the reins with clutched fists.

'Goodbye, Jaxom,' says Rue. The last drops of antidote have done their job and he is awake again, watching everything from over the Arukh's shoulder. 'It was nice meeting you.'

'Farewell, brave one,' says Jaxom. 'I *will* see you again. And it was an honour.'

With that he shakes the reins and turns his cart

around, riding off towards Icebark Forest. The bard is certain he saw tears in the warrior's eyes as he left.

'Well,' he says. 'That was a sad parting. But we can't stand around here all day. Let's get on to our hosts' village.'

'Can you carry on with the story?' Rue asks, doing his best version of a pleading look. 'It will help me stay awake as we travel.'

'Yes!' The girl Arukh attempts to pull the same face but with less success (more used, as she is, to twisting her features into terrifying battle-scowls). 'Tell some more!'

'While I'm walking up a mountainside?' says the bard. 'It's hard enough just managing to breathe!'

'Please!' say Rue and both the Arukhs together.

'Very well, then,' says the bard with a huff. 'But don't expect me to do the voices this time.'

And, as they begin the long trudge up the mountainside, he continues his tale.

Chapter Eight

Ambush

By the time they had scrambled their way between the palace walls, dashed along the brick passage to the Skullgardens and clambered down through the layers of tombs, every muscle in Uki's body burned and ached.

They stumbled into the Ghostburrow to find all the urchins and orphans tucked up in scraps of sacking and stolen blankets, lying in snoring bundles around the crackling fire. Only Rilda was awake, her long fingers playing over the scattered knucklebones before her. She must have read their arrival in them as she didn't even twitch her ears when they entered.

'Find what you were looking for?' she whispered, as they made their way across the wide, dark chamber.

'And some more besides,' said Uki. 'A travelling bard and a—'

'Bringer of death?' Rilda interrupted, picking up the skull of a shrew from amongst her tumble of bones.

'A good description, soothsayer,' said Zarza. She took a seat by the fire, after glancing carefully around the room. Yarrow was over by the stone table, fascinated by the statues of the first lords.

'This must be Cinder himself,' he was saying. 'And Nightshade, Thrykk, Argent . . . all the lords of the original clans! How fascinating!'

'There'll be time to stare at those in the morning, bard,' said Coal, dragging a blanket out of his pack. 'Right now, we need to sleep. I feel like I've been running for months.'

That wasn't an exaggeration, Uki realised. They had arrived in Eisenfell in the early evening and had spent the past eight hours or so sneaking, climbing and fleeing. He had never been so tired in his life.

With the last scraps of his strength, he also pulled out a blanket and nudged his backpack into a pillow shape. Kree made her bed next to him, but Jori remained standing, staring across the chamber to where the statue of Lord Nightshade sat, eating his eternal feast.

Uki knelt up to tug on her paw, while Kree rolled out some blankets for her. 'Come on, Jori,' he said. 'You need some sleep.'

'I failed,' Jori whispered. 'Failed my cousin, failed my clan. Again.'

'There was nothing you could do,' Uki said. Using some of his strength, he managed to pull her away from Nightshade's stone gaze. She sat down on her blankets slowly shaking her head.

'You can't blame yourself,' said Kree, grabbing Jori around the shoulders and hugging her tight. 'Venic wouldn't even have been there if he wasn't trying to hunt you down and kill you.'

'And he wouldn't have been doing that if I'd never left the clan,' Jori replied.

'But then you would have had to kill dozens of other rabbits by now,' said Uki. 'Would you rather that had happened?'

'Of course not!' The thought of it made Jori shudder.

'Then you made the right choice,' said Kree. 'You saved lives by doing what you believed. And Venic lost his by doing what *he* believed. There's no good crying over which way the wind blows, as we say on the plains.'

'And besides,' Uki added, 'I reckon Lord Nightshade *would* be proud of you. Of your courage, at least.'

'And of your amazing friends.' Kree gave Jori a final squeeze before collapsing on her bed. Finally, the older girl began to smile. She even managed a chuckle.

'Very well, you've convinced me,' Jori said. She curled up in her blankets before turning back to Uki. 'So, fearless leader, what's your plan? Did our trip to the palace give you any ideas?'

'Too tired . . .' Uki yawned. 'We'll talk about it tomorrow.'

In truth, what he had seen had given him more questions than answers. How were they ever going to get close to Mortix? Who were the two strangers they had met? What was Necripha up to? And the way she had known he was there . . . She must have been using one of her new 'tricks' – the ones she mentioned in Witherwitch. Somehow, Mortix had taught her to sense when he was near, rather than the other way round.

The thought of that shrivelled witch, sniffing him out like a bad carrot, made him feel sick. He curled up, clutching his belly, wondering if she could find him here, buried deep amongst the old bones of Eisenfell.

From the pile of blankets next to him, he heard Kree give a sad sigh.

'I hope Mooka is tucked up for the night,' she whispered. 'I hope he isn't missing me like I'm missing him.'

Uki opened his mouth to reassure her with some kind words, but before he could even get his voice to work, he had fallen into a deep, dreamless sleep.

*

He woke to the sound of chatter and the smell of breakfast wafting around the chamber. Toasted bread slathered with fresh butter and dripping with honey. So delicious it almost masked the dried-sewage stench of the Stinkers.

Sitting up and rubbing his aching muscles, Uki saw that Zarza and Yarrow had taken a spot by the campfire, next to Rilda and the other Bonegrubbers. They were all holding thick slabs of toast in their paws, sipping from steaming cups of nettle tea. Introductions must have been made and it looked as though Yarrow was questioning all of them, snaffling up every detail he could.

Standing apart, hidden in the shadows, were Ember and Sir Prentiss, ears pricked as they listened in on the news.

Jori was already stirring next to him, knuckling the sleep from her eyes. Beside her, Coal was fixing his hammer-arm back on, and lacing up the leather cuff that attached his wooden leg.

'What do you think of those two, then?' asked Kree, making him jump. She was peering at Yarrow and Zarza from a hole in her blankets, her voice too loud, as usual. 'That one with the skull mask – she gives me the shivers!'

'She's a bonedancer,' said Jori. 'We learnt about them in our training. They are an order of female rabbits who worship Nixha, the primitive goddess of death. They believe that they do her will by killing things.'

'What kind of things?' Uki asked.

'Anything. They hire themselves out as assassins. They're probably the best fighters in the whole of the Five Realms. Well, almost.'

'Are you saying dusk wraiths are better?' Kree smiled up at Jori, who just shrugged – and patted her silver-topped flask with a paw.

'Bonedancers are bad news,' said Coal. 'We should get rid of her as soon as possible.'

'What do you know of bonedancers?' Jori gave the wounded blacksmith a glare. 'You're a miner from Hulstland. Even *I* haven't seen one before.'

Coal was silent for a moment, making a show of testing his hammer-arm, almost as if he were lost for an answer. 'I've been around,' he finally said. 'Seen lots of things. All I'm saying is, you should be careful who you trust.'

'We trusted *you*,' said Kree.

'That's different,' said Coal. 'I'd never let one of you come to harm. Not ever. I swear it.'

'Swear on what?' said Jori. Her eyes were narrowed, distrustful. She was looking at Coal the way she had when they first met: as if she smelt an enemy.

'On my good eye,' said Coal. 'Without which I'd be completely blind, by the way.'

'It's fine, Coal,' said Uki, standing up and patting him on the back. 'Jori's just teasing. But I'm not sure I agree with you about the bonedancer. I think she could be useful.'

'You bet she could,' said Jori. 'Do you have any idea what it would cost us to hire an assassin like that?'

'As much as a poisoner from Clan Septys?' Kree poked her tongue out at Jori and then rolled out of her blankets before she could be slapped.

'Come on,' said Uki. 'Let's see what they have to say for themselves.'

*

They got to the fireside just as Yarrow, the bard, was finishing his questioning.

'Fascinating,' he said. 'So, Rilda here was already living in this … 'Ghostburrow'? And then the rest of you charming ragamuffins made your way down here when your parents went missing?'

'Some of us were already in the Underfell,' said Grit. 'I ran away from the orphanage when I was six. And we don't all live *here*. Just the Bonegrubbers. Us Scrappers are from the mines.'

'And the Howlers are from the docks,' said Lurky, puffing his chest out. 'The *best* place to live.'

Yarrow looked across the fireside to where the Stinkers sat, quietly seeping stench into the air. 'And what about your … more fragrant friends? Where do they live?'

'We're the Stinkers,' said one of the grubby rabbits. 'We live in the tunnels under Soilwallow. Where the tanneries and cess pits are.'

'I'd never have guessed,' said Yarrow, wrinkling his nose.

There was a pause, as all the gangs had finished telling their stories, and Uki took his chance to speak. He cleared his throat, drawing stares from all the rabbits. 'May we ask why you and your friend are here?' he said. 'And why you want to kill the emperor?'

There was a gasp from the room's corner, and Uki winced as he remembered Ember. But Yarrow was already bowing to Zarza, the bonedancer, motioning her to speak. Up until now, she had been sitting silently, firelight flickering across her carved bone mask.

'I am a servant of Nixha, the true goddess of death,' she said. 'This emperor who claims he is a god is nothing of the sort. His words are an insult. A blasphemy. Nixha herself has taken offence, and my order's leader has passed sentence on him. He must be destroyed.'

'Kether is the only god!' Lurky blurted out the words and instantly regretted them, as Zarza fixed him with the kind of look a buzzard might give a mouse just before it swooped.

'Kether was invented by your emperors centuries ago,' she said, her voice like a blade. 'All that nonsense about sacred numbers was made up as a way to control you. The only real gods are Nixha and her sister Estra. And their great foe, Gormalech.'

‘Gormalech is no god,’ Uki said, and then winced as Zarza shifted her killer stare on to him.

‘And how would you know this, chopped-in-half rabbit?’

Uki planted his feet and tried to look as fierce as possible. ‘Because I’ve met his brothers and sisters.’ He tapped the glowing crystals on his buckle for emphasis, and watched as Yarrow’s eyes boggled.

‘Do tell us more, old chap,’ the bard said, ears twitching. ‘Start from the beginning and speak nice and slowly. I’ve a feeling I’ll need to open up a new room in my memory warren for *this*.’

And so Uki, once again, told the tale of his night in Icebark Forest and the quest it set him on. He described the events in the twin cities of Syn and Nys, the battle in the Fenlands and the journey to Eisenfell. All the while Yarrow stared at him, unblinking. The gang members did, too, and even Zarza . . . Nobody dared breathe until he had finished.

‘Incredible!’ Yarrow shouted, as soon as he was done. ‘Apologies, dear Zarza, but this tale makes *your* quest seem like the drudgiest bedtime story in the history of drudginess! I hereby leave you to your own devices and attach myself to this fascinating young chap and his colourful band of merry friends!'

'I couldn't give a flying turnip. I never wanted you to come with me in the first place. If it wasn't for you, jabbering in my ear the whole time, we might not have got lost in the palace walls at all.' The bonedancer turned her head towards Uki. 'But it does seem that you and I both want the emperor dead.'

'I don't want to *kill* him,' said Uki, horrified. 'I just want to capture the spirit that's controlling him. I'm hoping he survives afterwards.'

'But you *do* both want the same thing,' said Jori, giving Uki a nudge. 'It would help all of us if we worked together.'

Zarza was silent for a moment, regarding Uki and the others with that cold, considering gaze. Finally, she nodded. 'Agreed. But even with a hundred more bonedancers, we will never get to the emperor in that palace. He is surrounded by soldiers and layers of stone walls. It would take an entire army to even scratch him.'

'*Nam ukku ulla,*' said Kree, punching one of her fists into her paw. 'How are we supposed to draw him out? Knock on the front door and ask if he wants to come and play?'

'I might have an idea.' A voice came out of the shadows where Ember had been carefully listening to all that was said. 'But I want a promise first.'

'A promise of what?' Zarza cocked her head as the princess and her bodyguard walked up to the fireside. It looked as though she was considering the best way to kill them both.

'That you will *not* murder my father,' Ember said. 'That Uki will try his best to save him.'

'The emperor's daughter!' Yarrow did a joyful dance on the spot. 'An actual princess! This tale grows more wonderful by the second!'

'Tell me the plan first,' said Zarza. 'Then I will decide.'

Ember narrowed her eyes and matched the bonedancer's stare. Then she glanced at Uki, who gave a slight nod. 'My father, or whatever is controlling him, will be leaving the palace shortly. Before I ran away, I overheard plans that he wanted to change the Cathedral of Kether into a temple to himself. There is to be a special ceremony with a procession from the palace. We would be able to surprise them when they enter the Skullgardens.'

'That would make a perfect place for an ambush,' said Coal, tapping his hammer against his paw.

'Yes,' said Jori. 'All those gravestones and tombs to hide behind. And we could escape back into the Underfell quickly, before the Deathless had a chance to react.'

Zarza nodded. 'Very well,' she said. 'I give my word that I will not kill the false god-emperor. At least, not until Uki has tried to strike him with his crystal spears. Now, tell us when this ceremony is to take place.'

Ember took a deep breath. Uki could see her battling the instinct to keep her father safe, gambling everything on the chance that he could save Ash from the clutches of Mortix.

'The Feast of Kether,' she said, shoulders and ears drooping as the words left her. 'He's going to destroy the old religion at dawn on the Feast of Kether.'

'Midsummer's Day,' said Yarrow. 'That's what it is in the *real* old religion. And it's in two days' time.'

Uki looked at the gathering of scruffy urchins, outcasts and strangers that stood around the

Ghostburrow. They really didn't look like an army that could stop a god-emperor and all his soldiers. Especially with only two days to prepare.

But it was all they had. And they had been in situations just as hopeless before. Their friendship and their bravery always carried them through. He clenched his fists.

'We'd better get planning, then,' he said.

*

Dawn on Midsummer's Day saw them crouching amongst the graves and lichen-covered tombs of the Skullgardens. They had crept up from the many hidden tunnels and passages below, finding spots to hide amongst the granite and ivy.

The sunrise was blazing off to the east, washing everything in an orange glow. Tendrils of mist clung to the ground high up on Cathedral Hill, snaking in between the tombstones which poked up through the wispy blanket – slabs of golden-daubed stone, mossy statues of robed and armoured rabbits, the tips of their ears snapped off by frost, the edges of their features rubbed smooth by centuries of rain.

Behind them loomed the Cathedral of Kether, so tall, so monumental, that Uki couldn't look at it without losing his breath. Spires towered upwards, like needles scratching the sky. So high that rooks and ravens were nesting up among the carved stonework. So high you could barely see the gold-plated numbers that decorated the topmost tiles.

Beneath their steep roofs, pointed arches framed windows of coloured glass, even taller and more intricate than the ones at Embervale. Stone creatures with grotesque faces leaned out into the wind all around, bat and dragon wings spread as if they were about to take flight.

A long nave stretched out from the main building, ending in a grand double doorway of oak. Its entire length was filled with more windows, flanked by rows of buttresses and topped off with as many pointed pinnacles as could be crammed on.

The place was big enough to fit every rabbit in Eisenfell inside, although Uki would not have wanted to try it. He didn't trust anything that big that hadn't been formed by nature. That many chunks of stone weren't meant to be stacked on top of one

another. Not without tumbling to the ground, or bursting open like one of the dams he used to build.

And yet it had stood there for many, many years. Long enough for the stonework to be painted all over with spatters of thick lichen. Long enough for the gargoyles to begin to crumble, their features worn blank, like pebbles on a beach.

There was a plaza in front of the cathedral doors. An open space of paved stone, surrounded on all sides by the clustered graves.

Although 'clustered' was an understatement.

All across the top of the hill, right up to the ramshackle wall that ran around it, the Skullgardens were squashed, crammed, crushed full of buried rabbits. More, even, than had been entombed in the endless crypts beneath it. Gravestones nudged and leant against each other like scales on a dragon's back. Like leaves on a stone tree.

There wasn't a spare scrap of earth that somebody's bones hadn't been planted in. So many dead rabbits, Uki marvelled that there were any still alive in the city below.

But there were. Thousands of them.

From up here, Uki could see the rooftops much clearer than before. They were crowded together almost as tightly as the tombs around him, draped in the same shroud of morning mist.

Chimneys poked up through the low cloud everywhere, just beginning to smoke as the city rabbits lit their fires to cook breakfast. Soon, the streets would be thronged with them, going about their busy lives. In the centre of Eisenfell, where the giant boulder of sky iron could be seen, nestled in its crater, hammers and picks would start to crash. Everything would carry on as normal, even though – up on this hilltop – Uki and his friends might be fighting for their lives. Sacrificing themselves to try and save them.

Would they hear the shouting and fighting down there? Would they look up and notice? Run to help, maybe?

It was too much to hope for, Uki supposed. Their battle plan would have to be enough.

They had spent the last two days working on it, honing it to perfection.

Zarza and Jori, along with Sir Prentiss, had come

up with the main strategy. They had even drawn an outline of the Skullgardens on the Ghostburrow floor, marking everyone's positions with chalk and lumps of coal.

Ember had told them that the procession would lead out from the palace, wind through the roads of Eisenfell and then climb the stairs at the north end of Cathedral Hill.

Ash and his retinue would walk through the Skullgardens, on to the plaza and then the god-emperor would knock on the cathedral door. This would be a sign for the new bishop and his rabbits to leave, giving up the holy space to its rightful owner. The official end of Kether and the beginning of the new religion of Hulstland.

The rag-tag army of gangs were all hidden amongst the graves, ears and noses tucked safely out of sight. They were armed with slings, stones and catapults – even a few bows that the Embervale Toffs had stolen from the palace armoury. Nikku had grabbed herself a particularly nice one, along with a quiver of red-fletched arrows.

Everyone was to stay hidden until Ash had

entered the Skullgardens. Then, before too many of his Deathless could follow him, the gangs would rain down a hail of missiles just behind him.

While his troops prepared to battle, Uki would dash out into the open, protected by Zarza, Coal and Sir Prentiss. They would buy him a few seconds in which to throw his spear, hopefully hitting Ash and capturing Mortix.

After that, well, nobody knew exactly what would happen.

Hopefully, all of the Deathless would collapse and then return to their normal selves, just as the Maggitches had done when Charice was caught.

If they didn't, then all Uki and his friends could do would be to run for the tunnel entrances and try to lose their pursuers in the Underfell.

As plans go, it isn't great, Uki thought to himself. *There's about a million things that can go wrong.*

And they probably all will, his dark voice added. **Especially with you leading everyone.**

I'm doing my best! Uki snapped at the voice. *And I didn't hear you coming up with any suggestions!*

The voice had no answer to that, and Uki felt

a bit silly for arguing with himself. He shook his ears and crouched lower behind a moss-covered statue of Kether, looking across to where the others were hiding. Apart from the odd curious nose, you couldn't tell there was a horde of armed, feral children, filling up the graveyard.

Crossing both sets of fingers, Uki settled down and looked across the city, towards the palace of Embervale.

*

It wasn't long before he spotted the procession.

Distant trumpets sounded and the dawn light glittered on the armour of hundreds of rabbits as they poured from the palace, forming themselves into a long column.

They began to parade down the zigzag steps of the palace hill, like a gleaming, steel-scaled snake.

'Here they come,' said a voice from one of the graves nearby. He recognised it as Kree's.

'Remember to hold until the emperor is inside the gates!' Sir Prentiss called out, loud enough for everyone to hear, and then there was silence as every rabbit scrunched themselves as still and quiet as possible.

The procession moved at a painfully slow pace, disappearing for a while into the maze of streets and houses, and then heading for the steep steps that led up the hill to the lychgate, the entrance to the Skullgardens.

Clank, clank, clank.

After an age of waiting, Uki could make out the faint sound of metal crashing against metal. The armoured suits of the Deathless as they marched closer and closer.

He tightened his grip on his spear, edging one eye around the statue so he could see the gate in the distance.

Clank, clank, clank.

Louder and louder until, finally, the top of a banner could be seen. Waving slightly as its bearer struggled up the steps, the whole thing came into view. The flaming star of the emperor, with a black heart added to its centre.

'Wait for it,' he heard Jori whisper. 'Wait for it.'

More steps, and an armoured figure appeared. It wore a full suit of sky-metal plate, gleaming like golden fire in the last rays of sunrise. Its head was covered by a helm, topped off with a plume of raven feathers and a black velvet cloak was draped from its shoulders.

Ash. The emperor.

Behind him were the first ranks of the Deathless. A line, four across, that stretched back, all the way down the steps. If they struck now, Uki realised, only eight or so would be able to defend their master. The rest would be trapped behind them, wedged in the narrow stairway, unable to do anything.

Uki looked across to where Jori was hidden, wondering why she hadn't given the order to shoot. The emperor kept walking, more of his metal-faced troops following him into the graveyard.

Now! Uki willed something to happen. *Now!*

As if in answer, he heard Jori's voice ring out among the graves, clear and fierce.

'Fire!'

The swish of twenty or more bows, slings and catapults came from all around, as a shower of arrows and rocks filled the air. They came tumbling down on the Deathless at the front of the line, bouncing off their armour with a clatter of metallic *pings.*

It didn't hurt them – didn't knock them to the ground or stun them, even – but it wasn't meant to. The soldiers panicked as they rushed to draw their weapons, turning this way and that to see where the shooters were hiding, finding nothing but rows of crumbling gravestones.

The few seconds of chaos were all Uki needed. Pushing himself to his feet, he ran out from behind the statue and began to sprint towards the emperor as fast as he was able. From the tombs and toppled graves around him came Sir Prentiss and Coal, roaring as they charged. Zarza was like a whirlwind of black ink as she somersaulted on to the path, a long, back-curved bronze sword in her paws.

Feet pounding, the four of them swarmed towards the armoured figure of the emperor, reaching him in the space of a heartbeat. Already, the closest of his guards had begun to step in front of him, protecting him with raised swords. Coal and Sir Prentiss crashed into them, slamming them aside and then swinging their weapons at those behind them.

Uki tried to ignore their struggles, honing his attention on the emperor, raising his crystal spear to strike.

But, even as he began to bring his arm downwards, another Deathless whirled across, blocking his path to Ash. Uki ducked as a sky-metal broadsword whistled over his head. He braced himself for another swipe, but in the next instant his opponent was gone, sent flying into the forest of gravestones by a spinning kick from Zarza.

'Do it now!' the bonedancer shouted at him, as she turned to face another Deathless.

Uki didn't need to be told. He was already slamming the spear at Emperor Ash, aiming for his armpit, the gap in his armour. The crystal tip slid past the plate steel and hit the chainmail undershirt. With Uki's boosted strength behind it, it punched through, jabbing into the flesh beneath.

Holding the shaft firmly, Uki braced himself for the sudden surge of power he felt whenever a spirit was captured. A rush of energy, a flood of new senses, the filling of the crystal . . .

But this time there was . . . nothing?

Frowning, Uki yanked the spear out and tried again, this time aiming for the eye holes in Ash's visor. The spear squealed as it entered the slot, bending the metal out of shape beneath it, shedding tiny splinters as it ground close enough to press against the face of the rabbit within, touching the flesh, ready to drink in Mortix . . .

. . . and still nothing.

Something was wrong.

Something was *very* wrong.

Only then, when it was too late, did Uki realise that his senses hadn't been jangling. This close to Mortix, he should have felt her chill, should have seen the ghostly shape of her true form, shimmering over the place where the emperor stood.

There's only one explanation, his dark voice sounded as horrified as he was. **The rabbit you've just speared . . .**

'. . . isn't Ash. Isn't Mortix.' Uki finished.

Already knowing what he would see, Uki pulled his spear upwards, taking the emperor's helmet with it, exposing the rabbit beneath.

A grey-furred teenager with black tips on his

ears. A familiar face, but with eyes of blank, clouded white.

'Venic!' He heard Jori shout from amongst the tombstones, where she was still firing arrow after arrow at the ranks of Deathless.

'It's not the emperor!' Kree yelled. 'We've been tricked!'

Then the laughter came. The evil, rasping cackle Uki had last heard at the bottom of a muddy pit in the Fenlands.

Turning around, he saw that the doors to Kether's cathedral were now open. Standing there, along with her hulking servant Balto and a squad of armed Deathless, was Necripha. She was dancing with joy, a wicked smile of triumph on her face.

'You stupid fools!' she cackled. 'Did you think I wouldn't know about your pathetic plan? Did you really think Mortix would walk herself into your trap?'

'Get her!' Coal shouted, turning from the guard he was attacking and preparing to hobble his way across the plaza towards Necripha and certain death.

'No!' Uki shouted. 'Run everyone! To the tunnels!'

'Capture them!' Necripha screamed at the same time, their voices overlapping. 'I want every single one of them caught and bound!'

From behind her, more Deathless began to pour out of the cathedral, where they must have been hiding all night waiting for the Underfell gangs to arrive.

The troops at the gate surged forward, running in amongst the graves, trying to grab the children.

Uki stared on in horror, seeing his new comrades being snatched by the arms and ears, hoisted into the air, kicking and screaming.

Not if I can help it, he thought. Slamming his useless spear back into his sheath, he looked around for the nearest thing he could use as a weapon. There was nothing. Nothing except tombstones.

Stones. He remembered his first meeting with Jori: how he had ripped a mighty rock from the ground and hurled it at the assassin who was stalking her. In a blink, he reached out and snapped the top half of the nearest gravestone off, just as if it had been a giant biscuit.

With a heave, Uki hurled the chunk of granite

at the armoured Venic, knocking him backwards, clanking and crashing in a mess of heavy armour. He tumbled into the Deathless behind him, metal smacking against metal.

Like a line of dominoes, they began to topple, all the way back to the lychgate and further on, down the steps.

'Run!' he shouted again to Coal and Zarza, who were still standing next to him.

Without waiting for a reply, Uki broke off another headstone and sent it flying towards the Deathless that were rushing out of the cathedral. They were less tightly packed together so only a few were knocked over, but it slowed them down, bought Uki and his friends a handful of seconds.

Shoving Coal before him, Uki headed for the nearest tunnel entrance, hoping, praying that all of his friends would somehow manage to escape as well.

With the sound of Mortix's guards clattering on his tail, he dragged Coal back towards the Underfell and started to run for his life.

Chapter Nine

Lost in the Underfell

Following a bunch of fleeing Bonegrubbers, Uki tore his way through a tangle of ivy and emerged into a long row of stone tombs. Shadowy doorways carved with columns – sealed off with gates of wrought bronze – stood on either side of a long, curving road of mossy, broken brick. A street of houses for the dead.

It was damp, sunless and silent, apart from the pounding of fleeing feet and the rasp of terrified breath. The ivy behind them was already rustling as several Deathless began to hack their way through.

Uki, still dragging Coal by the arm, chased the Bonegrubbers. They reached one of the tombs and wrenched the door open. Scrambling inside seconds behind them, Uki was just in time to see a pair of furry feet disappear through a hole in the floor.

'Hurry!' he said to Coal, pulling the big rabbit inside and slamming the bronze gate behind them. Inside the tomb it was dark, filled with the damp chill of lost centuries, and stacked all around with stone and lead coffins.

'What happened?' Coal managed to grunt, as he got down on his hands and knees and started to crawl through the small hole.

'I don't know,' lied Uki. 'Just hurry up! They're right on our tails!'

He could hear the clatter of metal boots on brickwork. The Deathless were through the ivy and moving down the street of crypts, peering through the gates of each one, like a horde of evil postmen.

Necripha, he thought to himself, as he watched Coal vanish into the darkness of the Underfell. *She* knew *about our plan. She was spying on me the whole time.*

You should have guessed she would do that, his dark voice scolded him. **You should have expected it. Now you've put everyone in danger.**

Uki couldn't argue. He had been so caught up in striking quickly. So sure they had an advantage with Ember's knowledge and Zarza's fighting skills. And Jori had seemed equally confident for once . . .

'How am I supposed to out-think an Ancient spirit?' he muttered to himself. 'I'm only a little rabbit. A child. It's not *fair.*'

Life isn't fair, his dark voice said, sounding like a stern parent. **Now stop feeling sorry for yourself and get down that hole. The guards are almost here.**

Uki slid, feet first, through the gap in the floor, finding a short drop into another crypt beneath. Coal was waiting there, holding a slab of stone. Once Uki was out of the way, he placed it across the hole, blocking it up.

'I doubt it will fool them for long,' he said. 'But it might give us a few minutes.'

Uki looked around, or at least tried to. With the hole sealed, everything was pitch dark. Only a thin sliver of light crept in from the edges of the blocked entrance.

'Where have the Bonegrubbers gone?' he whispered.

'Scarpered,' said Coal. 'Although I can't blame them.'

'But without them, we're lost!' Uki remembered Nikku's description of the maze-like cluster of crypts beneath the Skullgardens. They could end up wandering there forever, trapped and starving.

'Well, if we stay here, we're caught for sure,' said Coal. 'Let's walk on a way, then, when it's safe enough, I've got a couple of candles we can light.'

Uki swallowed, trying not to imagine the lightless, chill depths of the tombs all around him. A beehive of empty chambers. The dead rabbits in their graves, waiting to reach out and grab him with their cold, bony fingers . . .

'All right,' he managed to say. 'I'm glad you're here with me, Coal.'

'Me too,' said Coal. 'Me too.'

*

After ten minutes of stumbling through the dark, waving their paws around until they felt a stone wall or doorway, Coal decided it was safe enough to light the candles.

His flint sparked so brightly, Uki had to close his eyes, opening them again when Coal pressed a candle into his paw.

'I'm not sure how long these will last,' he said, frowning. 'We should look for those signs. And be quick about it.'

Holding up his candle, Uki saw they were in a small crypt, the centre of which was filled by a stone tomb covered in a heap of mummified flowers. A crack in the far wall was marked by the Bonegrubbers' cross-eyed symbol.

'There!' he said, running to the hole and squeezing through, emerging into another mining tunnel.

'They really dug the whole place clear of iron, didn't they?' Coal eased himself through the gap, stepping out beside one of the ancient joists, its wood blackened with age.

'Didn't you work in these mines?' Uki asked.

He shone his candle up and down the passage, wondering which way to go.

'Oh, yes. Yes, of course.' Coal seemed flustered for a moment. 'But not this part, obviously. In the new mines, right beside the Eisenrock itself. I would have … I mean, I *had* no idea there were tunnels inside the hills. Mind you, I didn't know there were so many tombs underground, either. Or that runaway children were living in them.'

Uki was about to ask more when he heard a noise. The echo of voices, bouncing their way along the shaft. Both he and Coal froze, staring at each other in horror.

'Blow out your candle!' Coal hissed.

'Wait!' Uki's senses, heightened by the darkness and the adrenaline that was cascading around his system, picked up a tingle along with the noises. The buzz of living things, faint but growing closer.

'It's not the Deathless,' he said. 'I can *feel* them. They're alive!'

'Some of the others?' Coal squinted into the depths of the tunnel.

'Hello?' Uki risked a shout. 'Jori? Kree? Is that you?'

There was silence for a long, tense moment.

'Uki? Uki?'

The faintest of voices, a whisper in the darkness.

'Yes! It's me!' Uki shouted back.

He and Coal watched the tunnel, waiting to see who would appear from the gloom. *Please let it be all of them,* he prayed. *Let them all have escaped.*

Soon, they could make out the sound of scampering feet, and then a glow of candlelight appeared. Seconds later, a crowd of rabbits came running down the tunnel. Fewer than Uki had hoped, but he could see Jori and Kree were there, along with Nikku and several of the Underfell urchins. At the back of the group, loping along, sword drawn, was Zarza. The light caught on her bone mask, making it look as though it was floating in the darkness.

Uki began to run towards them so fast that his candle blew out. He crashed into Jori and Kree's arms and the three of them hugged one another tight for a few moments.

'You escaped!' Uki said when they finally untangled. 'Did all the others get away too?'

'Not all,' said Jori. 'You bought us some time

throwing the gravestones like that. But they still managed to grab some of us.'

'Lurky!' Kree wailed. 'They got Lurky!'

'I thought you couldn't stand him?' Uki said, surprised.

Kree scowled, her bottom lip trembling. 'He's an annoying turnip-brain,' she said. 'But that doesn't mean I want him to be captured!'

She buried her head against Uki's chest and he patted it, awkwardly. All of this was *his* fault. If Necripha hadn't used him to eavesdrop on them . . . maybe the plan would have worked.

'I don't understand,' Jori said. 'How did they *know* we would be there? They must have been hiding in the cathedral all night! And Venic . . . his eyes. Did you see them?'

'That wasn't Venic.' Uki tried to reassure his friend. 'It was Mortix. Controlling him.'

'They must have realised we had the emperor's daughter with us,' said Zarza. 'They knew she would give away the ceremony plans. That it was our only chance to strike.'

'No.' Uki couldn't let them believe that. As bad

as he felt, as much as it hurt, he had to tell them the truth. Even if it meant they blamed him, hated him. 'It was me. Necripha must have been looking through my eyes. She saw and heard all our plans. *I* gave us away. It was my fault.'

'She can do that?' Zarza's voice sounded angry. Her grey eyes flashed behind her mask. 'Why didn't you warn us?'

'I . . . I wasn't sure . . . I didn't know . . .' Tears began to fall from Uki's eyes. 'I only thought she could speak to me when I was dreaming. Or when I tried to reach her. She must have a way to spy on me whenever she wants. Without me even knowing. Mortix must have shown her because she's never done it before.'

'So, she could be listening in on us right now?' Nikku stared at Uki, her eyes wide with fear. They were all looking at him like that. As if he were some kind of traitor.

'It's not your fault, Uki.' Jori put her arm around his shoulders, protecting him. 'You had no idea she was doing it. Blame *her*, not yourself.'

'But don't you see?' Uki stepped away, pressed

his paws over his eyes. 'I'm not safe to be around any more! I put all of you in danger!'

'We'll worry about that later,' said Coal. 'Right now, we have to regroup. Find a safe place to hide.'

Nikku nodded. 'The Ghostburrow,' she said. 'They'll all head back there. Although we might not have long before they raid it. They probably know where it is by now.'

'Does anyone remember the way?' Jori asked, looking at the ragged bunch of urchins that were with them. A mix of Toffs, Howlers, Stinkers and Scrappers.

'I do,' said a quiet voice. From amongst the crowd, a shrouded Bonegrubber emerged. The tiniest one of all, her little face smeared with ghostly white paint, black circles around her eyes.

'Coffin,' said Nikku. 'Walk with Uki and show us where to go.'

With a grim nod, Uki scooped her up in his arms, and they all began to run down the tunnel as fast as their paws would carry them.

*

They had just crawled through the gap, into the bricked-off corridor that led to the Ghostburrow when they heard it – the sound of grief-stricken sobbing.

Zarza and Jori drew their blades and stood either side of Uki, as Coal shepherded Coffin and the gang children into a group behind them. They all stood, breath held tight in their chests, waiting to see what was coming towards them along the tunnel.

The wailing grew louder, echoing backwards and forwards throughout the Underfell. It sounded like a lost spirit, a ghost from one of the tombstacks, howling in misery.

And then, in the flickering light of their candles, a pale shape appeared. All waving arms and legs, glowing in the dim light, stumbling along towards them . . .

'It's a ghost!' Kree shouted. 'I knew this place was haunted!'

Some of the gang rabbits began to shriek, but Uki raised a paw for silence. 'Wait!' he called. 'It's no ghost! I can feel life there. Lots of lives! There's more than one of them.'

Peering closer, they could now see there was indeed more than a single figure. There was a whole group of small, pale creatures, following behind a larger pair. As they drew nearer, Uki recognised the disc-pierced ears and hooded cloak of Yarrow. And he appeared to be supporting a staggering Princess Ember.

'It's our friends!' he shouted. 'It's Yarrow and the others!'

'Indeed it is,' coughed the bard. 'We are mightily pleased to see you again. We were just within a whisker of losing our lives – and for once, that is no exaggeration.'

Uki and the others ran to help them, discovering that they were covered head to foot in a thick layer of brick dust.

'What happened?' Uki asked. 'Why are you all dusty?'

Yarrow brushed clouds of chalk and grit out of his fur and off his shoulders, coughing and spitting and blinking as he did. 'That is a tale that would need quite a bit of telling. And, of course, I would need to compose it properly first . . .'

Jori took hold of Ember's arm and peeled her away from the bard. 'Could we perhaps have a short version right now? Why is Ember so upset?'

Uki looked at the princess and saw she was choking back sobs. There were streaks in the dust around her eyes where her tears had flowed, washing her black fur clean. It was then that he noticed Sir Prentiss was missing. A sick feeling of dread prickled his neck.

'We ran from the Skullgardens,' Yarrow began to explain. 'And we followed the Bonegrubbers. They led us back down to the Ghostburrow, where we thought we'd be safe . . .'

'We should have been,' one of the dusty gang rabbits spoke up. Uki thought it might be Rattle. 'But the Deathless were waiting for us. Rilda . . . she was lying on the floor . . .'

'They appear to have known about the hideout all along,' said Yarrow. 'Goddess knows how.'

'We have an idea,' said Zarza, shooting Uki a poisoned look. He cringed.

'Anyway,' Yarrow went on. 'There was a fierce battle . . . one which I *will* describe in detail once I have had a chance to compose myself . . . and the outcome was that Sir Prentiss stayed in the Ghostburrow to fight them off, while we all escaped.'

'Prentiss is dead?' Kree blurted out, far too loudly. Princess Ember instantly began wailing again, and even tried to push her way back down the passageway to the Ghostburrow.

'Well done, Kree,' snapped Jori, holding Ember back. She soon gave up resisting, and began to quietly sob again.

'It was a brave and heroic last stand,' said Yarrow. 'It deserves a song of its own. So noble! So selfless!'

'And why all the dust?' asked Coal. 'What happened to the chamber?'

'Rilda told us to weaken the walls, days ago,' said Rattle. 'We didn't know why at the time, but she must have seen this in her bones. We knocked out the pegs as we ran, and the Ghostburrow ceiling came down on top of her, Sir Prentiss and the Deathless. We all got away, thanks to them.'

'Kether's teeth,' Coal cursed. 'You had a lucky escape. But we can't stand around talking about it . . . there will be more of them after us. Every tunnel must be flooded with them by now.'

As if to prove him right, the sound of armour

clanking began to echo in the air. Faint at first, but growing steadily louder.

'Come on,' said Zarza. 'We have to move.'

'Where to?' Kree asked Uki, but he had no idea. Their only plan was in tatters. They were lost, helpless, outnumbered. And wherever they went, Necripha could simply look through his eyes and find them.

'I don't know,' he admitted. 'I have no idea. All we can do is . . .'

'Run?' Jori finished his sentence for him.

Knowing she was right, Uki took Princess Ember from her and began the long desperate sprint into the tunnels.

Chapter Ten

The Forge

They ran through the Underfell, tearing along abandoned mineshafts, wriggling through narrow half-dug passages, turning left and right so many times that Uki had no idea where he was or which way he was heading.

Different rabbits seemed to be leading them at different times. For a while, it was Rattle, then Scrag, then Grit as they passed through one gang's territory and into another.

All the while, Uki stared this way and that, just waiting to be ambushed by a squad of Deathless, or maybe even Mortix herself. With every step he wondered: *is Necripha spying on us right now? Can she see where we're going? Is she telling them where to find us?*

It was only after they had been sprinting for half an hour or more that he realised he was still clutching Ember's paw. The princess had stopped crying a while back. Instead, her eyes were blank and empty, her jaw slack. She followed where Uki led without even thinking, without knowing where she really was.

She's in shock, he realised. It was a state he knew well. The same thing had happened to him immediately after his mother died. His mind just went elsewhere for a bit, to save itself from shattering into pieces.

At the head of the group, Grit suddenly stopped. They all crowded around him, leaning against the tunnel walls, panting for breath.

'I can't . . . run much more . . .' Coal panted.

'I second that,' said Yarrow. 'My legs . . . they're about to snap like frozen twigs . . .'

Uki took advantage of the break in running to

look around. They were at a fork in the tunnel. To their right was another old mineshaft, to the left a scrappy tunnel that looked like it had been chewed out of the earth by a careless worm.

'We need to decide where to go,' said Grit. 'If we turn right, we'll pass the secret forge and then reach Scrapper land. If we head left . . .'

'We'll be in Soilwallow,' said one of the Stinkers. 'That's where we live! Next to the giant sewer and the underground rat-dung chamber!'

'*Pleasechooseright, pleasechooseright,*' he heard Kree muttering.

The Forge. It gave him an idea.

'If Mortix has pulled all her Deathless out to capture us,' he said. 'Who will be guarding the forge?'

'He's right!' Rainna clapped her paws together. 'We might be able to break in! We could free our parents!'

'A counterattack!' Yarrow heaved himself to his feet, eyes twinkling. 'How exciting! The daring urchins rescue their parents from the evil slave masters . . .'

‘We should get Ember to safety first,’ said Jori. ‘She’s in no fit state . . .’

Uki looked at Ember again. She was clutching his arm, staring into the distance. Her mouth opened and closed, as if she wanted to speak but had forgotten how. Jori was right – they really should get the princess somewhere safe and quiet. Somewhere she could piece herself back together.

But the looks in the other rabbits’ eyes . . .

Mention of their parents had filled them with a sudden, overwhelming hope. And if Uki could make some good come of the awful mess their plan had turned into . . . well, then maybe they wouldn’t blame him quite so much for it. It was selfish, he knew, but he couldn’t shake the sense that he had let everyone down. So much had been made of his powers, how important he was . . . and in the end it was all because of his connection to the Ancients that they had been foiled. He just wanted the chance to turn it around again. To feel as though he had helped these runaway rabbits instead of appearing and ruining their lives even further.

‘Maybe we could just take a quick peek,’ he said,

wincing as Jori glared at him. 'If the Deathless are there, if it's too dangerous ... then we can turn around and head deeper into the Underfell ...'

'And if they aren't, then we can storm in and rescue our families!' Uki didn't see which rabbit had shouted, but they were answered by a cheer.

Grit set off down the right-hand passage at a trot and everyone rushed to follow.

'You'd better hope they can save their parents,' Jori growled at him as she strode past. 'Or they'll have another reason not to trust you.'

Uki cringed as he led Ember after them. He'd only wanted to make everything better. Now he'd probably dug himself an even deeper hole.

*

The mineshaft was straight and clean, well-lit by lanterns in regularly spaced alcoves. All the rusted debris that filled the other disused shafts had been cleared away. This part of the mines was still being used. Deep ruts were gouged into the earthen floor, where carts had been driven. The mud inside looked brown and fresh, not dusty and fossilised like it did in all the other musty tunnels.

What are they doing down here? Uki wondered. *What is Mortix up to?*

They didn't have to walk much further before Grit motioned them to be quiet. He began to edge his way along, keeping close to the wall, snuffing out the lanterns as he went, keeping himself in shadow.

The other rabbits all copied him, slinking, silent as the graves in the Skullgardens. As best he could, Uki tried to make Ember do the same, but she wasn't even looking at him as he motioned her to crouch. Her feet scraped and stumbled at the earth as she walked.

The others looked back at him, annoyed, motioning him to hush, but there was nothing he could do.

Luckily, they didn't come across any guards. Not even when they reached a set of sturdy double doors that blocked the shaft. Uki noticed they were made of fresh wood, still smelling of varnish, hinges gleaming softly in the lamplight. They must have been put here only weeks – maybe just days – ago.

'This is it,' Grit whispered to them. 'There's usually deadheads standing outside.'

'Uki must be right,' said Zarza. 'They were all sent above for the ambush. This Necripha had no idea we would be coming here.'

'She will *now*,' said Rattle, glaring at Uki.

'Let's be quick, then,' said Coal. 'We don't want to get surprised down here.'

Scrag laughed. 'Quick? We've got to get through those doors first. You can bet they're locked tighter than a toad's undercrackers.'

Uki passed Ember's paw to Kree, who took it with a nod. He walked up to the doors, braced his feet against the floor and placed both paws on the wood.

'Surely he's not *that* strong,' he heard Yarrow whisper.

I hope I am, he thought, gathering all his strength, all his determination and sending it coursing through his muscles. He closed his eyes, put his head down and *pushed.*

The doors creaked, moving forwards a fraction, then jamming as the thick steel bolts that held them locked tight. Uki's feet slipped back, digging up the dirt, but he shoved harder. He used the anger he felt at Necripha – and at himself – channelling it into pure force. The wood began to crack on the other side, the bolts strained against their rivets, the steel bending, curving.

Whispers of amazement came from the rabbits behind him, which turned into whoops of joy when, with a whip-crack of snapping timber, the bolts and locks all burst out of the woodwork at once and the doors swung inwards.

They flew back, booming as they hit the walls behind them. The sound echoed around the room beyond, giving them a clue as to just how large it was.

Still, they were forced to pause and marvel at the sight, even as they rushed through the doorway. They clustered around Uki, looking up, every single one of them speechless.

Far above, lit by the distant glow of lanterns, was the bottom of the Eisenrock. It hung down into the cavernous chamber, bulging through the earth and rock like a colossal egg being pushed towards them.

Beneath it was a jumbled construction of wooden scaffolding, piled up in layers, in storeys, of lashed-together planks and struts. As high as the cathedral's tallest spire, it teetered beneath the rust-red iron of the Eisenrock. Chutes, ramps, cranes and pulleys jutted everywhere. There were lumps of iron in barrows and crates, freshly carved from the giant space rock, waiting to be winched and tumbled down to ground level.

'They're carving up the last of the rock,' Coal whispered. 'They're mining out the whole thing. As fast as they can.'

'I thought that was what happened in Eisenfell,' said Kree. 'This whole city is here because they're eating up all that iron, isn't it?'

'For the last two hundred years they have only been mining the fragments of iron buried in the ground when the Eisenrock fell from space,' Jori said. 'The rock itself is supposed to be sacred. Using it up is a last resort. Only the emperor is allowed to touch it.'

'Once the Eisenrock is gone, there will be no more iron in Hulstland,' Grit explained. 'But they have carved away tons of it. This is worse than anything else Ash has done.'

'But what are they using it for?' Uki asked. Whatever it was, it was bound to be horrid.

'*That*,' said Rainna, pointing to the far side of the cavern. The rabbits tore their eyes from the scaffolding and looked across to where a row of brick forges stood. Twenty or more, their chimneys quietly smoking, their doors opened wide like hungry chicks begging for food. In front of them were lines of anvils and stacks of tools. Metal buckets and tongs for collecting molten steel, moulds for it to be poured into; barrels of oil for quenching and cooling; wheeled carts for carrying whatever had been constructed.

And there, suspended high above the floor and covered in its own network of scaffold, was the object they were building.

It looked like a giant tube. Twenty metres long, at least, and two wide. Steel-grey, the metal lined with ripples where it had been Damascus-forged for extra strength, its mouth had been fashioned into the shape of a vast rabbit skull, the jaws gaping open.

At the other end was some kind of mechanism. Hinges for a door, cogs and ratchets and rivets. And it looked as though they were building a platform to hold it. Great trunks of oak were lined up, ready to be carved, and a stack of steel-rimmed wheels – each one taller than an adult rabbit – lay waiting to be fitted.

'What . . . what is it?' Uki asked. He had expected some kind of hideous weapon, but couldn't make out what this . . . *thing* . . . could possibly be used for.

'I have heard tell of a device like this,' said Jori, her voice quiet with awe. 'But on a much smaller scale.'

'Is it a fountain of some sort?' Kree asked. 'Or a pipe for a giant toilet?'

'They call it a cannon,' said Jori. 'You put a ball of iron in it, and then you fill the other end with a powder made of saltpetre and sulphur. The stuff explodes when you set fire to it, and the ball flies out at incredible speed.'

'Like firing an arrow?' Kree asked.

'Yes, but much more deadly,' said Jori. 'If it works, that is. There was an inventor developing one. He came to my clan warren – my family was interested in it as a way to kill, you see – but when he tried to light the fuse, the thing just flew to bits.'

'Ash must have perfected the design,' said Zarza.

Uki felt an icy chill begin to spread through his body. He was certain he knew where the orders to create such a thing came from. 'Mortix told him how to build it. She's the spirit of death. Imagine how many she could kill with this thing.'

'If it works,' said Jori, 'she could flatten entire cities with it. Nobody could stand against her.'

Coal was staring at the weapon, scratching his chin. 'With wheels, you could take it anywhere. That ratchet mechanism would let you raise and lower the thing so you could aim, and the door at the end must be where you load the ball . . .'

His pondering was interrupted by a shout from one of the gang rabbits.

'Look! Over there in the corner!'

Across from the cannon and forges was something they had missed. A block of cages, hidden in the shadows of the cavern's edge. Cages that were filled with huddled, exhausted shapes.

'Our parents!' Scrag shouted. 'It must be them!'

'They've locked them up while the guards are away.' Rainna and Rattle clutched each other in excitement. 'We can set them free! Come on!'

'I think not.'

A flat, cold voice echoed across the forge, making them all jump. It was followed by the clanking of steel boots as the speaker began to march towards them.

Whirling around, they saw two rabbits, one dressed in the splendour of the emperor's sky metal, the other in a crimson-tinted suit of armour with curved bronze spikes lining its forearms. Both wore the blank faceplates of the Deathless.

'Venic,' Uki said, reaching for a spear. 'And Needle.'

But the voice that had spoken was nothing like Venic's. It was female, for a start. Not to mention alien. Full of sinister, serpentine hisses, it sounded wrong, coming from a young rabbit's throat.

'Not anymore,' the Venic-thing said. 'These vessels belong to *me* now.'

'Mortix.' She was controlling them both, making them speak her words. Uki's voice trembled, but more with anger than fear. The spirit had him cornered, and yet there was no way to trap it. It was miles away, safe in the castle, nestled inside the brain of the emperor, using Venic's body as a mouthpiece.

'Release my cousin.' Jori spoke through gritted teeth as she stepped forward, sword pointed at the two armoured figures. Her other paw had thumbed open the lid of her flask, ready to take a dose of potion.

'Or what?' said Venic, with the spirit's voice. 'You can't harm me. You'll only kill your cousin's body. My real self is back at the palace now, safely guarded. Although, perhaps you might want to get rid of him, anyway. I saw his mind as I was eating it. He hated you with quite a passion, Jori.'

'And this one did too.' A voice came from behind the blank facemask of the rabbit in crimson armour. But it wasn't Needle's voice. It was the same hissing monotone that had just been spoken by Venic. 'In fact, it hated everyone. Everyone and everything. Such an angry, bitter soul.'

'We've seen your weapon,' Uki said, through gritted teeth. 'We know what your secret forge is for. Whatever you want to do with it, we won't let you. I will stop you like I stopped the others.'

'The others were idiots,' said Mortix, speaking through Venic and Needle's mouths at the same time.

'You can't stop me. Soon I will be everywhere. And any town or city that tries to stand against me will be smashed into rubble.'

Uki felt a paw gently nudge him. He looked up to see Coal, his face grim and fierce. 'We need to go,' he said. 'This place will be crawling with guards in a second.'

'Our parents!' Rainna cried, taking a step towards the cages. Venic moved to block her, drawing his sword. With his other paw, he pulled off his helmet, revealing the grey fur and ears that almost matched Jori's. Revealing the blank, white emptiness of his eyes.

'You'll have to kill these puppets first,' he said.

'With pleasure,' said Coal, raising his hammer.

'I will gift these bodies the blessing of true death,' said Zarza, pointing the tip of her curved sword at Needle.

'I'll . . .er . . . just take the younglings and stand back a bit,' said Yarrow. 'Just to observe things better, of course.'

As the bard ushered the crowd of gang members back into the tunnel, Jori pulled her flask from her belt and took a deep swig. 'Leave Venic to me,' she said. 'I'm just going to wound him. I can't let him be killed . . . he is my blood.'

Venic, or the thing that controlled him, laughed. 'It won't matter. You will never have your murderous cousin back. And this body can also use your nasty potion.'

As Venic stepped towards them, he pulled his own silver flask from a pouch at his waist. Popping the cap, he tipped the entire thing down his throat, gulping as it spilled from his mouth, trickling down his breastplate, smoking and steaming. A dose big enough to kill an army of dusk wraiths.

'Stop!' Jori shouted, knowing full well how dangerous the potion was. 'That's too much! He'll die!'

Venic – or rather Mortix – just threw back his head and laughed. It didn't matter to her what happened to Venic's body. In fact, Uki realised, she *wanted* him to die, just to upset Jori. She had plenty of other bodies to control. Such as Needle, for example . . .

As if reading his mind, the Shrike captain

suddenly leapt towards them, spiked gauntlets raking the air. Venic followed, swishing the emperor's sky-steel sword in wide arcs. Their charge was mad, reckless, as if they didn't care about dying.

Zarza and Jori met the attackers with their blades, but even with all their skill they were forced to fall back. Uki and Coal moved with them, waiting for a chance to step in. Uki knew he could help, but didn't want to get in Jori's way. If he hurt Venic, his friend might never forgive him. Although, with that much dusk potion inside him, it was only a matter of seconds until he collapsed anyway.

The forge was filled with the sound of crashing metal. Zarza parried every strike of Needle's, deftly keeping her blade from being snapped between the spikes on her armour. Jori, with the dusk potion beginning to flow around her body, began to move faster and faster, her sword whistling through the air as it blocked Venic's broadsword, then jabbed at the gaps in his armour, trying to wound his arms and legs.

Venic's movements should have speeded up too, especially with the amount of dusk he had drunk, but the heavy sword kept swishing back and forth at the same speed. Uki reached out to him with his senses, feeling that familiar gap of lifelessness. The potion wasn't affecting him, he realised.

'Jori!' he called out to her as the onslaught drove them back out of the forge and into the tunnel. 'The dusk isn't working on him! It's because he's not really alive!'

'It will still poison him, though,' said Jori through clenched teeth. Her attacks were now pinging off his armour like hailstones, but the sky-metal plate was impenetrable. Venic kept walking on, pushing them out of the forge and into the tunnel.

'Go for his head!' Coal shouted. 'Finish him!'

'I can't!' Jori shouted back. She was slicing at the joins in his armour, trying to get the tip of her blade through the chainmail undershirt, trying to trip or cripple him.

Next to her, Zarza cried out. Her blade had become lodged between two of Needle's spikes. The Shrike captain yanked her arm back, pulling Zarza off balance, and then jabbed at her with the other gauntlet. The cruel spikes ripped through Zarza's robes, jabbing into her shoulder.

'Look out!' Uki shouted. He barged Zarza aside and leapt towards Needle. Those spiked arms came down for him, but Uki saw them swooping and ducked underneath. He came up inside Needle's reach, almost as if she was about to hug him. For a second, he saw himself reflected in that blank steel mask. The fierce, furious look on his face surprised him, just before he put both paws against Needle's chest and *pushed* with the same force he had used to wrench the forge doors open.

She went flying back into the forge doorway, smashing the frame in two. A shower of mud and rock came tumbling down from the tunnel ceiling as twining cracks appeared. The whole thing was about to cave in.

Amongst the plumes of dust and mud, Jori and Venic were still fighting. The steel broadsword in Venic's paws *whooshed* back and forth, and Jori's smaller blade pattered all around it, stinging like a swarm of mosquitos.

'Finish him, Jori!' Coal shouted again. 'We're out of time!'

'Just a few more seconds!' Jori screamed, even as the clatter of armoured footsteps could be heard echoing from the forge. Mortix had sent reinforcements.

'Do it,' Zarza gasped, as Yarrow came to help her. Blood was pouring from her shoulder where Needle's claws had raked it.

Still Jori battled on, stabbing madly at Venic's elbows and knees. Shaking his head, Coal moved to the doorframe, raising his hammer to break the other side. A strike that would bring the tunnel roof crashing down, blocking off the forge completely.

'Our parents!' Scrag shouted, trying to dodge past the battle and run back into the chamber.

Uki stopped her with a paw, pushing her and the other children deeper into the tunnel. 'We'll come back for them,' he said. 'I promise we'll come back.' He seemed to be making a lot of promises today. Ones he wasn't sure he could keep.

'Do it now, Coal,' said Zarza, as Yarrow wrapped one of his scarves around her wound. 'Bring it down.'

'Please! Wait!' Jori shouted, but Coal was already striking. One, two, three blows of his meaty hammer-arm, and the doorframe splintered, just as it had on the other side. The ceiling of the tunnel gave out a low, tortured groan, cracks spidering out all across it. The joists above began to split and break as well. The whole lot was going to come down.

'Run!' Coal shouted, swinging past Uki on his crutch. The gang children and Kree began to sprint away down the mineshaft, but Jori was still desperately duelling with Venic. She was going to be buried alive.

Please forgive me, Uki thought to himself, reaching up to grab her by the collar. At the same time, he aimed a kick at Venic's armoured chest, knocking him back against the wall. With a roar that blocked out everything, the tunnel ceiling came down, even as Uki ran between the clods of falling earth and rock, dragging his friend behind him.

He ran and ran, eyes full of grit, stones bouncing off his body, until he felt clear air around him.

Then he turned, cradling the sobbing Jori and looking back down the mineshaft.

All they could see was a wall of rock and mud, splintered timbers jutting out of it.

The forge door was gone. Needle was gone.

Venic was . . . gone.

'Oh, Jori,' he said, tears filling his own eyes. 'I'm so sorry.'

Interlude

Rue is fighting to keep his eyes open as the bard speaks the last few words of the story. As he describes the death of Jori's cousin.

Despite the poison in his blood threatening to overwhelm him, the little rabbit reaches out a paw to Jori, who takes it in her own and squeezes tight.

'We must be nearly there now,' says the bard, who started to wheeze quite some time ago. They have just walked up a steep ridge, halfway to the peak, and are standing on a wide plateau, covered with straggly clumps of twisted trees.

'We are,' says the girl Arukh. She puts her paws to her mouth and gives out a cry: 'Chak-chak-cha-chak!'

It is answered later by another and three more Arukhs step out from behind a mass of bushes and boulders. They wave at the strangers, beckoning them to walk closer.

'You live behind those rocks?' the bard asks, leaning heavily on his staff.

'We do,' says the girl. 'But I think you will be surprised.'

And indeed, he is. And so would Rue be, if he had managed to keep his eyes open.

The unimpressive pile of rocks and gorse is just a screen. Behind it stands a wooden wall, lined with spikes and decorated with skulls bleached white by the icy wind. And behind *that* is a village, nestled in the shelter of the mountain wall beyond it. Twenty or so neat stone houses with roofs of thatch, including a longhouse in the centre. Standing before its open doors is a tall tree trunk, carved into the shape of a rabbit and painted with the familiar white and black fur of . . .

' . . .Uki,' Rue whispers, peering out from under heavy eyelids. 'It's him.'

'It is,' says Jori. The statue even has the harness

with its magpie buckle and crystals. At its feet are offerings of food and animal skins, beads and flint-bladed knives.

But the bard doesn't have time to be impressed by how neat and well-built the houses are, or how the carved totem looks so much like the young Uki. He can only think of his dying apprentice and the antidote he was promised. He is terrified that if Rue falls asleep again, he might never wake up.

'The ingredients,' he says to the Arukhs. 'We need them right away.'

'In a moment,' says the girl Arukh. She leads them towards the longhouse, while curious rabbits start to gather in the village centre, staring at the strange newcomers. The bard notices that all of them, even the children, have the same face paint. Half black, half white – like a crowd of Ukis, all different ages and sizes. Close to a hundred rabbits, each one with some kind of flint weapon in their hands or at their belt.

I should probably be terrified, he thinks. *This quaint mountain village must be the last thing many rabbits saw, right before they were . . .*

He doesn't get time to finish the thought, because the longhouse doors are swinging open. Stepping out, flanked by two fierce guards, is the largest Arukh warrior the bard has ever seen.

At least two heads taller than every rabbit around him, he is dressed in thick leather armour with plates of copper sewn all over it. His mane of long, wild hair is twisted into spikes, his ears pierced all over with gold rings. Around his shoulders is a cloak, its collar lined with magpie feathers, white on one side, black on the other. And, of course, his face is painted with the same colours.

'Chief Darkfire,' says Jori, kneeling before him and bowing her head.

The Arukh stares at her for a few moments, obviously trying to recall how he knows her. When he catches sight of the silver-capped bottle on her belt, his eyes widen in surprise.

'Can it be?' he says. 'Jori the dusk wraith? Companion of the Crystal Keeper? Stoneaxe, Brightwing . . . where did you find her?'

'They were in the foothills, Chief,' says the girl Arukh. 'I spotted them before Brightwing.'

'*I* helped you capture them,' says the boy Arukh, glaring at his sister.

'Enough!' shouts the chief. He motions Jori to get up. 'Dusk wraith. It has been many, many years. Why do you honour us with your visit now?'

Jori stands and points to the huddled body of Rue, still held in Brightwing's arms. 'My young friend,' she says. 'He has been poisoned. We need purple haircap and eagle mushrooms so I can make an antidote. Quickly.'

'Of course,' says the chief, making the bard sigh with relief. 'Bring what she needs! As fast as you can!'

Nearly all of the watching Arukhs turn and run, dashing in every direction. Darkfire himself beckons them all into his longhouse, from which the bard can smell a welcome fire and the scent of freshly baked bread.

'Not long, Rue. Not long now,' he says to his apprentice, following Brightwing as he carries him inside. Jori is already opening her pack, taking out her mortar and pestle and a metal cauldron.

I just hope we're in time.

*

They gather at the far end of the longhouse, beside a wide, stone fireplace where a blaze of logs burn. Jori hangs her cauldron on a metal hook over it, adds some water and then begins to grind her ingredients as they are brought to her in handfuls by a line of Arukh villagers.

Brightwing, the boy warrior who carried Rue up from the foothills, lays him down by the fireside and the bard, with help from Nikku, begins to pad him all around with blankets and cloaks, making him as comfortable as possible.

Chief Darkfire stands off to one side, watching closely, a frown on his terrifying face. The bard snatches looks at the mighty warrior while he fusses about Rue, noting the scars beneath his warpaint and on his broad forearms. Spotting the patchwork leather of his long cloak and realising it is actually made from rabbit ears.

'Are you sure they aren't going to kill us?' he whispers to Jori, hoping the crackle of the fire buries his words.

'Well,' she replies. 'I'm sure they aren't going to kill *me*.' She finishes grinding a batch of dried mushrooms and adds it to the mix in her cauldron. The stuff bubbles away, giving off a reddish steam and a bitter, musky smell. Like the roots of a rotten oak, or the damp mash of leaves hidden under a mouldering log.

'It's ready,' she says, at long last.

Nikku props Rue up and the bard opens his mouth, while Jori trickles spoonful after spoonful of the mixture in, blowing on each one first to cool it.

They feed him three cupfuls, most of it spilling down into the fur on his chin, but quite a lot slipping past his lips, where his tongue weakly moves as he swallows.

'Has he had enough?' the bard asks. 'Will it work?'

Jori prises open Rue's eyes with her fingertips and peers at his eyeballs. She listens to his breathing and gently holds his wrist to feel the strength of his heart pumping there.

'I think it's working,' she says. 'That first antidote we gave him helped, but it was a while before he had it. Crowsbane normally acts fast. The fact he's been fighting it off so well makes me think he only got a small dose . . . all these things are in his favour, but the Goddess alone knows what will happen. We just have to wait.'

So wait they do, all three of them watching Rue closely, while casting the odd nervous glance at the Arukhs around them.

The longhouse is full of them, standing in a semicircle around the fire. Children are pointing and whispering. Warriors are waiting with arms folded. Some paws are resting on the hilts of blades and axes. The bard feels their hungry gazes roam over his ears. His beautiful, tattooed, painted ears . . .

Stoneaxe, the girl who first spotted them, spends a long time whispering to Darkfire, standing on tiptoe while he stoops to listen. Every now and then he nods and looks over to the huddle of guests by his fireside.

The uncomfortable silence of a sickroom stretches on and on, broken only by the odd snap or shower of sparks from the fire.

'Come on, Rue,' the bard whispers, quiet as a breath. 'Come on, little one.'

And then, finally, thankfully, one of Rue's paws flutters. His long, speckled ears give a twitch and, best of all, he opens a brown eye, squinting up at Jori, Nikku and the bard as they all lean over him.

'What happened next?' he says, as if the story had paused only a second ago.

'Clarion's codpiece!' says the bard, beaming and slapping Jori on the back. 'Well done! For a trained killer, you make an amazing healer!'

'It looks like he's out of the woods,' says Jori, smiling wide herself. 'But he should probably sip another cup or two, just in case.'

'It tastes like a rat's underpants,' croaks Rue, sticking out his tiny pink tongue.

'Come on now,' says Nikku. 'Drink up. We want to make sure you're better.'

'Perhaps the bard will tell you the rest of Uki's story to take your mind off it,' Jori says, scooping out another cup full of mixture from the cauldron.

'Yes,' says Darkfire, his loud, gruff, growl of a voice making them all jump. 'Perhaps he will.' He steps towards them, two guards at his shoulders like particularly ferocious shadows. 'Stoneaxe tells me that you were also a companion of the Crystal Keeper. She says that you are a storyteller who knows Uki's tale. She says you told her some of it in order to save his skin.'

The bard, satisfied that Rue is comfortable, pushes himself to his feet, ignoring the creaks and cracks from his knees. He makes a show of bowing to Darkfire, while trying to keep his ears hidden from sight.

'Stoneaxe speaks true, great Chief,' he says. 'I have been telling her of Uki's battle against Mortix, the final spirit. A battle at which Jori and Nikku here were both present.'

'I am not convinced,' says Darkfire. 'The dusk wraith I remember, but you other rabbits . . . you will continue the story for me. You will prove that you know Uki. If we believe you speak true, then we will not punish you for walking on Magpie land without permission.'

'Certainly,' says the bard, bowing again. 'But perhaps I may ask a further favour?'

'Have we not done enough for you?' Darkfire growls. 'Be careful I do not decide to take your ears as payment. They would look good on my cloak.'

The bard swallows, trying not to look at the

patches of sewn-together ears, hanging from Darkfire's shoulders.

'Pardon me if I caused offence,' he says. 'I shall tell my tale as thanks for the medicine you provided for my apprentice. And, if you believe we are indeed friends of Uki, for the chance that you might grant my request at the end?'

'Very well,' says Darkfire. 'Companions of the Crystal Keeper are always welcome here. But others . . . not so much.' He snaps his fingers and his guards drag a chair over to the fireside for him to sit on. As one, all of the Arukhs in the room sit too, crossing their legs on the floor.

'Oh goody,' says Rue, looking up from his cup of antidote.

A story to save my ears, thinks the bard. *I've been in worse scrapes.*

He clears his throat and continues the tale . . .

Chapter Eleven

The Fugitive

'Are you still upset about Venic?' Uki asked. He knew it was a silly question, even as he said it. Being sad about someone dying wasn't like a sulk or a bad mood. It didn't go away for months.

Years.

Never, even.

But the silence was stretching on and on, and he felt he had to speak. Not being able to see made it worse, somehow.

'A bit,' Jori replied. Her voice came from beside

him, to the right. 'You must think me stupid. He was our enemy, after all.'

'He was your cousin, too.'

'He was.' There was a quiet snuffling sound, as if someone were wiping their nose. 'And even though he was awful to us, at the end, I still have the memories of growing up together. He was kind to me, sometimes. Just a few smiles and laughs. But it was more than anyone else in my family ever gave me. You can't imagine what it was like, Uki. Being in that clan . . .'

Uki's own childhood had been pretty grim. He had a good idea of how powerful even a smidgen of kindness could be amongst all the hate and spite. Like Nua, the young girl who had been the only one to play with him. He would have walked through fire to help her. And if anything bad should have happened to her . . .

'I understand,' he said. 'You don't need to explain. Not to me.'

'Thank you,' said Jori. Uki heard her sigh and lean against something wooden. A tiny, creaking sound.

He wanted to reach up and take off the blindfold

that covered his face just to see where Jori was, maybe put a comforting paw on her shoulder. It was maddening, not being able to look around, tripping over his own feet and walking into things. But he didn't dare. Necripha could be looking through his eyes right now. She would see where they were, and then tell Mortix. His own sight would betray them, again.

The blindfold had been his idea, after they had escaped from the tunnel collapse.

He had tied it on, right there in the mineshaft, and then told them what he wanted them to do.

Kree and the urchins were to take Ember and hide her away in the Underfell, somewhere deep and hard to find, in tunnels that only quick and nimble children could crawl through.

Coal and Jori suggested leading Uki up into the city. It was the opposite of what their enemies would expect, and they might be able to keep him hidden if they moved him around often enough. Zarza insisted on coming too. They would scout around the cramped buildings in patrols, finding spots to squirrel him away in. A few hours here, a few there, hoping to confuse Necripha if she was listening in on them.

Even though he knew it was keeping the others safe, Uki was filled with frustration. What good was running and hiding? How were they going to capture Mortix when they were sneaking around Eisenfell like outlaws? And it would surely only be a matter of time before they were caught.

He had never felt so useless in his life. Not even before he had powers, when he was just a frightened, bullied child.

'Tell me what you see, Jori.' He wanted to take his mind off the crushing knot of anger that was growing inside him. 'If you can do it without giving away any clues.'

'I can try,' said Jori.

'We're high up, above most of the rooftops. There's just a sea of chimneys, really. Threads of smoke everywhere, all joining up in a haze. The sun is going down, and there's lights coming on in the windows. Candles and lanterns, flickering yellow. In the distance there's the top of the Eisenrock, and behind that more houses. Then the black slab of the wall. Sorry, I'm not much of a poet.'

'That's fine,' said Uki. 'I can picture it in my head. Thank you. Can you see any rabbits?'

'Some. They're trudging about in the street down there. Going home for supper, probably.'

'Do they look worried?' Uki asked. 'Scared?'

'Well,' Jori thought a moment. 'They don't look happy, that's for sure.'

'It must be horrible, being trapped inside the city, knowing rabbits you love have been taken away. Seeing those scary guards stomping around everywhere.'

'Yes,' said Jori. 'There's lots of *them* around. And we're counting on the city rabbits being scared. If they're frightened enough, they might do something about it.'

'Like what?' Uki asked.

'Like rise up against Mortix,' said Jori. 'There's thousands of them. Many more than all the Deathless put together. Coal is getting the word out, while he looks for another place for us to hide. He's telling everyone about you. About the battle at the cathedral.

And letting them know the princess is safe. Ready to take over the empire from her mad father.'

'Stop!' Uki put his paws over his ears. 'Don't say any more! She could be listening!'

'Oh,' said Jori. 'Yes. I keep forgetting.'

'I hate it.' Behind the blindfold, hot tears stung at the corner of Uki's eyes. 'It's like I don't own my own mind any more.'

'I can imagine,' said Jori. He felt her paw on his. A gentle squeeze.

'But don't let Coal make the townsfolk attack. So many of them will be hurt! There *must* be another way to get to Mortix. If only we weren't so small and useless.'

'Being small has never stopped us,' said Jori. 'In fact, it's helped every time. Adults don't expect children to be stronger than them, or to know better. They underestimate us, and then we show them how wrong they are. Think of Valkus. And Charice.'

'We were there in time to stop them, though. Mortix has grown too powerful. My name won't be enough to make anyone do anything. We need some kind of heroic warrior. Like Sir Prentiss.'

Uki heard Jori give a sad sigh at the brave knight's name. 'He was a hero,' she said. 'But so are you. It doesn't matter how tall you are or how shiny your armour is. Sometimes it's a case of being just the right person the world needs at just the right moment. And that's you, Lord Maggety-Pie.'

Uki smiled at the nickname Ma Gurdle had given him. But it didn't make him feel any better. It didn't make any ideas pop into his head. He had the same feeling that always dogged him when things were going badly. That sense of uselessness. The thought that he would let Iffrit down, and everyone else who trusted him. The wish that he could be a better leader – strong and confident, like Coal or Jori.

Does it ever help you, feeling sorry for yourself? His dark voice sounded louder in the shadows of the blindfold.

No, Uki had to admit. *Focusing on everything that could go wrong doesn't help at all.*

Then stop it. Start thinking of a way out, before it's too late.

When his dark voice started to make sense, Uki knew things were really getting bad. But before he could even begin to plan, he heard footsteps outside the room door and the creaking of hinges.

'It's Zarza,' Jori said.

The whisper of soft feet slipped across the room. A floorboard gave the slightest squeak next to Uki and he heard the bonedancer's voice in his ear.

'We've found a new place for you. I'm taking you there now. Jori is to start scouting for another spot. On the other side of the city.'

'How will she know where to find us?' Uki asked. He was filled with the sudden fear he might not see his friend again, that he would forever be lost and sightless in this great, teeming warren of a city.

'I will whisper it to her. Cover your ears.'

Uki jammed his fingers into his earholes and hummed a tune for good measure. He hoped Necripha was listening in right now. He hoped she was screaming with frustration at not being able to eavesdrop properly.

He felt a tap on his shoulder and firm fingers gripped his paw.

'Come,' Zarza said. And then he was being led

out of the door and down several sets of wonky steps before he even had a chance to say goodbye.

*

Uki felt himself being pulled this way and that through the streets, his hood drawn down to his nose and Zarza's arm – strong as ever since Uki had used his power to heal the gash in her shoulder – looped around his.

Even though he couldn't see, he could hear and smell, senses which painted a picture of his journey. He caught snatches of conversation from groups of rabbits they passed. Low, worried voices, mostly telling tales of the latest folk to go missing. The muffled sound from an upstairs window of a mother rabbit singing a lullaby to her children.

He could tell when they passed the doorway of a shop or inn. The sudden sound of clinking earthenware, the rush of food smells that made his stomach rumble. Turnip soup, roasted parsnip, butter-glazed carrots with a sprinkle of fresh parsley.

Sometimes he caught the scent of old rat dung, blocked drains, or the stale stink of an outdoor toilet. Odours that could only be so strong in a city of thousands squashed together.

His feet padded over rough cobblestones, potholes and the smooth edges of doorsteps. More than once he tripped or stumbled over a loose rock or the corner of a building, but Zarza was always quick enough to catch him.

Every now and then she gave him a shove, squashing him behind a barrel or into a narrow alleyway. Each time, seconds later, he heard the clank of steel armour and marching boots. A patrol of Deathless, endlessly searching the city for him. He wondered if they were doing the same in the Underfell. If his friends were still safe.

Finally, he felt himself being led into a building. The air suddenly cooled, there were splintered floorboards beneath his toes, and he could smell damp mildew and rot. A derelict house, abandoned and empty. Far from prying eyes, he hoped.

'We're here,' said Zarza. 'Should be safe for a few hours. You can sleep if you want. Coal will be here soon, once he has found a place for you to stay next.'

Uki waved his paws back and forth in front of

him, trying to feel if there was a chair, a wall, a bed. In the end, Zarza came and helped him across to what felt like a pile of sacks. He flopped down on them, releasing a cloud of mould dust that made him sneeze.

Once he had coughed and spluttered his nose clear, there was a long period of silence. So long, in fact, that he thought Zarza might have left him on his own.

Finally, he heard a soft crunching sound, followed by the patter of something small and hard bouncing off the floorboards.

'What was that?' he whispered.

'I killed a beetle,' said Zarza.

Uki winced and pulled his feet up under him, imagining cockroaches crawling across every inch of the abandoned house.

'Relax,' said Zarza. 'It was one from my own pouch.'

'You carry beetles in your pouch?'

There was a rattling, as if a box of tiny pebbles was being shaken to and fro. 'Bonedancers carry them. Our beliefs are that we must kill every day.

The beetles are to make sure the rabbits around us do not die unnecessarily.'

Uki found he had no reply at all to *that.* He silently thanked the Goddess that Zarza hadn't run out of beetles.

There was quiet again for a long time. Uki got the impression that this mysterious killer rabbit didn't like him and he had a good idea why.

'I'm sorry,' he said, as a way to break the silence.

'Sorry for what?' Zarza had moved, although he hadn't heard a sound, and was now standing off to his right.

'For ruining the ambush. For not realising Necripha would be spying on me.'

More silence. Then Zarza spoke again, this time from the left. 'No need to apologise. You were not to know how devious this creature is. If, as you say, she is kin to Gormalech, then she may be very dangerous. He is as cunning and deadly as a rattlesnake.'

The words brought Uki relief. He had thought Zarza blamed him for what happened.

'You fought Gormalech?' he asked. 'The one who was tricked by the goddesses?'

'We did.' Zarza's voice sounded even more fierce than usual. Each word dripping with hatred. 'Him and his army of rabbits. The Gorm.'

'Were they like the Deathless?' asked Uki. 'Did he take over their minds, as Mortix has?'

'Not quite like that,' said Zarza. 'He changed their whole bodies. Poisoned and twisted them with his iron. They became his slaves, but he didn't speak through their mouths or see with their eyes. At least, not as far as I know.'

'What happened in your battle?' Uki asked.

Zarza sighed. 'We defeated him. Or his army at least. A very brave young rabbit – about the same age as you – and his sister and brother collected and used magic Gifts. They struck a mighty blow against their leader, Scramashank, and the Gorm were all wiped from the earth. But many good rabbits were lost in the fight.'

'A rabbit my age? Defeated an army?' Uki remembered the tale of three young rabbits and their bravery from the puppet shows he had seen with the Strollers. But he had thought it was just made up. A bedtime story.

'Indeed.' Zarza made a quiet noise that might have been a chuckle. 'So, you shouldn't doubt yourself so much. The goddesses seem to like using children as their heroes.'

Uki cringed. 'Me? I'm not a hero. And I don't think the Goddess even knows I exist.'

'Oh, she does. Believe me, she does.'

Hearing that other young rabbits had managed to beat their enemy kindled a blazing spark of hope in Uki's belly. But then he remembered he was talking to a death worshipping killer. The servant of a goddess that ended rabbits' lives, perhaps as cold and cruel as Mortix herself.

'And what about your goddess?' he asked, a slight tremble in his voice. 'Does she know of me, too? Is she . . . taking an interest in what I do?'

'I would think so,' said Zarza. It was probably the most sinister thing Uki had ever heard. 'Does that worry you?'

'Well . . .' Uki chose his words *very* carefully. 'She is a goddess of death, isn't she? What makes her different from Mortix?'

'The two could not be more different!' Zarza

snapped, making Uki flinch. 'Mortix claims to rule death, but wants to create a kingdom of it. She wants to use her evil weapon to wipe out life completely. But life is a part of death. They go together, like the twin goddesses. To live is to die, and to die is not cruel – not when it is your time.'

Uki thought he understood, harsh as it sounded. 'And when you are ready, Nixha comes for you?'

'Yes. She comes with her bow and quickly, gently ends your life. Then you are free to move to the Land Beyond. To be at peace. It happens to every living thing.'

Uki thought of his mother, of her cold body lying in the graveyard back in the Ice Wastes.

'She came for my mother,' he said, his voice almost a whisper.

'Mine too,' said Zarza, as softly as Uki had ever heard her speak. 'And we will see them both again, when Nixha calls us. And in the meantime, as long as you hold your mother in your heart, she is never really gone. She is a part of you, and will be part of your children, and their children after. If there are rabbits that know your name, you are never truly dead.'

'I would dearly love to see her again,' said Uki. 'Dying wouldn't be so bad if I knew she'd be there, waiting for me.'

Zarza's paw brushed his fingertips, making him jump. Again, he hadn't heard her move a step. 'She will. But all in its time. You have a lot to do first. And when you move on, I have a feeling there will be many rabbits to remember you.'

Uki was about to ask for more details about the Land Beyond. To try and get an idea of what it might be like, what kind of place his mother was in right now. Could she see him? Was she proud of what he'd become?

But sounds outside the door made him swallow his words. He held his breath, hearing the silky hiss of Zarza's sword being drawn from its sheath.

Clomp-clunk, clomp-clunk, clomp-clunk.

'I think it's Coal,' Uki whispered, recognising the sound of his friend's wooden leg. Sure enough, the door creaked open and the blacksmith's familiar voice was heard.

'Don't skewer me with that thing, will you? I've brought you some dinner.'

Uki heard the door shut and the sound of Coal's crutch as he hobbled over to him. His nose was filled with the delicious smell of hot pastry as a crumbly pasty was pressed into his paws.

'Thank you, Coal,' Uki said. 'I'm starving!'

'Zarza?'

There was a rustle of robes as the bonedancer moved closer. Taking a pastry from Coal, Uki guessed.

'I will eat this elsewhere,' she said. 'Someone should be watching the street.'

'Perhaps you should take your mask off,' said Coal. 'They might be looking for a bonedancer.'

'I *never* take my mask off!' Uki heard a rustle, which he guessed was Zarza pulling up her hood, and then the door creaked open and shut once more.

'Kether's teeth,' said Coal. 'She's terrifying. Were you all right in here with her on your own?'

'I was fine,' said Uki. 'She seems nice, really. Once you get used to the skull mask and all the killing.' He lifted his pastry to his mouth and took a bite. It crunched and flaked, crumbs sticking to his lips. Inside was creamy tomato sauce and chunks of carrot and potato. He could taste a hint of basil, thyme and bay leaves. It might have been the best thing he had ever eaten.

'Bonedancers give me the creeps,' said Coal, his mouth also full. 'All those black robes and bone faces . . .'

'Glad she's on our side,' said Uki, in between bites. 'She says she fought against another creature of the Ancients. Gormalech the iron god. Apparently, he was beaten by a young rabbit, just like me.'

'Gormalech beaten, eh?' Coal grunted. 'I wouldn't believe everything you hear. Gods are hard things to kill.'

'But I'm fighting against similar things,' said Uki. 'Don't you think I have a chance of winning?'

'That's different,' said Coal. 'You have me on your side. You can't see it, but I'm flexing my muscles right now, and they are *impressive*.'

Uki laughed, spraying crumbs all over the place. Coal seemed a lot more relaxed now he was out of the Underfell. Perhaps it was being back in the streets he had once called home.

'Have you seen anyone you used to know here?' Uki asked. 'Any of your old friends. Or maybe . . . your wife?'

'No.' The spark suddenly vanished from Coal's voice. 'I haven't seen anyone. And they wouldn't recognise me if I did. I don't look anything like the rabbit I was before . . . before the accident.'

'I'm sorry.' Uki had said the wrong thing again. *Stupid of me.* Of course, remembering his lost wife would upset him. He still carried her hair in his locket. He'd wanted it buried with him, back in the Fen. Being here must be a reminder of everything he once had. *Change the subject,* Uki told himself. *Quick. Think of something else to ask him.*

'Jori said you'd been spreading word about me and Ember in the taverns. Do you really think it will help?'

'Can't hurt.' Coal smacked his lips as he finished his pastry. 'The rabbits here are all terrified. Trapped and scared. But there's anger, too, bubbling away under the surface. And every new rabbit that goes missing makes it stronger. At some point they might decide to rise up – especially if they know there's someone to get behind. And a princess to rule the empire properly, too.'

'Do you really think they could defeat all the Deathless if they did?'

'Why not?' A creak of wood as Coal sat down. 'There's thousands upon thousands of rabbits in Eisenfell. Much more than all of Mortix's troops put together. Now's the time for them to rise, before too many get . . . changed.'

Uki imagined all the simple smiths, shopkeepers and craftsmen going up against the ranks of armoured Deathless. It would be a massacre. 'So many would get hurt,' he said.

'You can't make soup without peeling a few turnips,' said Coal. 'And it might be our only option. We're not going to get at Mortix while she's keeping the emperor cooped up in the palace. Not when that Necripha creature is watching our every move through you. Unless . . .'

'Unless what?'

'Well.' The wood creaked as Coal shifted his weight. 'Have you thought about just taking the blindfold off and letting her come for you?

If we could get *her* out of the way, we'd have a better chance.'

Uki couldn't believe what he was hearing. Coal was normally a voice of reason, but this plan . . .

'If I did that, they'd *all* come for me,' he said. 'I'd be captured in an instant!'

'Of course, of course. Forget I said anything.' Coal's voice sounded strained. 'Stupid idea. Just thought you might be able to turn her spying against her, that's all.'

Turn her spying against her, his dark voice echoed. **Why haven't you thought of that?**

Would it be possible? Uki wondered. Could he somehow give Necripha the wrong information? Get her to believe a lie that would let him get close to Mortix?

There was the sound of something hard tapping against glass. Coal grunted in surprise.

'That's funny,' he said. 'Two flipping great magpies pecking at the window! Shoo! Get out of it, you flying rats! Must be after our pasties . . .'

Magpies. Uki remembered seeing the birds before, in the Gurdle village and when they were stuck outside Valkus's fortress. They seemed to turn up whenever he was thinking of an idea that might help him. Like a message sent to nudge him on to the right path. A sign from nature, or maybe the Goddess. And, this time, they had come at just the moment his dark voice told him to trick Necripha.

'Coal,' he said, speaking slowly so as not to chase his hunch away. 'Get Zarza. I think I might have had an idea . . .'

Chapter Twelve

Broken Chains

'Uki! It's so good to see you again!'

Uki felt familiar arms squeeze tight around his waist. His eyes were still hidden behind his blindfold, but he recognised Kree's voice. Besides, nobody else that tiny could hug with such ferocity.

'Hello, Kree,' he started to say, but then his nose was hit by a waft of stench that made him gag. The reek of an open sewer on a hot summer's day, right after a diarrhoea epidemic.

'What's that stink?' he gasped.

'It's the fragrant odour of the place we've been hiding, unfortunately.' Uki heard Yarrow the bard's voice. It sounded worn with stress. 'My nose will never be the same again. I shall have to spend the rest of my life surrounded by incense to recover.'

'You were hiding in a toilet?' Uki gently prised Kree away and moved her to a safe distance.

'As good as,' said Yarrow. There was a chorus of grumbles and moans from behind him. Uki guessed it was the Stinkers. 'Well, you can hardly take offence when you choose to live in the smelliest part of the city, young fellows.'

'Soilwallow is the safest part too,' said a Stinker.

'You tell 'im, Ponger,' said another.

Uki was about to warn them not to give away any information, but then he supposed it didn't matter any more. Not if his plan worked the way he hoped.

They were gathered in the Underfell again, in a tunnel Uki assumed was close to the secret forge beneath the Eisenrock. He had no way of actually knowing, though, as the details had all been left to his friends. Because his ears and eyes could not be trusted, he'd had to tell them his plan in a way that wouldn't reveal what he was doing.

Telling someone an idea without actually using any words was almost impossible, he'd discovered.

The germ of the idea – to trick Necripha by showing her just what he wanted her to see – came from Coal and the magpies. The rest of it, Uki had to figure out himself. And it hadn't been easy.

What he wanted was for Mortix to leave the safety of the palace and come out into the open. To get her in a place where he could use his spear to trap her. But how under earth would he be able to do that?

To make it even harder, he couldn't ask anyone for advice because, if he did, Necripha might overhear and know what he was up to.

They have to think we are weak, he realised. *They have to believe there is no risk of themselves being captured.* That part would be easy – there were only a handful of them left, anyway.

And they will only leave the palace for a good reason. To kill me, maybe? Or to capture Princess Ember? And what if they thought we were going to destroy the cannon they are building? Would there even be a way to use all three?

He would have to choose what he showed Necripha very carefully. She would have to hear and see just the right things, and Uki wouldn't be able to say *anything* else. Which meant he also needed a secret way to communicate to the others. A silent language he could use while blindfolded . . .

*

After the magpie's visit, back in the city above, he had waited until he, Jori, Coal and Zarza were together. As they sat, squashed up in a cramped attic, he felt the familiar itch of Necripha's presence and had signalled to them by flapping his paws, trying to let them know he had something important to say.

'What's the matter?' Jori had said. 'Are you trying to learn how to fly?'

'Coal just had a terrible idea,' Uki began. 'He said we should let Necripha *see where we were*, so she would come for me and we could attack her.'

'What?' Jori and Zarza spoke together.

'It was just an idea!' Coal protested.

'A terrible idea,' said Uki. 'I can't let her *see or hear our plans.*'

Kneeling on the floor, he began to draw with his finger in the dust. He made a circle with two lines for ears and three dots for eyes. Without being able to see, it was impossible to know what marks he was making, but he hoped it looked a bit like Necripha.

'But,' he had continued. 'I have a really good plan that I think I should risk telling you. I really hope she's *not* listening.'

At the word 'not' he nodded his head frantically. At the same time, he drew an arrow pointing towards the Necripha picture's ears and next to it the Hulstland rune for T. The sign for a trap that the Howlers had used in their tunnels.

I want her to hear this because it's a trap, was what he was trying to say. He hoped one of them would understand.

'No! Don't!' Zarza snapped. 'We don't want her to know!'

'Oh!' a sound came from Jori's direction, as if she had just clicked her fingers. 'I see! Well, perhaps it's worth the risk, just this once. Go ahead, Uki. Tell us the plan.'

'What?' Coal said, but his voice was cut off by a thud and a grunt. Uki couldn't see, but he imagined Jori had just kicked him in the shin. *She's got it,* he thought. *Thank the Goddess.*

'Well,' he said. 'Now that Kree, Yarrow and all of the gang rabbits have *run away*, leaving us *all on our own*, there's no way we can attack Mortix head on. The only thing we can do is destroy her weapon. That might stop her in her tracks, at least for a bit.' It felt strange, speaking such lies, especially about brave and fierce little Kree, but if Necripha thought there were only the four of them, she would become very confident of her victory.

'Good idea,' said Jori, speaking slowly so the others would catch on. 'Curse Kree and the others for leaving us, just when we needed them! I thought she was our friend.'

'So did I,' said Uki. 'I'm so angry with her.' He hoped he was being convincing. 'And I think we should strike at the weapon *soon*. If the city folk are about to rise up and burn Eisenfell down, it might give us the distraction we need.'

'Good thinking,' said Jori. 'When shall we attack?'

'In *five days*,' said Uki. He held up three fingers as he said it, waving them around. 'That should give us time to prepare.'

'Five days it is then,' said Coal, finally catching on. 'I'll make sure there are riots all over the city at the same time. It might just be enough to defeat the empire.'

Behind his eyes, Uki thought he felt a writhing, tickling sensation. Necripha had heard and would now be spilling all to Mortix. Telling her that their army could wait five days to ambush them at the forge, when they would be there in three. That they should station many of their troops up in the city, waiting for imaginary riots that never came.

And then an attack on the cannon in just *three* days would lure Mortix and Necripha out in a hurry, before they were properly prepared. If they dashed to the forge with a smaller force of Deathless and were met by all the gangs . . . that might just give Uki the chance to launch a spear at the emperor's body and capture the evil spirit inside.

It seemed like too much to hope for, but it was the best he could do. And then, for the next three days, he had to keep his mouth shut as he was led from place to place around the city. Three long days trapped behind that thick, itchy blindfold. Seventy-two endless hours of blackness, of being led around by the paw, of trying to resist the temptation to peel the scarf covering his eyes back just a *smidge* . . . It had been torture. He couldn't even ask if his friends had properly understood. He had to trust that they would be able to put the rest of the plan into place themselves while, up in the palace, Necripha and Mortix would be feeling smug, thinking they had plenty of time to prepare their next move.

It was the longest, darkest, loneliest wait of his life. And then, finally – when he thought he might never use his eyes again – they took him to a cellar with a trapdoor that led to the Underfell, into the familiar twisting tunnels of bare earth.

*

'I suppose it's safe to ask where we are now?' Uki said. He must have been brought underground because they were about to spring their attack. It wouldn't matter if Necripha was listening in. In fact, they wanted her to.

'We're in a tunnel right next to the secret forge,' said Kree, her voice bubbling with excitement.

'The one that collapsed when we fought Venic?' Uki asked. Surely that would either still be blocked or bristling with guards.

'No.' Jori's voice was right by his ear. 'A new one. Turns out the Scrappers are expert miners. They've dug us a tunnel leading right up to the forge.'

'We's even been in a few times,' came a gruff voice. Uki thought it belonged to Grit, the Scrapper leader.

'Into the forge?' Uki couldn't believe how risky that was.

'Yes,' said Kree. 'It's just like going on a scouting patrol. Most of the tin bonces are on the door, or up in Eisenfell, hunting for *you*. There's only a few of them actually in there, whipping the slaves about and making sure everyone's working themselves to death. We even stole a keg of their exploding powder.' She took Uki's paws and pressed them against a wooden surface. He could feel the curved sides of a barrel banded with metal. Someone levered open the lid and a sour smell, not unlike rotten eggs, wafted out.

'It stinks,' Uki said.

'That's the sulphur,' Coal explained. 'We've stacked more underneath the cannon itself, without anyone noticing. All we have to do is run a trail of powder away from it to a safe distance and then set the end alight. It'll burn along, quick as a whip, and when it hits the barrel stack . . .'

' . . . *bang*,' Jori finished. 'No more cannon.'

'Can we do it now?' Kree asked, jumping up and down. 'Can we?'

'Not yet,' said Uki. He was waiting for that familiar tickle behind his eyes that told him Necripha was peering in. He needed to get all of his enemies rushing down to the forge in a panic, desperate to stop him from destroying Mortix's pride and joy.

'Why don't you take your blindfold off?' Coal said. 'That might bring them running.'

'Maybe,' said Uki. 'But I think we should be in the forge first. And the gangs should stay hidden. If our plan has worked, she still thinks it's just us four.'

'*Nam ukku ulla,*' said Kree. 'I spent all that time doing our warpaint for nothing.'

Uki risked lifting the edge of the blindfold, just for a split second. It was the first time he'd seen light – bright, gleaming, wonderful *light* – for days, so he squinted a bit, but he could make out the faces of Kree and the others, lit up by candles and lanterns. They were all smeared with grime and sewage, but they had stripes of red paint criss-crossing their noses and ears. Even Yarrow had outlined some of his tattooed spirals with lines of crimson.

'Highlights,' he said, tossing his ears.

Seeing everyone again, even for an instant, was like Uki's eyes having a Lupen's Day feast after a long, bleak winter. 'You all look very fierce,' he said. 'Like real warriors.'

He spotted Ember there, as grubby and tattered as the other urchins. She gave him a nod and a smile. Her eyes looked sad still, but that terrible emptiness had gone. She was herself again.

He quickly pulled his blindfold down and turned away before the gangs could see the grim look cross his face. *Warriors.* They were just children, most of them, excited as if this was some game. But Uki knew that Mortix was the spirit of death. She wouldn't be happy until they were all lifeless and cold. This was anything *but* a game. This was risking their lives.

Just as his blindfold fell, as luck would have it, he felt a mosquito-bite niggle behind his left eye.

She's here.

He shot out a paw, grabbing hold of Jori's arm and squeezing. Silence fell in the narrow tunnel. This was it – time to bait the trap.

With trembling fingers, he reached up and pulled the blindfold from his face. His sight was still blurry, but the earth wall in front of him slowly swam into focus. That, and the barrel of stolen gunpowder propped against it.

'Are we ready for the attack?' he asked Jori, knowing Necripha would hear every word.

'We are ready,' she said. Uki could feel the group of gang urchins behind him, trying desperately not to breathe. He prayed that nobody moved or sneezed.

'Let's go,' said Coal. 'Time to *destroy the giant cannon.*'

Uki felt the itch in his head begin to burn. It had worked. Necripha had heard just what he wanted her to. She now knew the attack was coming early, but had hopefully missed seeing all the gang rabbits. They needed her to believe it was just Uki, Jori, Coal and Zarza.

He had the flicker of a vision – the twisted old witch running along a palace corridor as fast as her withered paws could carry her. In her panic, the walls that blocked him were slipping and she had allowed him a glimpse.

Jori hefted the barrel under her arm, just as Zarza knelt down and moved a wooden covering aside from the corner of the tunnel. Torchlight flooded in, along with the sounds of hammering metal, the crack of whips and the moaning cries of slaves.

'Into the forge,' Jori said.

Crouching, crawling, Uki entered the giant chamber again. The curved bottom of the Eisenrock still hung above, threatening to fall in and crush them all under its iron weight. The rickety wall of scaffolding still stood underneath it, as did the slave cages and the forges. The metal behemoth that was the

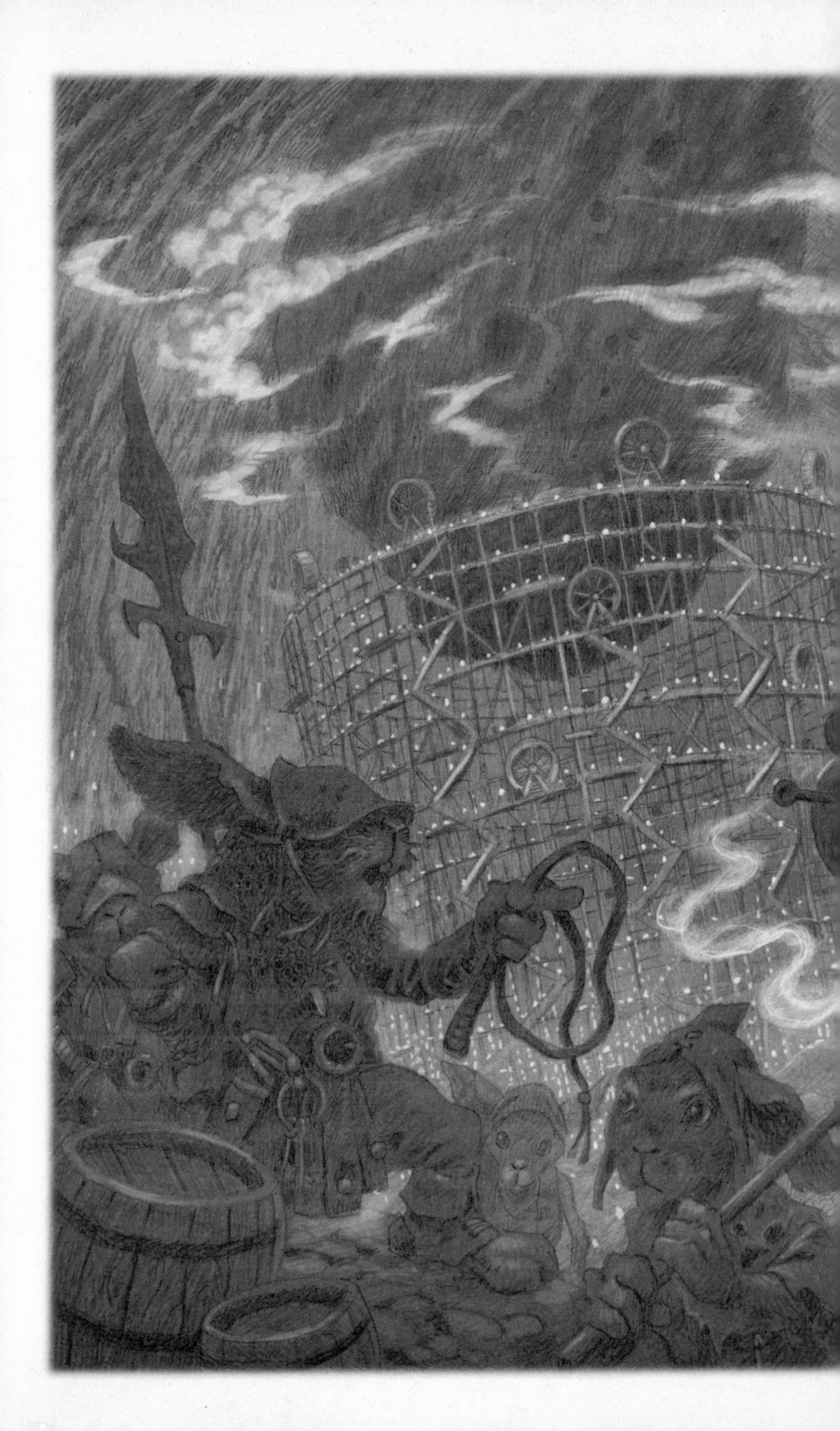

cannon still hung, partly finished, mouth open ready to bellow out destruction on the whole Five Realms.

But the rest of the forge was very different from their last visit. Now rabbits were everywhere, bustling about like a nest of ants under a suddenly lifted stone.

Most of them were slaves. Scrawny sacks of fur and bone, half-starved and whipped. They were chained in lines and were busy lifting molten iron from the forges, chipping metal from the surface of the Eisenrock, or ferrying it in baskets up and down teetering ladders.

Amongst them were several slave drivers, flicking whips against bare backs and screaming insults. And watching over everything (with Mortix seeing through their eyes) were five or six Deathless.

'It should get their attention when we take *those* out,' Jori whispered in his ear.

'How are we going to do that?' Uki whispered back. 'There's more of them than I thought.'

Jori just winked. Then she ran off towards the cannon, laying a thick trail of gunpowder on the floor behind her.

I hope they have everything planned, Uki thought. Tunnelling up to the forge had been a brilliant idea, as had stealing the gunpowder. But if they were overwhelmed by Deathless before Necripha and Mortix got here, then it was all for nothing.

He risked using his link to Necripha to try and see what she was doing. His eye was itching like a nest of tiny bees and he saw another flash from her viewpoint. This time she was running into the throne room of the palace. Emperor Ash was sitting there with a line of victims before him, all waiting to be changed . . .

'She's about to tell Mortix,' he whispered to Coal. 'The Deathless will know we're here any second.'

Sure enough, the silver-faced guard closest to them suddenly stopped watching the slaves and span on its heel, searching the forge for Uki and his friends. Uki reached for Coal's arm, trying to drag him into cover, but instead the blacksmith stood up, in full view.

'What are you doing?' Uki hissed. 'They'll see you! It's too early!'

Coal ignored him. He cupped his good hand around his mouth and bellowed, as loudly as his fire-scorched lungs would let him. 'Now! Rise up everyone! The time has come!'

All of the Deathless in the room turned towards him, swords raised. The forge doors, newly repaired, swung open, letting in several more.

I think your friends have messed up, Uki's dark voice sounded scared for once. **You shouldn't have trusted them.**

Uki was about to agree, but then a noise erupted from all around him. It echoed about the colossal cavern, shaking the scaffolding, making the guards flinch. For a second, Uki had no idea what it was. The cannon blowing up? The walls falling down? And then he realised it was voices. A tide of them, furious and desperate.

It was the slaves themselves. The stolen, chained rabbits of Eisenfell, taken and forced to labour on Mortix's engine of destruction. They were all, every single one of them, roaring at the top of their voices, smashing their chained wrists and ankles with their hammers and picks.

And then, one by one, the chains fell away. Close to a thousand rabbits, instantly freed, charged at the slave drivers and Deathless, screaming even louder, waving sticks and clubs and pickaxes in rage.

'What . . .' Uki stuttered. 'How . . .?'

Coal whooped and laughed, pausing to club a fleeing slave driver to the ground with his hammer. 'We've been planning this with them for days,' he said. 'We sneaked up to the cages at night. We gave them files to cut through their chains and told them to listen for the signal. Now they have broken free and are ready to fight!'

'Your very own army!' said Jori, returning from the cannon, holding out a flaming torch. 'Shall we blow it up now?'

'Not yet,' said Uki. He watched as the hordes of freed slaves swarmed over the Deathless, beating them unconscious and wrapping them in their cast-off chains. The itch behind his eye had stopped for a moment – Necripha must be too busy marching towards him to spy – but the air around him had suddenly grown colder. 'I can feel Mortix coming. I have to pick a spot to stand. A place where she can come for me, but that stops most of her troops from getting through. I need to be close enough to use a spear without getting killed . . .'

'We could use barricades, maybe?' Jori suggested. 'With a gap in the middle, so they can only come through one at a time?'

'As long as we don't make it too obvious,' said Coal. 'We don't want them to know that's what we're doing.'

'Do it quickly,' said Uki. 'I don't think she's watching me now, but she could look in at any second . . .'

Their planning was interrupted by a series of shrieks. They all jumped at the sound, weapons ready, but soon realised they were screams of joy.

The gang children had come running out of the tunnel, straight into the arms of the parents and grandparents they had been missing. All around the cavern, reunions were going on. Howlers, Toffs, Scrappers – and even Stinkers – were being whisked off their feet and whirled in the air, or just clutched and held tight. Tears of joy were being shed, whoops and shouts echoed around the forge instead of moans and screams.

Uki spotted Kree, holding hands with Lurky, dancing round and round and laughing. Then they both realised they were supposed to hate each other and let go, sticking their tongues out instead. And then they doubled over, laughing at each other and started dancing once more.

'This is lovely,' said Uki. 'But we don't have time. How long before they get here from the palace?'

'We got Nikku to run the tunnels,' said Coal. 'It took her half an hour.'

'Then we'd better get those barricades up,' said Jori.

Coal nodded. He picked up a nearby shovel and beat his hammer against the blade. The clanging rang out like an alarm bell, and the celebrating rabbits gradually fell silent.

'Listen up!' Coal shouted in his husky voice. 'We're very happy you are with your children again, but we need your help! Mortix – I mean, the emperor – is on his way here now with more of his soldiers! Do you want to be truly free? Do you want to stop this great city being turned into a prison? Because we have a plan to do just that!'

Silence fell for a moment. But then it was broken by a whoop from every rabbit in the forge, even the most broken, exhausted slaves.

Coal would make a good leader, Uki thought, feeling a pang of jealousy. *Much better than me.*

As if hearing his thoughts and deciding to prove him wrong, Coal pointed his hammer-arm at Uki and bellowed again. 'This is the rabbit you need to listen to! This is the one who will save you! Tell them what to do, Uki.'

All eyes were suddenly upon him. Even his friends were staring, expecting him to say something inspiring.

'Um. Hello!' he began. Probably the worst start to a speech in the history of rabbits. **Just tell them, you idiot,** said his dark voice. Uki took a deep breath.

'It's true. I am here to try and free your city.'

The rabbits cheered again and Uki felt his confidence grow a little. 'I know I just look like a young, clueless rabbit with unusual fur – and that's exactly what I was until a few months ago – but this thing that is controlling your emperor: I have fought against creatures like it before. I have defeated them every time and taken their powers for myself!

'Each time I thought the odds were too high for me – that it would be too difficult. And each time I came through and won. Not because I am a hero, or anything special, but because I had the best friends around me. Because I had rabbits that loved and trusted me by my side . . . just like you all do right now.'

The escaped slaves squeezed their children tight and Uki felt Coal slap him on the shoulder. The words began to flow from him now, almost without him having to think.

'Your children have been so brave while you have been trapped. They fought on and survived when they had to, like my friends and I had to when *we* found ourselves alone. They have also learnt how strong they can be together, how they can achieve things they never thought possible when they have someone who believes in them. And now we ask *you* to join with us, to believe in us. For just one more battle, we ask for your help.

'We need to build a barricade across the chamber.

We need to stop them getting to the cannon before we can blow it to pieces. We need to fight hard and hold the Deathless back. If we work together, we can stop the emperor. We can make sure you will *never* be made into slaves again!'

To his surprise, the rabbits cheered him. They whooped and yelled and raised their clenched paws in the air. Some of the gang children started calling his name and then it swelled into a chant that filled the forge.

'Uki! Uki! Uki! Uki!'

He felt the hair on his neck stand up. He felt a warm tingle of pride fill him from ear to toe. *Maybe I* can *be a leader,* he thought. *Maybe I can be as confident as Coal if I just believe in myself.*

'Great speech, son,' Coal whispered in his ear. 'Much better than I could have done.'

Jori nodded and beamed at him. Then she took hold of an imaginary skirt and did a pretend curtsey. Uki laughed, full for a moment with relief and joy and love . . . that was until the oncoming presence of Mortix sent another icy wave rushing over him.

'Quick, everyone!' He broke the celebrations with another shout. 'They are almost here!'

Everyone sprang into action, running towards the crates, barrows and ladders, dragging them to the centre of the forge and piling them on top of one another. Uki could feel Necripha scratching behind his eyes again. He made sure she got a good look at the barricade and the pile of knocked-out Deathless. He looked down at the trail of gunpowder leading to the cannon, the stack of barrels underneath it. He even added in a glance at Ember, in case that encouraged Mortix to rush to the forge in person.

Jori watched him moving his eyes, saw the way he was deliberately showing Necripha what he wanted her to see. Uki tapped his head a few times, just to make sure she knew what he was doing.

Nodding, Jori headed off to supervise the barricade-building. Coal stayed put, slapping the head of his hammer against his meaty paw. 'We need to get you out of danger, Uki,' he said, risking a quick wink. 'If they find out how weak we really are, if they get to you, then it's all over.'

Uki knew the words were just for Necripha, but

it was still hard to hear them. He looked around the chamber with frightened eyes. Where was the best place to make a stand? Where could they lure Mortix to, so the other rabbits wouldn't be hurt?

His gaze rested on the scaffold, on the platform below the Eisenrock. Just big enough to hold a few rabbits. Just the right size for a last stand.

'There,' he said. 'We can hide up there.'

The needling in his head told him his words had been heard. The frosty chill creeping over his fur meant Mortix was getting steadily closer. There was nothing left to do but put their pieces in place and wait for the game to play out.

Chapter Thirteen

Ka-boom

Uki looked down from the top of the platform, seeing the miniature figures of his new army scuttling around beneath him.

The barricades were now built. Nikku and Rainna stood by the trail of gunpowder holding torches, ready to light the fuse at his signal. Amongst the other rabbits he could see specks of bright silk clothing that were Toffs, smudges of grimy brown that were Stinkers, and the glinting copper helmets of the Scrappers, all standing with their parents, ready to fight, ready to lose them again, maybe. He prayed it wouldn't come to that.

Jori and Kree stood on the platform with him, as did Zarza and Yarrow. Coal had just finished his gruelling climb up the ladders and steps. It had been tiring enough for Uki, even with his spirit-enhanced strength. Goddess knew how hard it was with one arm and one leg.

Princess Ember had come with them. As the next in line to rule the empire, she was too important to risk being captured. And Uki had a glimmer of hope that some part of Emperor Ash might still be there, inside his body. Seeing his daughter on the scaffold might convince him to climb up. Either that, or Mortix might want her out of the way – if the rabbits of Eisenfell did decide to rise up, Ember would be the one they chose for the throne.

This small group, Uki thought. *A handful of us to face the spirit of death, to finish the task.* He hoped it would be enough. But even if it wasn't, he couldn't think of any finer rabbits to meet his end with.

Goddess keep them safe, he prayed. *If anyone has to fall, please let it be me.*

His mind turned to Zarza's talk of the Land Beyond. He wondered if his mother was watching him now. He wondered if she was waiting for him, knowing he'd be with her soon.

Stop thinking like that, his dark voice scolded. **The whole Five Realms needs you now. Needs you to win, not die.**

Uki nodded. He was being frightened, imagining the worst. He couldn't afford to do that, not when so many rabbits depended on him.

'They look so small down there,' Jori said, moving beside him and peering over the edge.

'*Pok ha boc,*' said Kree, edging up on his other side. 'Rabbits aren't supposed to be this high up. It's not natural.'

'Where's your boyfriend?' Jori asked, with a smirk.

'He is *not* my boyfriend!' Kree glared daggers but Uki thought he glimpsed a blush beneath her bristling fur. 'Lurky is down there with the others. I've told him to go and find Mooka when this is over. If I don't . . . well, if I don't see him again.'

'You'll see him,' said Uki, quickly. 'I promise you will.'

'Don't peel your carrots before they've grown,' said Coal, finally getting his breath back. 'If Mortix does come up here for us, she's going to be bringing as many Deathless as she can. We're in for a hard fight.'

'There's Necripha's servant as well, don't forget,' said Jori. 'The one that looks like a mountain in a tunic.'

'Balto,' said Uki, remembering the times that hulking rabbit had already tried to kill him.

'I'm looking forward to giving him flying lessons,' said Kree, brandishing her adder-fang dagger. The thought of her taking on a behemoth like Balto made Uki wince.

'Maybe you should stand back with Yarrow and Ember,' he said. 'Be our second line of defence.'

'Defence? Second line?' The bard was hiding behind a barrel at the far edge of the platform, his tattooed ears poking out. 'I'm just an observer! Nobody mentioned fighting!'

'If we need *you* to come and save us, we're doomed,' said Zarza. She was moving through a range of combat stances, weaving her way across the wooden platform. Ember was copying her, a dagger in her elegant black-furred paw.

'Nobody is doomed,' said Uki, trying to sound confident. 'We're going to—'

He was interrupted by a muffled booming sound, then another and another.

A cheer went up from the rabbits down below, and Coal waved his hammer in the air, laughing.

'What was that?' Uki asked.

'Traps in the tunnels!' Coal said. 'We couldn't tell you in case Necripha was listening in. But we've laced the passages from Embervale to the forge with pitfalls and cave-ins. Tripwires, spiked pits . . . everything we could think of.'

'Thinning their numbers,' said Jori. 'We wanted to make it more of an even fight.'

'Well done,' Uki said. He hadn't thought of that himself. *I knew I was right to trust them with the plan.*

'And there should be fires blazing in the city as well,' said Coal. 'I don't think I talked enough rabbits into rising up, but they might think that's what is happening anyway. Mortix will have to send some of her puppets there, just to see what's going on, at least.'

'The fewer of them, the better,' said Uki. He shivered as a sigh of icy wind seemed to flow over him. The feeling of creeping frost rising up from his toes. 'Mortix is coming,' he whispered.

Before anyone could speak, a horn sounded, sending echoes bouncing off the cavern walls. The rabbits on the barricades below ducked down, dragging the last few baskets of rocks and iron lumps with them to use as missiles. Uki felt his every muscle tense. Beside him, Jori snapped her flask from her belt, thumbing open the cap.

'Here we go,' she said.

The sound of the horn died down, was replaced by a jangling, a clanking. A roar of noise like a wave dragging pebbles down a beach.

And then the wave broke. From the forge doorway it poured – a tide of Deathless in their steel armour, dusty, dented, caked with mud and clay. They had staggered and clambered through collapsing tunnels and booby-trapped mineshafts, losing bits of their metal shells along the way.

But still they came.

Only four could fit through the doorway at once,

so they pushed and shoved, battling with each other to get inside the forge.

Gone were the neat, ordered lines of controlled marching. They were desperate now, hungry to reach Uki and his friends. Each one had a fragment of Mortix's mind raging inside them. And it looked like they had made her seriously, dangerously angry.

Clambering and grappling over each other, they streamed into the room, right into an onslaught of hurled rocks and clumps of raw iron.

There was already a pile of them in the doorway, shoved down and crushed by the force of all the others behind. More fell now, knocked unconscious by the shower of missiles that clanged against their steel faceplates.

But, however many dropped, there were more to replace them. Even though there must be scores of senseless bodies in the tunnels, whole squads of Deathless fighting fires in the city above, there were still swarms of them stumbling their way into the forge. More than they could hope to fight off with their rag-tag army.

Uki looked down on the scene below with

mounting horror. The gangs and their parents were still raining down rocks on the enemies' heads, but it wasn't enough to stop them.

The ground between the doorway and the barricade was quickly becoming covered with a carpet of armoured, unconscious bodies, but very soon the rest would reach the scrappy walls of crates and barrows, and then the brave rebels would be cut down by the blades of the Deathless. They wouldn't last five minutes.

'We should have stayed down there,' Uki said. 'We should be fighting with them. They don't stand a chance without us!'

'Hold,' said Coal, laying his paw on Uki's chest before he could take a step towards the ladder and climb down. 'Here comes the emperor.'

Tearing his eyes away from the barricades, Uki looked towards the doorway. The last of the Deathless had poured through, and they were forming themselves into a wall to protect their master.

The clog of bodies at the entrance parted, and three rabbits that Uki knew well stepped through. The looming hulk that was Balto, the bent, withered crone, Necripha, and the gleaming, armoured emperor – although all Uki could see was the ghostly shape of Mortix blotting him out completely.

'Show them Ember,' said Jori, beckoning to the princess to come closer.

Ember stepped up to the platform edge, standing beside Uki. There they waited for one of their enemies to spot them, hoping they would take the bait.

Sure enough, the dead, black eyes of Mortix roved around the cavern, scanning the rabbits at the barricades before moving up the tower of scaffolding to rest on Uki at the top. She raised a pale-skinned arm to point, at the same time as her puppet – the emperor – raised his gauntlet.

'Bring me those rabbits!' Mortix's voice, coming from the emperor's mouth, echoed around the chamber. 'Bring them to me, and leave my cannon untouched, and I may spare your feeble lives!'

'Blow it up,' Jori said.

Uki looked down to where Nikku stood and raised one of his crystal spears. She saw the signal and set her torch to the trail of gunpowder.

It sparked alight instantly. A living speck of brilliant light that whizzed its way along the black trail, heading for the stack of barrels underneath the giant weapon.

All the gang members and the freed slaves dived for the ground, clapping their paws over their ears.

Mortix could only stare on in horror. Seeing through all the eyes of the Deathless under her control. They watched as the flame hit the mound of gunpowder and then . . .

CRA-KA-BOOM!!

A supernova of brilliant light swept out. A wall of force and sound that shook the walls of the cavern.

Every rabbit standing was knocked off its feet, even Uki and his friends on top of the scaffold. The rickety wood rocked and trembled, many pieces of it splintering or ripping away. Somehow the platform at the top remained standing, although it teetered to and fro like the deck of a storm-ridden ship.

The cannon itself was thrown upwards, its steel shape twisting, bending, ripping, until it smacked into the cavern roof with enormous force and tumbled back to earth in fragments, in shards, in ribbons.

The rock walls of the forge cracked and crumbled. The Eisenrock itself shivered and seemed to drop an inch or two, sending showers of earth pouring down like waterfalls.

For a good minute or more there was complete silence, then Uki realised it was because his ears had stopped working. He pushed himself up from the platform, brushing drifts of dry mud and flakes of rust from his shoulders, and crawled to the edge to look down on the devastation.

As his hearing returned – just a long, low ringing at first – he watched the clouds of dust clear.

The cavern below was a wasteland. The cannon was broken beyond recognition. The forges were blown into piles of brick. The barricade was hidden under a bank of loose mud, and there were crumpled bodies of Deathless everywhere.

As Uki watched, movement began in the drifts of earth. The gangs of the Underfell were slowly rising, getting up from where they had sheltered to avoid the worst of the blast. One by one they stood – brushing dirt from their faces, shaking their heads to clear them – before moving to help their friends and parents. Finally, when all were upright, even though they still tottered from the force of the blast, Uki saw Nikku, Rainna, Scrag and some of the others look up to the platform, trying to see if anyone was still up there.

Uki raised his spear again, to show them he was all right. Then he pointed with it, aiming towards the entrance of the secret tunnel they had dug.

'Go!' he shouted, not sure if any of them could actually hear him. 'You've done enough! Go now!'

Nikku waved back, then began to usher the others, slaves and urchins alike, towards the tunnel. They staggered over, as quickly as they were able, and began to crawl inside one by one. Soon they would all be out of the forge, off into the Underfell, away from any Deathless that might pick themselves up and want to carry on the fight.

Uki smiled to himself, knowing they would be safe at least.

But his smile didn't last long.

Over on the far side of the forge, sheltered by a row of armoured soldiers, the figures of Balto, Necripha and the emperor had begun to move.

If Mortix was angry before, she would be blazing now. Uki could feel every scrap of heat being sucked out of the chamber as she forced the emperor's body to its feet. The flames of the crushed forges flickered out. Fern-shaped patterns of white frost began to form on the cavern walls.

Balto and Necripha were up too, kicking the bodies of the Deathless, making them rise as well. Within minutes, there was a small force of fifteen or more and they marched, hungry for revenge, straight towards the scaffold that held Uki and his friends.

Chapter Fourteen

Beneath the Eisenrock

Uki staggered over to the bodies of his friends which littered the top of the platform. They were stunned, motionless. Covered by drifts of mud and red-tinted rust from the Eisenrock above. One by one, he brushed the dirt from their faces and shook them until they stirred.

'Wake up!' he cried. 'They're coming! They're climbing up the scaffold!'

Even as he was working, he could feel the wooden structure begin to tremble with the heavily armoured rabbits beginning their climb. How long before they reached the top, he wondered? Five? Ten minutes?

Zarza was on her feet first, shaking her head to clear it. Uki helped Jori and Kree up, then went to lift Coal. The big rabbit had trickles of blood coming from his ears. He slapped the sides of his head.

'I'm deaf!' he shouted.

'It only lasts a minute,' Uki mouthed at him. He could hear well enough now himself, although there was a high-pitched ringing sound buzzing in his head.

Jori moved to peer over the edge. 'They're coming!' she called back. 'I count ten – no, twelve – deadheads, with Necripha and the others at the rear.'

'What?' Coal shouted. Uki grabbed his paw and pulled him over so he could see for himself. 'They're coming!' he said, his voice much too loud.

'Uki's just told us that, you *bulba boodah*!' Kree shouted at him, waving her dagger, but luckily he didn't hear her.

'Stay back, Kree,' said Jori. 'Protect Ember and Yarrow.'

'I will deal with them as they come up this

ladder,' said Zarza. She pointed to the other end of the platform with her sword, where the top of another ladder jutted. 'Jori, you take that one. If they get past us, Uki and Coal are the second line.'

'Can't we just chop the ladders down?' Yarrow asked.

'We *want* them to come up,' said Jori. 'At least, we want Mortix to. Then Uki can capture her with his spear.'

'Ah yes, of course. Silly me.'

'Do you think you can really free my father?' Ember asked, her eyes filled with hope.

'I'll try,' said Uki. Although he had a nasty feeling it might not be so easy. And even if he did, there was a whole city of rabbits who blamed Emperor Ash for everything that had happened. He might walk out of the Underfell free of Mortix, only to be attacked by his own subjects.

Think about that later, his dark voice chided. **They're almost upon us.**

Uki felt the platform juddering as the first of the Deathless started up the ladder below. Wood creaked and the entire scaffold listed to one side. The blast must have weakened it badly.

'Steady on!' Coal cried, trying to keep his balance. The sound of splintering wood came from beneath them.

'Kree,' Uki called. 'Can you look under the planks? See what the damage is?'

The plains rabbit scampered to the back of the platform and ducked her head under. Then she jerked it back with a screech.

'Uki! He's coming!'

Uki spun around, wondering what she meant, just in time to see an arm like a slab of meat slap itself over the side. Another paw came up, then the hump of a monstrous back and a pair of stubby ears. A face with a thick chunky brow and spiteful piggy eyes followed. Uki's fur bristled as he recognised who it was.

'Balto.' He turned to face him, spear at the ready. 'He's trying to flank us. Get back, Kree! I will deal with him.'

'Deal?' Balto grunted as he swung a leg up and heaved himself on to the decking. 'With me? This time I'm going to kill you properly, maggot.'

'Nam ukku ulla!' Kree shrieked. 'Don't touch my friend!'

Balto, still getting to his feet, hit Kree with a back-handed slap that sent her sliding across the platform. She almost toppled over the edge, but Yarrow grabbed her and cradled her in his arms.

'No!' Uki shouted, and charged at the Endwatch thug, hoping to knock him back off the scaffold before he could stand. He might have succeeded, if two Deathless hadn't chosen that moment to leap up from both ladders at the same time. They met the blades of Jori and Zarza, and then crashed down on to the deck, defeated, making the whole structure teeter to one side. Uki stumbled and, instead of barrelling into Balto, he went down on one knee.

'Ha!' The motion of the scaffolding helped Balto stand, throwing him towards the toppling Uki. He hit the little rabbit with a punch, right between his eyes, and Uki found himself collapsing backwards, looking up at the great craggy lump of sky metal that was the Eisenrock.

Lights sparked across his vision and his head swam, but he knew if he lay there, he was finished. Kicking his legs up and under, he flipped himself upright. Balto blinked in surprise. A punch like that should have killed a small rabbit, and here was Uki, up and ready to fight again.

'Is that all you've got?' The anger at seeing Kree hurt had made Uki brave. More than that, he wanted to teach this great bully a lesson. He had chosen the wrong set of rabbits to pick on.

'Die!' Balto shouted, drawing a dagger from his belt and swinging it at Uki.

Uki saw it coming and ducked underneath, time seeming to slow as Balto's thick arm swooped through the air above him. He leapt as close to the Endwatch rabbit as he dared, bringing the butt of his spear up into Balto's stomach, using all of his spirit-given strength.

The blow was strong enough to lift Balto off his feet. The blunt end of Uki's spear bashed the big rabbit's stomach up and under his ribcage, knocking every last scrap of air out of his lungs.

Uki danced away again as Balto came down, a ton of muscle, flopping on to the splintered planks like a freshly caught whale.

The shock sent the platform swinging the other

way, nearly toppling everyone over. Uki heard a cry from behind him and snatched a glance over his shoulder.

He saw Zarza send a Deathless cartwheeling from the ladder. There were three or more lying at her feet already. Jori was kicking one backwards as it clambered up. She paused to swig from the dusk potion in her flask.

'Kill them!' Zarza shouted at her, swinging her sword around to take on another. 'Don't just wound or knock them down!'

'Not my style!' Jori shouted back. Another Deathless popped its head over the edge, swinging a blade at Jori's feet. She leapt above it, coming down to trap the sword beneath a boot. Her other foot kicked at the blank steel of the Deathless's face, caving the metal in and sending it toppling backwards, out of sight.

Uki turned his attention back to Balto. The winded rabbit was trying to get up, croaking as he sucked air into his bruised lungs.

'Oh, no you don't,' said Uki. He jumped forwards and punted the big rabbit in the side.

With all Uki's magical strength behind it, the blow was enough to send Balto rolling off the platform. Gone.

'Hurrah!' Yarrow shouted. Uki looked over to see the bard pumping his fist in the air and was relieved to spot Kree doing the same. She looked a bit ruffled, but Balto's slap hadn't seriously harmed her.

For a second, a heartbeat, Uki dared to think things were going well . . .

. . . and that was when he heard the scream.

Back at the ladders, Zarza had been hit. She crumpled to the ground, clutching at her thigh, and a Deathless with a bloodstained short sword clambered up on to the platform.

Quickly, Coal stepped forwards, swinging his hammer as he moved, cracking it against the Deathless's head.

The rabbit toppled backwards, knocking into another that was climbing up behind it. But the scream had distracted Jori as well. She was forced back by a second Deathless, parrying blows, trying to find a gap in which to strike.

And behind her, on to the platform, came the unmistakeable figure of the emperor – his gleaming, ornate armour rimed with frost, steaming with cold.

Mortix was upon them.

*

'Fall back!' Coal shouted. He was dragging Zarza with his hammer, trying to keep balance with his crutch as the platform swayed. Jori was still battling with the last Deathless, swords crashing against each other left and right, sparks flying.

Emperor Ash was stepping forward, reaching down to draw his own broadsword. Uki could see the cold white light of Mortix swirling about his body. He caught glimpses of the spirit's face, her long black hair flowing as if it drifted beneath some icy lake. The image blinked in and out: Ash-Mortix-Ash-Mortix.

There didn't seem to be any more Deathless coming up from the ladder beside Uki. He moved forwards, spear at the ready. Would it work if he threw it now? Or would it just bounce off the emperor's armour? Just how close did the crystal have to be for the trap to function? With all the other spirits he had touched the fur and flesh of the rabbits that carried them. But they weren't wearing plate armour of solid sky metal.

Aim for a joint, he decided. *Get the spear tip in as far as it will go. Even if there's chainmail underneath, you should be strong enough to push through. Don't take any chances.*

Uki moved closer, but Mortix was ready for him. The face of the spirit swam into sight, seeming to hover above Emperor Ash's head.

'You won't get me that easily.' Her icy, dead voice echoed from within Ash's armour. The emperor drew his sword and pointed it at Uki.

She doesn't know how fast I am, Uki thought. *I could dodge that blade and get in close. I might be quick enough to jab her under the armpit, where the armour joins.* If only he could use Charice's power on her as well. Poison her or slow her down.

The thought gave him an idea. He couldn't touch Mortix or the Deathless she controlled. But he *could* use his healing on his friends.

Even as he took another step towards Ash/Mortix, he reached out with his mind, sensing the living bodies of his comrades.

Zarza was a pulsing red streak, gasping with pain from her slashed thigh. He sent her calming waves of energy. He made the edges of her wound start to knit as fast as they were able. A few more minutes and she might be up, fighting again.

Jori was there too, her heart pounding away at three times its normal speed. Uki helped it with a boost of energy to her muscles, making her strikes as powerful as they were fast.

Snap! She sheared through the Deathless's sword with her next blow, then followed it up with a kick to its ribs that knocked the creature to its knees. Then she brought the pommel of her sword down with both hands, slamming it against the back of the Deathless's head, knocking it senseless.

Now there was just Mortix. There was no way the spirit could fight them both off. Uki and Jori closed in together, stepping carefully, waiting for the chance to strike.

Now! Uki's mouth was just about to form the

words, when a scream from the other side of the platform stopped him.

He looked across to see Balto, clambering back up from below.

'Whiskers!' Uki cursed himself for not checking the brute was properly finished. Although it didn't matter. Coal was there, striding across the decking to whack Balto, *clunk,* on the head. Hard enough to crack the thick boulder of his skull. Hard enough to send him plummeting from the scaffold, crashing against the wooden struts all the way down.

But that wasn't where the scream had come from.

Uki looked over to where Yarrow still cradled Kree, where Zarza lay clutching her leg as it healed.

And he saw the one rabbit he had forgotten in all this. The hunched, withered, witch with her knotted headscarf hiding her disgusting third eye. *Necripha.*

She must have clambered up the same way Balto had, and now she stood amongst his friends, clutching Princess Ember in an arm lock, a curved knife blade at her throat.

It was Ember who had screamed, as her shoulder was wrenched and her neck almost sliced open. Now

Necripha peered over at Uki, her face twisted into an evil, triumphant smile.

'Put your spear down, brat,' she said. 'And tell your friend to drop her sword. Or I slice the princess open.'

'Don't do it!' Ember shouted, then gasped as Necripha bent her arm harder. 'Father! Please stop this!'

The armoured figure of the emperor shook its head. Mortix's voice came, echoing from inside.

'Your father can't help you. He's gone from this body. Now do what the witch says. Drop your weapons.'

Uki and Jori looked at each other. Both knew they could still attack Mortix. They still had a chance to capture her inside Uki's spear.

But if they did, then Ember would die. As surely as if they had plunged their weapons into her instead.

Jori raised an eyebrow.

Uki shook his head.

No. We can't do it.

'Even if it means we lose?' Jori said.

'Even that,' said Uki. And, despite his dark voice screaming at him not to, he dropped his spear on to the wooden floor.

Chapter Fifteen

Gods and Monsters

There was silence on the slowly rocking platform. Just the sound of Uki's spear rolling to the edge of the planks and then dropping to the level below. A sad, hopeless clattering.

And then Mortix began laughing. The sound echoed inside the steel shell of the emperor's battle helm, and Necripha's vile cackle joined in.

'You came so close,' Mortix said. The ghostly image of her face swam above the emperor's body, looking down on Uki with those empty, black eyeballs. As cold and dark as the lightless depths of the deepest sea cavern.

'We've put our weapons down,' said Uki, teeth gritted. 'Now let Ember go.'

'Not likely.' Necripha still held her tight. She gave her arm a sharp twist, making the princess yelp.

'No, I have plans for her,' said Mortix.

'What plans?' Uki asked. His mind was racing, looking for an idea, a way out. Something, anything.

'Well.' Mortix drove her sword tip into the wooden flooring, leaving it standing upright, within reach. Then she made the emperor bring his fingers up, opening the catches at his neck and lifting his helmet free. Beneath was the face of a black-furred rabbit, eyes that might once have been deep brown like Ember's, now blank and empty.

'I would imagine the rabbits of Eisenfell are quite angry with their ruler.' The emperor's mouth moved but Mortix's voice came out. 'Especially after you have been busy putting word out about a rebellion. They will be quite keen for his daughter to take over. Which she will – with me controlling her, of course.'

'You can take my body.' Ember strained to speak

against the knife at her throat. 'As long as you let my father go free.'

'Oh no,' said Mortix. 'He'll have to die, of course. We'll blame this Uki. Nobody will want to follow him when they hear he killed the emperor. Folk get quite offended about strangers murdering their leaders, even if they were horrid tyrants in the first place.'

'And I suppose you'll kill me too,' Uki said. His paw went to the crystals on his harness buckle. 'It won't be that easy.'

'Wrong again,' said Mortix, her mouth twitching into a smile. 'You'll have to be locked away in a dungeon. If you died, then my siblings in your prisons there would escape. I don't want them coming out and spoiling my wonderful new world. They have such strange ideas about what to do with it.'

'You'll share it with Necripha though, will you? Do you think she can be trusted?' Uki looked across to where the spiteful old witch was still clutching Ember. *If I can get them to fight one another, I might have an idea*, he thought.

Mortix was looking at her too. 'I'm sure she

can't,' she said. 'Although she has been very useful. Especially in telling me all about what *you* were up to. I suppose I can share my planet with her. As long as she keeps *completely* out of my way . . .'

'Oh, I will, Your Majesty,' Necripha simpered. 'You won't see me at all.'

'And what sort of planet will it be?' Uki asked. He risked edging a paw just a hair's width upward, towards the last spear in its harness on his back. 'What sort of world will it be if everything is dead?'

'A perfect one!' Mortix laughed again. 'Imagine a place free from all life. So pure. So simple. So peaceful. When the Ancients made me, they wanted me to kill viruses for them: mistakes in their computing engines. But if there were no engines, no life . . . then there would be no problems. The perfect solution.'

'Killing everyone is a solution? Is that what your cannon was for?'

'Of course.' Mortix looked down to the pile of twisted, blackened shards that had once been her secret weapon. 'It was to have been the first of many. An arsenal of weapons powerful enough to wipe this rabbit-world clean. Now I shall have to start again. An inconvenience, true, but once *you* are out of the way . . .'

She paused and snapped her head round to Uki, who froze in mid-grab.

'Are you moving?'

Uki shook his head, trying to look innocent.

'Do you really think I'm that stupid?'

'I wasn't . . .' Uki stammered. 'I wouldn't . . .'

Mortix grinned. One of the emperor's steel-clad arms shot out and grabbed Jori by the collar. 'I think such impudence should be punished!'

'No! Don't!' Uki went to take a step forward, but Necripha yanked Ember's arm so hard she screamed. He froze, not knowing what to do.

'Look at me, girl.' Mortix turned to Jori, pulling her face closer. The emperor's other arm came across, gauntleted fingers prising open Jori's eyes.

'Stop! Please!' Uki felt his insides turn to ice. There was already a thin stream of white mist flowing out of Jori and rolling towards the open mouth of Mortix. The spirit was devouring his friend and there was nothing he could do. If he moved to stop her, then Necripha would kill Ember. It was the princess's life, or his friend's. An impossible, terrible choice.

Ember will be killed anyway, whatever you do. His dark voice sounded in his ear. **Mortix will kill them both. If you save Jori, at least one of them will live.**

But could he do it? Doom the princess, just to save his friend?

He looked across at Ember. She stared back, as if she knew what he was thinking. Her head made the tiniest of nods, giving him her blessing, her permission. Then she closed her eyes.

Uki swallowed. He tensed every muscle, ready to reach for his spear. More and more of Jori's essence was seeping out with every second but still his feet were frozen, knowing that taking a step was as good as cutting Ember's throat himself.

And then, from the corner of his eye: a movement.

The smallest rabbit on that platform, the tiniest, the least significant. Brave Kree, an expression of fierce defiance on her warpainted face.

Necripha hadn't noticed her lying next to Yarrow.

Probably hadn't thought she was important. The witch had hardly bothered to look down – her glittering eyes were fixed on Uki, even as Kree slid her adder-fang dagger from the folds of her cloak. Even as she raised it, oh-so-slowly, edging herself closer, closer . . .

. . . and then she struck – just like the snake that had once grown the fang her dagger was made from – slamming her blade down into Necripha's unprotected foot. It sank deep, jabbing through fur and flesh, making the old witch scream in agony.

And then – in that short heartbeat of time– everything moved at once.

Ember, feeling Necripha's grip loosen, twisted herself away from the knife, yanked her arm free and ducked out of danger.

Coal stepped forwards, dropping his crutch and shooting his paw out to grab Necripha by the throat, hoisting the scrawny rabbit from her feet.

And Uki . . . Uki moved fastest of all, snatching his last spear from his back, flicking it in a powerful throw, sending it streaking towards the body of Emperor Ash.

It hit him on the side of his unprotected head, piercing his cheek.

As soon as the crystal point touched his flesh, the power of the prison took over, drawing Mortix in, sucking her down like a whirlpool.

Uki saw a look of sheer surprise cross her face just for an instant, and then she was gone. The air rippled with white light as every trace of her was drawn into the crystal and all the essence she had stolen from countless lords, ladies, guards and soldiers escaped her clutches.

Still moving, Uki grabbed the spear haft and wrenched it free, then twisted off the point. He didn't want to waste a second, to risk the chance that their victory might be foiled a second time.

Slamming the crystal into the final slot on his harness, he felt a wash of pure energy flow over him. The orange flames of Iffrit were everywhere – all over his body, covering his face. They raged around the four crystals, sealing them, locking them. Trapping them, forever this time.

And in Uki's head he heard a voice, distant, but familiar. The same voice he had heard in that frozen graveyard, what seemed like an eternity ago.

'I knew I was right to choose you,' it said. *'You did me proud, Uki. You did your mother proud.'*

'Iffrit,' Uki muttered, as the flames burned, painless but so bright.

'My task is done,' Iffrit's voice said, growing ever fainter. *'But yours is just begun. I am sorry for this. So sorry . . .'*

Sorry for what? Uki wondered. But then realised he knew. He had always known in the back of his mind. Perhaps in the memories that Iffrit had shared with him.

The crystals had to stay bound. They had to stay together, protected. And that was Mortix's power. The final piece of the puzzle. There would be no dying for Uki. He would always have to be the spirits' guardian. From now until the end of time.

The flames went out and Uki collapsed to the floor. His powers were sealed, his life was saved. But the price was never being able to visit the Land Beyond. Never having that reunion with his mother when Nixha finally came for him.

'Mother …' he whispered her name, tears beginning to form in his eyes. Until he saw the crumpled body of Jori in front of him.

Scrabbling, clawing, he got to her as quickly as he could, rolling her over and looking into her face.

He dreaded seeing those blank, dead eyes staring back at him, but instead there were Jori's steely grey ones, filled with relief, gratitude and a twinkle of mischief.

'You took your time, didn't you?' she said.

'Jori!' he shouted, wrapping her in his arms. A second later, Kree was there too, crushing them both in her grip, smearing red warpaint all over their fur.

'Kree!' Uki hugged her back. 'You were brilliant! You saved us all!'

'I know!' Kree gave a whoop. 'I hope Yarrow puts that in his story! I don't have any powers or secret potions, but I was the one who saved us all! I'm the hero of the Five Realms!'

'I can't believe it's over,' said Uki, tears of pure happiness spilling down his cheeks. 'We did it! We actually did it!'

'With a little help from some friends,' said Kree.

Uki remembered Yarrow, Zarza, Ember and Coal. He turned to thank them, to celebrate with them.

And that was when he saw it happen.

*

Coal was standing, apart from the others, still holding Necripha by the throat, her feet dangling above the floor.

Has he killed her? Uki wondered. *He wouldn't have . . . surely.*

But Necripha wasn't moving. Her jaw hung open, tongue lolling. Her eyes were glazed, lifeless. And there was a look on Coal's face – a mixture of anger and sorrow. As if he had done a terrible deed. Awful, yet important. A job he'd never wanted, finally fulfilled.

But that body is just the puppet of an ancient spirit, Uki realised. And he knew what happened when they had to change their hosts.

'Coal!' Uki held out a paw, trying to warn him of the danger. 'Put her down! Move away! Before she leaves the body!'

Coal turned to Uki, his mouth set, his eye glinting with a hint of tears. He made no attempt to drop Necripha's body, even as the core of the spirit inside her appeared. A tiny speck of purple light that rose up from the witch's forehead, from that spot under her headscarf where her third eye had grown.

'COAL!' Uki shouted again, louder, more desperate. 'Don't let that glowing thing touch you! It will take you over! You will become Necripha yourself!'

Still, Coal made no move to get himself clear. He just stared at the point of purple light as it rose, glowing across his scarred face, his eyepatch, the tattered scraps of his ears.

A spear, Uki thought. *I can trap Necripha in it like I did the others!* But his only remaining spear had rolled off the platform. It was lying somewhere beneath, maybe at the bottom of the whole scaffold. There was no way he could reach it in time.

Turning back to Coal, Uki watched as he finally dropped the lifeless body he was holding. But the glowing purple speck remained, floating in the air, level with the blacksmith's face. And then, instead of moving away, Coal began to fumble inside the collar of his jerkin, pulling out the golden locket that held his wife's fur.

What is he doing? Uki couldn't understand. *What does his lost wife have to do with this?*

Now Coal was flicking the locket open, holding it up towards the gleam of light that held Necripha's terrible essence. And instead of a lock of fur, a twitching, wriggling strand of silvery grey substance appeared. It moved from side to side like a worm, like a serpent sniffing out its prey. The purple glow made it sparkle, as if it was made of metal. Living metal.

'I'm sorry, Uki,' Coal finally spoke. Gone was the light and laughter in his husky voice. He sounded like a rabbit condemned. 'I have to do this. I don't have any choice.'

'I don't understand,' said Uki. 'What are you doing? What's going on?'

'I *have* to do it,' Coal said again. 'My master commands it . . .'

There was a gasp from the other side of the platform where Yarrow still crouched behind his shelter of barrels. He was staring at Coal, wide-eyed,

tattooed ears beginning to tremble. 'It can't be,' he said. 'You can't be *him* . . .'

And then a sound from Zarza, half groan, half shriek.

'*Scramashank!*'

She pointed at Coal. 'We never found his body! We thought he'd been destroyed!'

What are they talking about? Uki shook his head. None of this made sense. That name . . . Zarza had used it when she talked about her battle with Gormalech. She said he had been the leader of the Gorm army. That he had been beaten . . .

'Coal,' he said. 'What's happening? What are they talking about? Is it true?'

Coal, his friend, stopped lifting the thing in his locket towards the bead of light that was Necripha's essence. He looked at Uki again, and this time the tears did spill from his eye.

'It's true,' he said. 'I'm not who I said I was. But – you have to believe me – I never wanted to lie to you. I would never do anything to hurt you.'

Uki couldn't understand what he was hearing. 'You're not from Eisenfell? Not a blacksmith?

What about your lost wife? The explosion in the mine?'

Coal choked back a sob. 'Not true,' he said. 'None of it.'

'Everything you said about helping us, though . . . all the things you did for us . . .'

'I did them because I wanted to!' Coal shouted, his voice echoing around the chamber, bouncing back at them from the Eisenrock above. 'Not at first, maybe. When I met you in Reedwic . . . I sensed the power of your crystals. I couldn't understand what they were . . .'

'You wanted to take them for yourself!' Jori spoke up, the edge of a snarl in her voice. 'I *knew* we shouldn't have trusted you!'

'No!' Coal shouted again. 'Listen . . . I am – I was – the servant of a god. A creature just like the ones you've been hunting. Gormalech. He controlled me for years – made me do things. Terrible things.

'And then he was beaten. And I was wounded. Badly. I almost died. But he came to me, with the last of his strength, and healed me. He sent me out into the world, searching for his sister. Necripha. So he could devour her. Use her power.

'I became a hunter. Wandering Hulstland, following a trail. The blood of my master was still part of me. It could trace her presence – just a glimmer. Just enough to lead me.

'When I met you, I could tell you had been touched by the same magic. And then I learnt that Necripha herself was after you . . . I knew if I stayed by your side, she would come to me eventually.'

'You used me . . .' Uki whispered, too shocked to properly speak.

'No!' Coal reached out to Uki with his hammer. 'Well, perhaps at first. But then, the way you trusted me, laughed with me . . . The way you were kind to me without asking anything in return . . . Nobody has ever treated me like that. Not even before – when I was just a normal rabbit, back in my warren. I would give anything just to stay as your friend, Uki. I would give anything to lay down my duty. To forget I ever met Gormalech!'

'Then do it!' Uki pointed at the locket in Coal's paw. 'Throw that thing away! Let me trap Necripha in a crystal! You can stay with us. You can be Coal the blacksmith. Just him and nothing else!'

For a second, for one endless moment, Uki thought he might do it. He stared into Coal's eyes as the two sides of him fought. As his friend tried to step away from the monster he had been, from the master who still crawled through his veins, calling him, commanding him.

Coal's whole body shook with the effort. His jaw creaked, tears streamed down his face. But the power of Gormalech was woven through his every cell. His bones were filled with it, his blood ran thick with strands of living metal.

It was a battle no rabbit could win.

Uki watched his friend's lips move, even as his head turned away. 'Forgive me,' he mouthed. 'Uki, forgive me.'

The locket moved upwards, the sliver of metal touched the speck of light, whipping itself around it in hungry tendrils, drawing it close.

'STOP!' Zarza screamed, leaping up from the floor, swinging her sword. But her leg hadn't quite healed and it buckled, tipping her sideways. The killing blow – one which might have saved so many lives, so much torment – fell short. The tip of her blade raked down Coal's chest, breaking the skin, drawing blood, but only wounding him.

Coal bellowed. A roar which rose, louder and louder, filling the cavern until it seemed like the very walls themselves were screaming.

And then, just as Zarza brought her sword around for another blow, the chamber roof split open. All along the edge of the Eisenrock, a gaping crack appeared, and from it shot a tentacle of that same writhing iron that had been trapped in the locket.

The same, but a thousand times larger. Big enough to wrap itself around Coal – or Scramashank, as he was once again – covering him from head to foot in its embrace. Then, with the sound of a whip cracking, it flicked away, shooting up into the cavern roof and disappearing: rabbit, locket, ancient spirit and all.

Gone.

'After them!' Yarrow shouted, pointing up at the rock. 'Catch him! Kill him! We can't let him escape!'

Uki stood up. Jori and Kree as well. Was there a way? Could they follow? Catch up with that metal *thing* and free their once-friend?

They never found out. With a scream of breaking

timber, the struts that held the platform finally gave way and suddenly they were all falling, crashing, tumbling downwards amongst a mess of poles and planks.

*

They fell three or more levels – Uki clutching Jori and Kree in his arms, trying to cushion them with his body – and then came to a sudden stop, half buried in a mess of planks, torn rope, broken poles and splinters.

Luckily, it was only the topmost section of the scaffold that had been dangerously weakened. The rest stood firm, creaking under its tumble of shattered wood.

Uki sat up, pushing pieces of smashed carpentry away from his legs. He clambered to his feet, helping his friends stand, and then went to check on the others.

Nobody was hurt in the fall, thank the Goddess, but they were all stunned by what had just happened. Yarrow was trembling, his eyes bulging. He pulled at his ears over and over, whispering to himself: 'It can't have been him. It can't. It can't.'

Zarza was in shock as well. She kept shaking her head. Stared at her bronze sword as if it had failed her.

'All those times,' she said, as Uki helped her stand on her bad leg. 'All those moments I stood next to him. I could have killed him a hundred times over. Why didn't I know? Why wasn't there a sign?'

Uki had no answers. He still couldn't understand what had happened himself. He should have been dancing around the cavern, filled with joy at having completed the task. The ordeal that had seemed so gigantic, so impossible. And yet, here he was instead aching, feeling empty. Bruised with disappointment. As if Coal had punched all the air out of him with his words.

There was a rattling of wood as Kree clambered over to him. In her paws was his lost spear. She had found it, jutting from the wood pile. Too late now to do any good. She looked at him, eyes full of concern. 'Are you all right, Uki?'

'I think so,' he said. 'I'm not sure. I don't feel like I know anything any more.'

'I can't believe it, either,' she said. 'I know I was

rude about him, but I actually liked Coal. Except that wasn't his name, was it?'

'Scramashank.' Yarrow moved to stand next to him, still pulling at his ears. 'His name is Scramashank.'

'What did he do?' Uki asked. 'I know he was a servant of Gormalech, that you beat him in a battle. But why are you so scared of him?'

Yarrow stared blankly for a moment before answering. 'He was the leader of the Gorm. An army of rabbits, ten times worse than the Deathless you've just seen. Twisted, cursed things that were once normal. And he was the worst of them.'

Uki couldn't believe it. Couldn't match that description with the blacksmith who had begun to be like a father to him.

'What did he want with Necripha? Why did this Gormalech need her?'

'To break the Balance again.' Zarza came and stood next to Yarrow. They leant on each other like rabbits in the deepest grief. 'Gormalech was trapped under the earth by Nixha and Estra. Last time, he used the power of a sacred Gift to break free. But we destroyed it and sent him back. If he devours Necripha, perhaps that will give him strength enough to return again.'

'Or to capture another Gift,' said Yarrow. 'There are still some out there, don't forget.'

'Podkin,' said Zarza. 'We have to warn him.'

'You have to rest first,' said Jori. 'And we should get down off this scaffolding. I'm not sure it's going to stand much longer.'

As if in answer, the structure gave an ominous creak. The rabbits hurried over to Princess Ember, who was crouched by the body of her father.

'Princess?' Uki put a paw on her shoulder. 'We need to climb down. How is the emperor. Is he . . . ?'

'He's alive,' said Ember, although her brow was creased with worry. 'But he seems so weak. Is he going to die?'

Uki bent to examine Emperor Ash. He didn't need his senses to see that he was in a bad way. His body was weak, his heart beating feebly. And there was a hole in the side of his cheek where Uki's spear had pierced him.

Placing a paw on the emperor's forehead, Uki cleared his mind and sent a wash of healing energy over him. The strength of it was surprising. As was the ease with which Uki was now able to use his power. Almost without thinking, he stitched Ash's cheek shut, then went about his body, fixing the damage caused by Mortix, rebuilding and restoring everything, until the emperor's eyes flickered open.

They *were* brown, Uki saw, just like his daughter's. She looked into them as she helped him sit.

'Where . . . where am I?'

'You're in the tunnels under the city, father.' Ember took his paws in hers and squeezed. 'A terrible creature took over your mind. But it's gone now. This rabbit and his friends saved you.'

The emperor looked around him, blinking as if he had just woken from a deep sleep. 'That was real?' he said. 'All those rabbits with the steel faces? The cold? The darkness?'

'Yes, father,' said Ember. 'And now we have to go back. We have to fix everything that's happened to Eisenfell.'

With Uki's help, they got the emperor standing and began the climb down to the cavern floor. All around them, the Deathless that had been stunned by the blast were struggling to their feet, casting their steel helmets aside. Underneath were ordinary rabbits – groggy, dazed, clutching their pounding heads, but ordinary.

They stared at Uki and his friends as they went past, as they walked into the tunnels outside the forge. A few staggered after them, picking their way through the mineshaft with its crumbled walls and broken joists. By the time they emerged to stand at the foot of the steps up to Embervale, there was quite a crowd.

Up on the hill was the palace, the Cinderthrone, the empire. It had been bruised and battered by Mortix and the spirits, but it had survived, just as it had for hundreds of years.

All that history, Uki thought. *All those stories of lords and heroes and battles. And now we're a part of it, too.* He smiled at Jori and Kree, imagining them being stitched on to a tapestry, or drawn with pieces of coloured glass in a palace window. Shaking his head at how strange it would be.

And then he started up the steps, following Emperor Ash himself.

Chapter Sixteen

Farewell

It surprised Uki just how quick the city was to begin healing. Although, after centuries of routine and tradition, he supposed it was easier to roll back to the way things had always been. More comfortable. Like a pair of worn leather boots.

The rabbits who had been turned into Deathless handed in their armour and went back to their previous lives as guards, knights and clan lords. Everything they had done and seen while under the power of Mortix was just like a bad dream to them. One which might wake them in the night, sweating and shouting, but was always gone again by the time the sun rose.

The fires Coal had set had been small ones in a few deserted warehouses. Put out almost before they had started. *Was he really trying to help us?* Uki wondered. *Or was it just part of his plan to get to Necripha?* He supposed he would never know. And that he would now have to question everything Coal had done or said. His betrayal had poisoned every memory Uki had of him.

The rabbits that had been enslaved returned to their families. The children that had run wild as the gangs of the Underfell returned, too. And, in all the days after, they hugged each other a little tighter than before. They cherished all the ordinary moments they had together a little more, knowing what it was like to lose them.

Word about the cannon and the secret forge had spread around every house, hut and hovel in Eisenfell. Probably before Uki and the others had even finished the long climb up the palace steps.

There were tales too about a black-and-white furred rabbit and his strange friends. About spirits and magic and monsters. About battles in the Underfell with witches and curses and explosions.

The emperor and his bishops had to act quickly. They decided to blame it all on Ash himself. The plots of a power-crazed ruler were quite familiar to the rabbits of Hulstland. And besides, Kether was supposed to be the only being with powers of any kind. What would happen to their churches and priests if stories about ancient gods started spreading around?

It was announced, on the day after Mortix's defeat, that Ash was abdicating immediately. He would be giving up the throne to his daughter, Ember, who would repair all the damage and keep the empire ticking over, just as before. And then he would quietly disappear to a country warren in the middle of nowhere, safely avoiding any more threats of revolt and riots.

Everyone seemed most pleased with that. And even more pleased when the city gates opened and traffic began flowing in and out, bringing goods, trade and coins with them.

Although there was still the strange matter of

the mysterious rabbits who had helped them. The patchwork hero, the dusk wraith, the plains rabbit, the bard and the bonedancer.

*

After sleeping for ten hours straight, Uki was woken by a servant bringing breakfast to his room. A tray heaped with hot porridge, bread, honey and wild berries. A steaming pot of nettle tea, a pile of blueberry pancakes slathered with melted butter and a jug of fresh blackberry juice. More than he could possibly eat in a week.

He uncurled himself from his luxurious feather bed, ate, washed and dressed before being interrupted by another knock at his door.

Opening it, he saw Jori and Kree, along with a servant in imperial uniform.

'We've been summoned,' said Kree, puffing herself up with importance.

'By who?' Uki asked.

'Ember,' said Jori. 'For some kind of ceremony.'

The servant led them down several staircases and along many corridors, all lined with tapestries and statues. Uki couldn't help wondering about the secret passageways behind the walls – whether anyone was watching him through a peephole right now, in that dusty darkness full of cobwebs.

They were taken to a room not quite as large as the throne chamber, but still big enough to fit in a small village. Yarrow and Zarza were there already, along with Ember, who sat on an ornate chair. She was dressed in layers of black silk, which set off her fine velvet fur. Now she looked every inch the princess, so different from when Uki had first met her, cowering in an underground tomb, fearful for her life.

'Good morning, Your Highness,' he said, attempting to bow.

'Please,' she said, frowning at him. 'Call me Ember.'

'You wanted to see us?' Jori said.

'To give us a ceremony?' Kree added. 'Maybe some chests filled with gold?'

Uki nudged her in the ribs.

'I don't know about the gold,' Ember laughed. 'But yes, I was planning a ceremony. There is much talk about the "heroes of the Underfell" in the city, and we have decided to honour you on the same day as my coronation. I want to make you knights, and for you to become my personal bodyguards, if you are willing.'

There was a long moment of awkward silence before Yarrow spoke.

'Your Imperial Highness, we are most honoured,' he said. 'But unfortunately, Zarza and I have decided we must leave for Gotland immediately. Our friends there are in great danger because of the events that followed your father's rescue. We must warn them, so that they can prepare for the return of their old enemy.'

Ember smiled. 'I thought you might say that,' she said. 'So, I took the liberty of having your medals prepared early.'

She beckoned to a servant, who came forward bearing a cushion. On it were two falling stars made from sky metal, each etched with the imperial crest.

'Wearing these will mark you as one of my chosen servants,' Ember said. 'And a knight of the realm. Please take them, along with my eternal gratitude.'

Rising from her seat, she carefully pinned them to Yarrow and Zarza's chests. They bowed in return.

'And what of you three?' Ember turned to Uki and his friends. 'Do you have urgent plans, or may I tempt you to stay in Eisenfell?'

Uki looked at Kree and Jori's faces. He had an idea of what he should do next, but he didn't want to spoil his friends' chance at this noble and important life.

'Well,' he said. 'I can't speak for the others, but . . .'

'Hey!' Kree interrupted. 'We're the outcasts, remember? Everything we do is together!'

'It is,' agreed Jori. 'Tell us your plan, Uki.'

Everyone was looking at him expectantly, making him squirm a bit. 'I was thinking,' he said, 'that, even though Necripha has gone, her Endwatch remains. I believe I know where their base is, their tower. And I would like to find it and burn it to the ground.'

'Count me in!' said Kree. Jori nodded.

'But,' Uki continued, 'I think there is a task I – we – should do first. I believe we should travel with Zarza and Yarrow. We should help bring warning to their friends. After all, Coal was there at the end because of us.'

'His deeds were not your fault,' said Zarza. 'We had just as many chances to stop him. But your company would be very welcome.'

'I suspected you would say that as well,' said Ember, a sad smile on her face. She beckoned to another servant, who brought three more medals across.

One by one, she pinned them on to Uki, Jori and Kree's chests.

'Does this mean . . .' Jori began to say.

'It means you are under my protection,' said Ember. 'And I have already written to your father in the Clan Septys warren. He is to accept your decision to leave. And any attempt to harm you will be dealt with by *me* personally. You are welcome to join my clan, Clan Hulst, or to start your own, if you wish. The choice is completely yours.'

'Thank you,' Jori whispered. 'Thank you so much.' There were tears in her eyes and her ears shook with emotion. Uki took her paw and squeezed it. 'It's over,' she said to him. 'It's finally over. And I'm free.'

'You see?' Uki smiled at her. 'You were right to

stand up to them. You were right all along. And it paid off in the end.'

'It did.' The tears spilled over, running down into her fur. 'All because of you two. You're my clan now.' She ran her fingers over the steel star, just as Kree was doing. The little rabbit looked as though she was about to burst.

'When will you be leaving?' Ember asked.

'Today, if possible,' said Zarza. 'We cannot waste any time.'

'I understand.' Ember nodded, and more servants hurried over to attend her. 'Let us gather outside the palace after lunch. I have an idea there are some friends who would like to see you off.'

*

They found, when they stepped out on to Embervale's grand courtyard with their bags all packed, a group of rabbits waiting for them by the far gate.

But before they could take a step, a large bundle of fur on two spindly, springy legs, bounded out of nowhere, almost knocking Kree back into the palace.

'Mooka!' she screamed, loud enough for some

of the freshly restored guards to reach for their weapons in alarm, 'Mooka! It's you!'

The jerboa hopped up and down with glee, pausing to turn to Uki and slap a wet, pink tongue across his face, covering him with drool.

'Hello, Mooka,' Uki said. 'We missed you.'

'I'm never leaving you again!' Kree shouted, climbing on to his back and burying her face in his fur. She showed him off to Zarza and Yarrow, beaming with pride. Daisy, the farmer, had kept him well fed and groomed, his coat sparkling in the sun.

Once their reunion was over, Uki turned his attention to the rabbits who had come to see them off.

It took a while to recognise them without their uniforms of bright silk, winding sheets, copper helmets and grime, but he eventually realised they were all the gang members: washed, scrubbed and dressed in new clothes. Scrag, Nikku, Rainna, Grit, Coffin, Rattle . . . they were all there, beaming and waving as Uki and the others walked over. And at the front was Lurky, looking up at Kree as she balanced on Mooka's back.

'I hear you're leaving,' he said to her.

'Yes,' she replied. 'On my beautiful jerboa. Amazing, isn't he?'

'He's all right, I suppose.'

Kree laughed. 'Are you going to miss me, then?'

'No.' He poked out his tongue. 'I still hate you completely.'

'I hate you too,' Kree replied. 'But I might be back in a month or two. After we outcasts have done our important missions.'

'Oh,' said Lurky, looking away. 'Good.'

And then he wiggled through the crowd to hide at the back. Uki and Jori shared a secret smile before stepping forward to say farewell to everyone.

One by one, they shook hands with their new comrades. It took quite a while, and there were many hugs and tears along the way.

'I don't know how to thank you all,' Uki said. 'We would never have done it without you.'

'You gave us our lives back,' said Rainna. 'That's thanks enough.'

'Although it will be strange going home,' said Nikku. 'Nothing to fight. No secret passages to sneak down. And not being allowed to steal whatever we want.'

'I've been thinking about that,' said Yarrow. 'And it occurred to me that, although this Necripha is gone, her network of spies remains at large. Uki has plans to deal with their headquarters, but they must have agents scattered all over Hulstland. The whole Five Realms, maybe.'

'And you want us to hunt them down?' Scrag asked, with a fraction too much enthusiasm. 'Drag them back here and throw them in a dungeon? With a bit of torture added in? I bet they've got lots of spiky, poky, stretchy machines in the palace . . .'

'Not quite that harsh,' said Yarrow, with a chuckle. 'But we should definitely have a network of our own. A way to guard against them.'

'I'll be a guard!' said Nikku, followed by similar shouts from all the others.

'Very well,' said Yarrow. 'I shall give it some thought, and send word through one of my fellow bards to organise everything. Or perhaps I shall come back myself, one day. If I survive the return of the Gorm, that is.'

Everyone had begun to discuss what their guard might be called and the heroic deeds they might do, when Empress Ember arrived. She was flanked by two knights in steel armour like that of Sir Prentiss. It made Uki think of that brave warrior who had given his life to save them. Word had it that his body had been rescued from the Ghostburrow, and was to be buried in a splendid tomb of its own, complete with a statue. Along with the ballad Yarrow was writing about him, it was an end that would have made him proud.

'Farewell, dear friends,' Ember said, reaching out to hold paws with Uki, then Jori and Kree. 'If ever you need Hulstland's – or my – help, don't hesitate to send word.'

'Goodbye,' said Uki. 'We'll see you all again, we promise.'

The crowd of rabbits all cheered and kept on cheering as Uki and his friends walked through the palace gates and down the steps to the streets below. The sound rang in his ears as they made their way through the bustling city, towards the Cindergate, the main entrance to Eisenfell, and beyond that, Gotland.

New roads, new adventures . . . a new life.

The threat of the spirits had left him. That nagging dread, the constant, gnawing fear that he would fail, that the quest set him had been too hard. All gone.

He felt like he could breathe – properly breathe – for the first time since he'd woken up in that graveyard. As if, ever since, part of the pile of stones his dying mother had covered him with had still been there – pressing down on his chest – and only now had it fallen away.

He had succeeded. Him. Uki. A tiny scrap of a rabbit. An odd thing that had been shunned and cursed at for most of his life.

He had brought down four of the deadliest creatures to walk the Five Realms. He had beaten warlords and shadow clans and emperors. He had used his strength, his courage and his wits to outplay all of them.

And, even more important than that, he had made two of the best friends any rabbit could hope for along the way.

He sneaked a quick glance at them now, marching beside him with the midday sun glinting on their new medals. He wondered if they felt as proud as him. If they knew how much he loved them both.

Reaching out, he took their paws, one on each side and squeezed. They squeezed back, Jori giving him a wink and Kree grinning down at him from Mooka's back.

The outcasts, he thought. *Saviours of Hulstland. Knights of the realm.*

His mother would never have believed it. She would have been so proud. And the old rabbits from his village . . . he had half a mind to go back and show them how wrong they'd been.

The thought made him laugh out loud, and he waited for his dark voice to disagree. To make a cruel or spiteful comment. To drag him back down and break his spirit into shards.

But it didn't. It was completely silent. Gone, even.

After all, how could it possibly still exist?

There was nothing left for it to say.

Chapter Seventeen

Jerboas of Gotland

The bard finishes his tale, dips his head, spreads his paws wide . . . and waits.

There is silence for a minute, and then Stoneaxe begins to clap. Her brother too, followed by more and more rabbits. Soon the whole crowd of assembled Magpies – even Chief Darkfire – are applauding wildly.

Rue still has a bowl of antidote clutched in his paws, so he can't join in, but he nods along. The pain in his chest has gone, replaced by a warm, woolly feeling that is stuffing his body with fuzz, clogging up his head. His brain is telling him to go to sleep, to heal more, but he has *questions* ... Although it appears he is not the only one.

'A fine tale of the Crystal Keeper,' says Darkfire. 'And one full of detail. Very convincing. But you are not the bardic rabbit in it, are you? So how did you know Uki? And how do you speak of his adventures as if you were there?'

'I met him in the years after,' says the bard. 'When I was very young. And Yarrow was my master. He taught me the tale himself. And as for the rest ... well, Jori filled in some gaps for me.'

'We are in the presence of three rabbits who knew the Crystal Keeper,' says Darkfire to his tribe. 'We are honoured. We should mark this day with a feast. Perhaps a whole week of feasting!'

When the cheers from the Magpies have died down, the bard clears his throat to speak. 'That is very kind of you, Chief. But it brings me to the request you promised to grant.'

Darkfire grunts, beginning to look displeased. Rue holds his breath, praying that his master's ears are safe.

'Like Uki, we are on a quest,' says the bard. 'My

companions and I are in a hurry to get across the mountains and into Gotland. Once my apprentice is fully rested, perhaps you could escort us through the pass? Someone very dear to me – my brother, in fact – is in danger from the same Endwatch that once threatened the Crystal Keeper.'

At this, Darkfire sits up, his paw going to the flint knife at his belt. 'The Endwatch still exists?' His snarl is matched by growls from his tribe. A feral sound, more like a pack of wolves than rabbits.

'They do,' says the bard. 'In fact, they were the ones who poisoned young Rue here. And we must hurry to stop them. My brother's guardians could be fighting them off as we speak.'

Darkfire nods. 'Then we shall take you in the morning. Any enemy of the Crystal Keeper is an enemy of ours.'

Rue smiles. Although being shot was by no means a pleasant experience, it means he is tied to the story even tighter. A victim of the Endwatch like Uki himself. His eyes start to close, he begins to drift off, but then Darkfire's next question makes him snap awake again.

'Before we stop the tale telling, there is something I wish to know. A question for the dusk wraith.'

Jori looks at the chief long and hard before nodding, and Rue fights to keep his eyes open, wondering if Darkfire will ask the thing that he dared not.

'We met you, the Crystal Keeper and Kree of the plains when you burnt the stone towers of the Endwatch to the ground.'

'You did,' says Jori. 'I remember being found by you yourself on a scouting patrol. You nearly took our skins until Uki showed you his powers, then you decided to worship him as your tribal god.'

'We did,' says Darkfire. 'And we were right to do so. But then, some months later, the Crystal Keeper returned. He was on his own and about to venture off into the Ice Wastes. Neither you nor Kree were with him, and yet you were supposed to be his companions. Why was this? What happened between you?'

This is it, thinks Rue. *Just what I wanted to know.* His sleepy eyes threaten to close, the moss and mushrooms make his blood flow sluggish and heavy.

It is with sheer force of will that he manages to keep himself awake, for just a few more seconds . . .

'What you ask is very personal, Chief Darkfire,' says Jori. 'But, out of respect for you, I will answer.

'There was no bad feeling between us, if that is what you are thinking. When our tasks in the Five Realms were all done, Uki decided that his powers were too great. That many rabbits might be tempted to try and take them, or to use Uki himself for their own gain. So, he decided to leave these lands behind. To go into the Wastes, and perhaps beyond. To keep the spirits as far away from the Endwatch and their like as possible.'

'Why . . .' Rue manages to croak. 'Why didn't you go with him?'

'That,' says Jori, 'is complicated. Kree and I both felt we had a life to live. We weren't sure we were ready. I think Uki sensed that, and he didn't press us to go with him. And then, one morning, we woke up to find him gone. I could have followed him, I suppose. I could have come back here to pick up his trail. But I didn't. And then it was too late.'

Don't you miss him? Rue wants to ask. *Will he*

ever come back? And what happened to Kree? Is she still alive?

So many more questions, but his mouth refuses to move. The murmur of rabbits around him becomes a woozy hum of noise and he falls fast asleep.

*

Rue awakes from a dream about earthquakes, about giant waves rocking him up and down. He opens his eyes to find himself outside, strapped into some kind of papoose, swaddled up like a baby on the back of Brightwing.

All around him are his friends, and they are walking through a narrow crack of rock in between two mountains. The air is thin, and so cold it makes his eyes water. Breathing it in sends spikes of icy pain into his lungs.

'Ah,' says a familiar voice. 'You're awake.' The bard's face swims into view as he pulls the hood of Rue's cloak back to inspect him. 'We wanted to leave in time to get to camp before nightfall. We didn't want to disturb you. How are you feeling?'

Rue thinks about that for a moment. The fogginess in his head has gone, so has the pain in his arm and chest. Mostly he just feels hungry, and annoyed at being strung up like a helpless infant.

'When's breakfast?' he says.

He hears the rabbits all around him laugh, and they carry on marching. Nobody offers him any food, and by the sound of all their panting, they are all putting too much effort into walking to even tell him a story. He closes his eyes and decides to have another doze.

*

That night, they stop and camp inside a small cave in one of the rock walls. There is a fire, some hot spinach soup and a mournful Arukh song from Stoneaxe, and then everyone falls asleep. Every part of Rue is toasty warm in his papoose, except for his nose, which feels as though it is about to freeze. After an hour of struggling, he manages to free a paw and uses it as a nose warmer before he, too, drifts off.

*

The march continues all the next morning, until their path begins to veer steeply downwards, just before lunch.

Another hour or two, and they emerge from the mountains and on to a broad slope, covered all over by chippings of flint and straggly grass.

It is here that Brightwing and Stoneaxe, their guides through the pass, wave farewell before vanishing into the mountains again. Almost instantly invisible.

The others carry on, until the flinty foothills have turned to grass plains, thick with clover and bright yellow buttercups.

'Can I get out of this stupid papoose now?' Rue asks. He has been passed on to Nikku's back and has had more than enough of being trussed up like a bale of wool.

'Are you well enough to walk?' the bard asks.

'Of course!' says Rue. And proves his point by leaping out of his bindings and doing a merry jig.

'An amazing recovery,' smiles the bard, handing Rue his staff. 'You had us all worried there!'

'I knew I would be fine,' lies Rue. 'Especially with Jori around. And besides, it was worth it for the story I can tell!'

'No story is worth nearly dying for,' says the bard,

conveniently forgetting that he was once nearly fed to a giant weasel because of one.

'Talking of stories,' says Rue, 'there was another bit to your last tale that I had a question about.'

'Oh, yes?' The bard raises an eyebrow. If the jig hadn't convinced them Rue was back to normal, the questions certainly would.

'It's for Jori, though,' says Rue. 'About what happened after. You said Uki went off to the Ice Wastes, and you stayed behind in Hulstland. But what about Kree? What did she do? Is she still alive?'

The bard laughs. He points ahead of them with his staff to where some animals are grazing on the hillside. 'There's your answer,' he says.

Rue stares at the creatures, unimpressed. 'Sheep? How are sheep the answer to anything?'

'Look closer,' says the bard. And, as they walk a bit further on, Rue notices the 'sheep' have long, tufted tails. Also, enormous ears and huge, bouncy legs.

'Jerboas!' Rue shouts. 'I didn't know there were jerboas in Gotland!'

'There weren't,' says Jori. 'At least, not until thirty years or so ago.'

Now Rue can see some figures on the hill, walking amongst the jerboas, brushing and caring for them. One is a large lop rabbit with brown spots and a belly straining at his tunic. The other is about half his size, dressed in a leather jerkin decorated with beads and tassels.

'Is that . . . ?' Rue blinks. 'Could it be . . . ?'

'It's her,' says the bard. 'She moved here quite a while ago. Set herself up as Gotland's first ever jerboa breeder.'

'And who's that with her?'

'Who do you think?' Jori says. The figures have seen them now, and the smaller one is waving both paws in the air, grinning from ear to ear.

'Lurky?' Rue says. 'Did she marry Lurky after all?'

'Of course she did,' says the bard. 'Wasn't it obvious? And they have about ten children, I believe. Never could keep count.'

The tiny figure of Kree, sandy fur now flecked with grey, has started to run towards them. She is shouting, the words growing clearer as she bounds through the long grass.

'Jori!' she yells. 'My old friend, Jori! And Nikku! Lurky – it's Nikku!'

'Kree!' Jori yells back.

And then the rabbits are all running towards each other, the years falling away until they are just like children again, sprinting to meet their dearest friends.

'Can I go too?' Rue asks, hopping from foot to foot.

'If you want,' says the bard.

'Hooray!' Rue shouts. He takes a step, and then remembers something very important.

'Don't forget your promise,' he says.

'Which one was that?' says the bard, rolling his eyes.

'You promised to tell me the rest of Podkin's story! And now I know that Scramashank comes back! You have to tell me what happened. I want to know *everything*. Will you have time to tell it between here and Thornwood?'

'Perhaps,' says the bard. 'Are you sure you want to hear it? It's quite scary. And sad.' He thinks of the fighting and the danger. The lives that were given up and the tears that were shed. The blood and the sorrow.

'Of course!' Rue shouts over his shoulder. 'I *always* want to hear your stories!'

And then he is gone, running so fast down the hillside each step nearly turns into a tumble. The bard watches him, half tempted to follow, except he would probably break both of his ankles.

Instead, he looks out, across the wide expanse of fields and trees and lakes between him and Thornwood warren, where the Endwatch may be upon his brother even now.

'I'm coming, Podkin,' he whispers into the wind, towards the rolling plains of Gotland, towards the great, green sweep of Grimheart Forest and beyond. 'I swear by the Goddess, I'm coming as fast as I can.'

And he hears – or imagines he does – an answer on the breeze. The hint of words in the rustle of the grass, the branches of scrub rubbing together.

'Hurry,' it says. 'Please, hurry.'

Collect the whole Five Realms series!